Legends of Clover Talamh:

Unravel

by Shannon-Lee Morrissey

DORRANCE
PUBLISHING CO
EST. 1920
PITTSBURGH, PENNSYLVANIA 15238

Dorrance Publishing Co
585 Alpha Drive
Pittsburgh, PA 15238
Visit our website at *www.dorrancebookstore.com*

ISBN: 979-8-88729-354-7
eISBN: 979-8-88729-854-2

Prologue

How did our lives fall apart so fast?

Today is August 23rd, my eighteenth birthday. Well, mine and my sister, Caitlin's. We never kept photos of our parents, but Aunt Megan sometimes tells us how we look like our dad when he was alive. We both have red hair, but mine is pretty messy while Caitlin's is long, about waist-length. We also have light blue eyes that Aunt Megan is constantly comparing the sky to. For the longest time, or for as long as any of us can remember, it has always been just Aunt Megan, Caitlin, myself, and our three younger sisters, Brigit, Nora, and Alison.

Brigit is fifteen with brown, doe-shaped eyes and long, jet black hair and is somehow even paler than everyone else in our family. She's a very smart girl, but incredibly introverted. Hell, she gets looks from random strangers just because she wears black all the time. Her classmates think she hates everyone just because she's quiet. Too bad they never take any opportunity to actually get to know her.

(Actually, she's pretty quiet at home, too.)

Nora is seven with olive skin, red hair, and brown eyes and has a gift for sarcasm...and pointing out your insecurities and flaws. I mean, the kid has *got* to be the child of Satan.

Alison is the youngest, being only five. She has long black hair just like Brigit, olive skin, and hazel eyes. She's very sweet, but does have the tendency to repeat whatever she picks up, so we try to not swear around each other.

Aunt Megan is in her late forties with long deep red hair that's graying a little bit with brown eyes. She took us in after we lost our parents. Some sort of accident. We don't know what happened, what caused it; never got any answers.

The day started out simple: I woke up at seven and went downstairs to find Caitlin watching *9-1-1* and drinking coffee. As usual, she woke up at six in the morning, because she's always been an early riser. Nora and Alison came down about thirty minutes later with Aunt

Megan while Brigit slept in for a few more hours.

Aunt Megan paid the bills while Caitlin and the girls ate their cereal before going to work. Today was my day off from the diner in Prospect and Caitlin's from the thrift store in Cheshire. Brigit was the only one of us who had to work, so I dropped her off at the dollar store and came back home to be greeted with Nora and Alison giving me birthday cards. The four of us went outside to the pool since it was literally ninety degrees outside. Soon, Aunt Megan and Brigit got off work and came home together with ice cream cake and soda.

Just as Caitlin and I blew out the candles, a storm rolled in. The news said nothing about a storm today, or for the rest of the week. It came out of *nowhere*.

First the power went out and then the house began to shake. Violently.

The windows shattered, allowing the howling wind to rip the curtains off, nearly knocking me out. The furniture went flying before smashing into splinters or just fell apart entirely. We were all screaming and freaking out, especially when the house lifted high up on its side and out of its foundation. We all went sliding across the house while trying to grab hold of anything *and* simultaneously dodging shards of glass and heavy objects. The door to the basement flew open as the wind grew stronger, to an unbelievable point.

I couldn't make out what was happening, it was so quick. I was just trying to reach out to

my aunt and sisters. I had no idea how we were going to get out of this… I was the first to fall into the basement. Then I blacked out.

When I woke up, I found myself in the middle of a forest clearing. My head spun as I pushed myself up and looked around.

"Aunt Megan! Girls!" I called.

All I heard back was the sound of my own voice echoing in the distance. I shook my head, trying to clear my vision. Everything was so...dizzy. How could I be in a forest anyway? I live in Connecticut, but there weren't any woods close enough to our house for me to have landed in. How was any of this happening? How was I even alive?

And where is my family?

I took a few steps forward, ready to look for a way out, to find my family. We couldn't be too far apart. But I didn't get very far. I was thrown to the ground, landing with a hard *THUD* on my stomach, forcing the wind out of me. Someone grabbed my arms and pulled them back forcefully before tying me up.

"State your name and business, boy!" a man growled.

There's two of them?

I grunted as my assailant pulled me to my feet, squeezing my forearm. Panting, I got a better look at the two men who ambushed me. The one who just spoke was a man old enough to be my father: mid thirties, early forties. His hair was black, as was his goatee. His eyes were dark and tired, reminding me of when I've had long, hard days at work. The man was wearing a suit of armor that has seen better days. Parts of his armor were dented and broken and his gloves looked a bit worn. But what snapped me out of my dizzy spell was the fact that the man in armor had a very long, sharp sword gripped tightly in his hand.

At first, I didn't know what to say. I thought maybe I was still dreaming. The man behind me shoved me by my lower back. I snapped my head around, expecting to see a face inches from mine...and then I looked down. A dwarf was wearing the same kind of armor as the man in front of me. His hair was long and blond as was his beard. Both had to be almost as long as he (four-foot). His eyes were blue and he had an ax in his other hand. He glared hard at me.

"Answer, boy!" the dwarf growled.

I stammered, racking my brain for something, but all I could say was, "...the hell?"

The man in armor took a step closer, raised his sword, and aimed the pointed end only inches from my Adam's apple.

"Your name and business," the man ordered. "Now."

These two can kill me if they really wanted to. How the hell did I get in this mess? What was even going on?

"Don't hurt me, please," I said, trying not to shiver. "There was a storm... my family and I were separated. I'm trying to find them."

The man's eyes softened, only a little, but enough to tell me he was sympathizing. His sword remained near my throat. "Your name?"

"Garrett Sullivan."

The man's face quickly went from firm and business-like to complete disbelief as soon as I told him my name. He immediately lowered his sword and flickered his eyes to my captor.

"Bruce, let him go," the man said, breathing heavily.

The dwarf hesitated before scoffing. I heard him unsheathe his dagger before slicing right through the ties. Once I was free, I rubbed my wrists, and nodded my thanks to the man in armor.

"Uh, thanks," I said awkwardly. "C-can you guys help me—?"

Before I could even finish asking my question, the man in armor knelt on one knee and bowed his head, sticking his sword in the ground. I stared at him, unable to speak.

"Lord Garrett, please forgive us," the man said. "We were only patrolling our borders. We had no idea it was you."

I was too stunned to say anything. Lord? Did he just address me as *Lord?*

The dwarf—Bruce—scoffed again. "Charles, stop making a fool of yourself! How do we even know he is who he claims to be?"

Charles looked defiantly at Bruce. "I *know*. He and his family have been gone five years, Bruce, and all of a sudden, a boy with red hair arrives with family in the apex of a war—"

I held my hands up. "War? Wait a second, okay? What is going on here?"

"The boy plays the fool quite well," Bruce commented as he circled around me.

Charles got to his feet. "Bruce, *look* at him. Look at him and tell me you don't see who I see in his face!"

Bruce ignored his comrade. I stared at the two of them expectantly. "Excuse me, sirs, but I'm still confused. What are you two even talking about?"

Charles sheathed his sword and held his hand out towards the forest. "Come with us and we will explain everything, Milord."

Everything in me was telling me not to go further into the woods with two strange men I just met. Caitlin forced me enough times to watch crime documentaries with her to know what could happen. But the urge to get my family back won out.

"Alright," I said. "Please lead the way."

Chapter 1

Garrett

Charles and Bruce took me on a journey through the forest, with Charles leading the way and Bruce staying close on my tail. He probably thought I'd make a run for it. I admit, the thought crossed my mind. There were bells going off in my head to not go, but I forced those thoughts away and only thought of my family. I had to. If there was any chance of seeing them again, I had no choice but to trust these men.

It was getting dark, which only made the woods look a lot scarier. I swear, I thought I heard crunching leaves in the distance and whispering in the air.

But that was impossible.

We took a narrow path leading downhill until we came upon a waterfall. Careful not to slip, I stepped across the wet rocks and leaves and followed Charles into a cave behind the waterfall. The rushing water was deafening and powerful. I knew that it could probably knock me on my ass if I wasn't careful enough. I pressed my palm against the freezing cave wall and steadily continued on. It was pitch black, but I could still hear Charles's footsteps in front of me.

Besides him, all I heard in the cave were drops of water hitting the floor.

"Are we getting close?" I asked.

"Why? We are not going fast enough for ya?" Bruce demanded.

"Peace, Bruce," Charles said firmly. "We are almost there, Milord. Just keep going straight."

I kept my mouth shut and did as I was told. I was getting very tired of Bruce snapping at me, but in the end, he was the one with the sword.

Eventually, I saw a light at the end. Okay, so it was a tunnel within a cave. Cool. It wasn't a bright light like a lit torch. It was moonlight. Squinting, I could also make out branches covered in long green leaves ahead. Charles brushed the leaves away and held them back for me and then Bruce.

I realized that Charles and Bruce had taken me to a village just outside the entrance. There were houses made from logs close to a few gardens. In the center of everything was a fire pit. Something was tied to a stick roasting just a few inches above the fire. Upon closer inspection, I could make out a few rabbits. People were walking all around the village, some pushing wagons, others carrying game or sacks of fruits and vegetables. They stared at us suspiciously as we made our entrance.

No. Not us. Me.

Nervously, I looked back at Charles. He cocked his head forward, offering me a small smile. "It's alright."

Charles led the way to the fire pit which made the villagers stop in their tracks and turn to him. So Charles is the one in charge? Makes sense.

"Everyone hear me," Charles said, his voice booming. "While on patrol, Sir Bruce and I came upon this young man—" he gestured to me "—in the forest alone. We first thought him to be an enemy; whether that would be of Scathe's or Jotnar's, we weren't sure. But he has revealed himself to be Lord Garrett Sullivan of the Witch Domain!"

Everyone went silent, exchanging shocked looks with each other. I gaped at Charles.

Wait, what? Witch Domain? What's a Witch Domain?

I quickly stood beside him and looked at the villagers. "Whoa, whoa, whoa! Hold on! I never said I was part of this Witch Domain! I never even said I was a lord! I just wanted to—!"

"You are eighteen, are you not?" Charles interrupted. "As of today, August 23rd? You said you and your family have been separated?"

This was way too much. "Yes, but—"

"You have an aunt, yes?" Charles interrupted again. "Megan O'Dwyer... She's your caretaker, no?"

Okay...maybe he just heard me call her name? He and Bruce were close enough to hear before jumping me.

"Yeah—"

"You have four sisters, correct, Milord? One of them is your twin? Caitlin?"

I never told him my sisters' names. How could he possibly know? I said nothing in response. I don't understand...

"Sir Charles, it doesn't seem as though the Witch Lord remembers us," someone in the crowd said sullenly.

"I agree," someone else said.

Sir Charles acknowledged their words, but his eyes remained determined. "Regardless, this young man is our Lord! He has come to reclaim what Scathe and Jotnar have stolen from all of us!"

Before I could argue even further, a young woman stepped out from the crowd. My heart stopped immediately. The woman looked to be my age with snow white skin, icy blue eyes, and wore a lavender tunic with black pants and boots. She was beautiful, like an angel.

"You don't remember any of us, Milord?" the woman asked gently.

Her eyes looked somber, like she couldn't believe any of this, either. I studied her features. Something about her looked familiar, like something out of a dream that I had a long time ago.

"I can't say I do and I'm sorry," I said quickly. "I just—Five years ago, my family and I had been in an accident; my sisters and I lost our parents and our memories—"

"Strange how you and your sisters have lost all your memories prior to five years ago," Bruce said gruffly.

I stared down at Bruce. "That's what our aunt Megan told us. She would never lie to us about that."

"Perhaps not with malicious intent," Sir Charles pointed out.

I glared. "Are you calling my aunt a liar?"

"Watch your mouth, boy," Bruce growled as he reached for his dagger.

Sir Charles held up a hand to stop Bruce. "Do not threaten our lord, Bruce. Milord, if I may, five years ago, not long after Princess Alison was born, you six disappeared. You vanished during the siege of the Capital."

I did a double take. "*Princess?* Wait, so...I'm so confused..."

"May I explain what happened?" Sir Charles asked politely.

Doing my best to hide my shaking, I nodded once and crossed my arms.

"Jotnar and Scathe are the two who are at war in our world," Sir Charles began. "They are witches as well...but they are *far* from good. They are monsters—tyrants. They have been at war with each other even before you disappeared. The Witch Domain, you see, is the Capital of Clover Talamh, our kingdom. It is made up of different domains."

"The Human Domain," Bruce listed, "the Dwarf Domain, the Fairy Domain, the Dragon Domain."

I snapped my head at him. "Dragons?"

Bruce rolled his eyes before sitting on a log before the fire pit.

"You see, your mother had left your father and remarried a few years after Lady Brigit was born," Sir Charles went on. "Lady Amelia Sullivan married King Eluf Helvig of the Witch Domain. Not long after, she gave birth to Princess Nora and then Princess Alison."

Suddenly out of breath, I crouched down on one knee. I...I couldn't believe any of this. My mother *remarried?* Why didn't any of us know about that? It's not like I care that Nora and Alison have a different father than Caitlin, Brigit, and I; it's just the fact that none of us *knew*.

"H-How did we disappear?" I asked.

"That, we don't know," Sir Charles explained. "The castle—your home—was suddenly attacked weeks after the birth of Princess Alison. Your whole family, exempt from the Lady Megan, your sisters, and yourself, were murdered."

We had more family? It wasn't just us? Why didn't we remember?

"Months went by after the siege, but none of you could be found," Sir Charles continued. "Jotnar and Scathe's war went on. Their armies spread violence and fear throughout our lands. Homes were destroyed and people were tortured and killed. Scathe would leave his prisoners to rot and die while Jotnar would torture his prisoners. Children were forced to become either their servants, experiments, or they were forced to become part of their armies."

I swallowed the bile that rose up in the back of my throat. Innocent people were tortured and *killed* by these monsters. CHILDREN!

"But why?" I asked quietly.

"Do either really need a reason?" Sir Bruce asked harshly.

"We are the few that managed to escape," Sir Charles went on. "We are the survivors of the Human Domain, which borders the Witch Domain. Sir Bruce had just joined our Brotherhood not long after the siege happened."

Bruce wouldn't look at me. His jaw was clenched, like he was trying to keep himself from snapping at me further.

"As for why you have no memories, that could be due to a spell," Sir Charles said. "It could be an effect of your disappearance or perhaps your aunt spelled you to forget."

No... No, she wouldn't...she wouldn't…

Caitlin

My head was spinning. I was cold and lying against something flat and hard and wet. I was in and out of consciousness and I felt like I was floating on something. I thought I was hearing things, like waves moving around me.

Eventually, I heard voices. They were far away and deep. Again, my world went to sleep.

Suddenly, I felt lighter than before. I was being lifted up somewhere. No, I wasn't floating. Something long and rough was lifting me up. I tried lifting my head, but it felt so heavy.

My head rolled to the side and I went to sleep once more.

Next thing I knew, I heard feet moving on wooden floors. They sounded heavy like boots. There were people talking, too. Were the girls watching TV or something? Why can't they keep the volume down? It's too loud.

When did I fall asleep? Was the storm just a nightmare?

Then I felt the back of someone's fingers brush my cheek. This touch sent a shock through me, a feeling I *really* didn't like. Heart leaping from my throat,

I gasped and smacked the hand away, now wide awake. Ignoring the pounding in my head, I scooted backwards, putting as much space as possible between me and whoever this creep was.

It was a woman in a gray tunic with a black ascot holding a bowl of water in one hand and a cloth in the other. She was pale and about 5'6" with a brunette pixie cut.

"Wh-Who are you?" I demanded.

The woman opened her mouth to speak when someone interrupted her.

"My nurse, Sheila," the voice said.

I looked up at the stairs as a woman approached. I instantly froze. I'm on what looks to be a pirate ship and the woman looking at me now, based on how she's dressed, is the captain of this ship. She was a dark-skinned woman with black dreadlocks swept over on one side, big brown eyes, and wore a black shirt with a long purple tailcoat and hat with a long white feather sticking out from the side. She wore long golden hoops and a black pair of pants with a sword sheathed in her belt.

The captain cocked her head to the side, dismissing Sheila, and looked back to me. I realized I was lying on a long wooden table, just a couple of feet from the side of the ship. The captain stood over me.

"So you're awake," the captain said. "That's good."

I hesitated. "Yeah, I guess, but I have no idea where I am."

The captain chuckled, taking a seat beside me. "You're on my ship, sweetheart."

I blushed. "N-No, I mean...Where am I exactly? What's your name?"

The captain gave me a confused look. She looked just as weirded out as I felt. "I am Captain Raina Murphy, captain of this ship, the Crimson Kraken. Currently, we are sailing through the Raven Ocean."

I stared at Captain Raina in disbelief. "I-I'm sorry. I still have no clue where I am."

Captain Raina's eyebrows shot up. "We are heading towards Asmund Rock, west of the kingdom known as Fenrir-Himinn."

I blinked a few times before breaking out into nervous laughter. "Yeah, uh, I'm really sorry. I still have no clue where I am."

Captain Raina tilted her head to the side curiously. "You don't know at all?"

I shook my head. "I guess I hit my head harder than I thought."

"But how? Were you on another ship? Can you remember anything at all? Was there an attack?"

I shrugged.

Captain Raina sighed. "Well, I am just glad that we found you when we did. You were floating on a board in the middle of the ocean."

My eyes widened. "The ocean?"

The captain nodded once. "Do you recall your name at all?"

"Caitlin," I said. "Caitlin Sullivan."

Something in the captain's eyes changed once I told her my name; something shifted.

Then a smile appeared on her face. "Caitlin Sullivan?"

My heart started racing. "Yes. Why do you ask?" The captain raised a brow.

I lowered my eyes. "Why do you ask, Captain?"

Captain Raina smiled again, followed by a humorous chuckle. "You, Caitlin, are the key to my revenge."

Revenge?

"Revenge for what?" I asked.

But the captain was already up and picking up some rope. I immediately knew where this was going. I jumped off the table and started running only to be blocked by a man (at least six feet tall) with two swords in his hands. He stared down at me just as more members of the crew formed a wall on either side of him. Another tall pirate grabbed me by my shoulders and turned me around roughly. Captain Raina took deliberate steps forward, a gleam in her eye. "Come now, Treasure," Captain Raina said. "There's no need to run." What the hell have I gotten myself into?

Chapter 2

Brigit

I rolled onto my stomach, something I did unconsciously while sleeping. I didn't think anything was out of the ordinary. I did have this crazy fucking nightmare, though. It was my older brother and sister's birthday and just as they blew out their candles, a goddamn storm rolled right the fuck out of nowhere and we all died.

I still don't know why I dreamt of a crazy storm. And right as they blew out their candles?

It was like magic. But magic isn't real and dreams are weird like that, right?

Then tell me why...as I roll onto my side...my eyes flutter open...and I see a huge-ass forest miles underneath me...and that I'm lying on the side of a *fucking cliff*!

I let out a scream so loud that birds *yeeted* themselves out of the fucking trees and flew away so fast, you'd think it was the end of the world. I pushed myself backwards and scooted away as far as I could. I thought I was gonna have a heart attack!

What the *fuck*?

Adrenaline pumping, I climbed to my feet, careful not to trip, and looked around. I was on the top of a mountain and there was a forest right behind me. The sky was getting dark and there was nothing else around except for more mountains on the horizon.

The wind blew hard. I wrapped my arms around myself and looked around. How the fuck…?

Was…was the storm not a nightmare after all? Did we all die in the storm? Oh, God! Am I dead?

My breathing became shallow like someone just punched me in the stomach. Sweat dripped down my forehead as I crouched to the grass. Tears pricked my eyes as I tried to steady my breathing.

This can't be real! This can't be real! This can't be real! This can't be real!

Maybe I'm still dreaming! Maybe this is all just one big nightmare!

Suddenly, the earth began to shake. I looked straight ahead, just towards the edge of the cliff. What I saw scared the living shit out of me. (Even more, I mean.) The mountain was *crumbling*. It was crumbling into pieces of grass and soil, melting like ice cream and catapulting to the trees below. The ground continued to shake as I turned and ran into the woods behind me. I had no idea what the fuck was going on, but I sure as hell wasn't going to stick around and find out.

My lungs felt like they were on fire and my throat was drier than any desert you could think of. My legs turned to Jell-O, but I knew stopping was not an option, especially since the ground behind me was disappearing rapidly.

It was catching up to me! I knew right then that I wasn't in a nightmare. This was fucking *real* and I was about to die!

Or so I thought.

"Hold on!" a man yelled over the crumbling earth.

I couldn't even react because I was literally swooped off the ground and into the air. I let out another scream and clung on to whoever grabbed me. It was a boy, not much older than me, with tan skin and long black hair. He was wearing different shades of green clothing and had…pointy ears…?

…And we were swinging on a rope…shot from an arrow?

Maybe this is some crazy fever dream, after all?

The two of us swung higher up into the air just as something in the corner of my eye caught my attention. It was getting closer, whatever it was. The elf let go of the rope and the two of us fell—only for a second—before landing on something big and soft. I looked down at whatever was carrying us and…

"Holy shit!" I exclaimed.

The animal we were riding on was a fucking griffin! Its fur was sandy brown and its wings were long and dark chocolate brown. They were so long! Each wing had to be almost seven feet wide! The front of its legs were actually talons, just like a bird, and its back legs and tail looked just like a lion's! The head did look like a bird's, but there was also a pair of ears on either side of its head. It was incredible!

I clutched to the elf's shirt, now sitting behind him. I was breathing normally again, but I was still shaking like a leaf. He looked back at me. His eyes were brown and striking. It was like I was looking at two moons.

"Are you alright, miss?" he asked.

I was about to answer when something overtook me and I blacked out once again.

Megan

The first thing I did when I came to was beginning my search for finding my family. We had all somehow been separated when the portal swallowed us. I don't know how it was possible, but we were back. We were *back* in Clover Talamh.

Magic doesn't exist in the Other Realm. Someone knows. Someone knows about us and who we are—that we're from this world—but who? The only way we could have been brought to this world is if someone from our homeland summoned us on this side.

No matter. That can wait until later. I woke up underneath a willow tree in a meadow and am now heading towards a forest. Which forest this is, I don't know. I haven't lived here for five years...not since Alison was born.

All the trees looked the same to me, but I kept going. My intuition was telling me not to give up, to continue in this direction. My only living family was out here somewhere and they had no idea about any of this. Alison and Nora were too young to remember any of this and the older three just *don't*.

Luckily, I went hunting enough times with my father as a child to find my way out of the forest. Unfortunately, the sun was nowhere to be seen and the stars had yet to come out. Instead, I mentally took note of each landmark I passed: some boulders, rotting wood, sometimes even a feather or two.

Then I came across a slope—a downwards slope. I walked steadily down it (which was a miracle, considering how much of a klutz I've always been), my feet crunching the leaves and twigs. Soon, I heard running water. I thanked the Gods silently before hurrying towards the sound. If I can just get to it…

Sure enough, the river was in my line of sight in a matter of seconds. There were a few rocks as long as my waist further down as well as a few leaves floating past.

"Yes! Yes!" I cheered.

I was only a few yards away before my ankle gave out and I fell on my side. I saw white and gasped for air.

Dear GODS! That hurt!

I rubbed my ankle, chastising myself for being such a fool. For a few seconds, I couldn't move—didn't want to, but I thought of my nieces and nephew. They need me. I know they're alive, I can feel it. But I can't get to them if I'm in no shape to walk. Straining, I crawled the rest of the way down the hill, simultaneously ignoring my screaming ankle. Once I was only a few inches from the river, I held my hand out, reaching for the water. My fingers began to tingle. I imagined the water floating in the air, like it was defying gravity. The water did just that, turning into a long arm-like being before reaching out to my fingers. The water floated around my wrist and over my shoulder, swirling down like a cat's tail all the way down to my injured ankle. I felt the coolness of the water as it wrapped itself around my ankle before settling gently on it. The pain subsided as soon as the water vanished into the air. Carefully, I moved my foot left to right.

No pain.

I pushed myself up, stifling a groan. I am officially too old for this.

But the feeling of using my magic after five years felt great! Better than great! I looked down at my hands, in time to see the glowing sky blue magic fade away.

My head shot up at the sound of twigs being snapped. I looked across the river to see two figures getting closer. I put my hands out, ready to summon my magic again when the two figures came into view. They were wearing armor and carried axes. One was a man with dark hair and the other was a woman—slightly taller than her companion—with short light hair. They saw me and stopped. The woman pointed her ax at me.

"Who are you?" the woman asked.

My hands tingled, warming up as sky blue light began to glow on my palms. Their eyes widened.

"I should ask the same of you," I said.

The two exchanged a look before turning back to me. "Are you Lady Megan O'Dwyer?" the man asked.

I tilted my head to the side. "Who are you to ask?"

"We'll take that as a yes, then," the woman said. She stepped into the water and walked towards me. "Do you know who you are?"

"Yes, I know who I am. Now, if you would, please tell me where I am exactly. I know this is Clover Talamh, but I would like to know my exact location."

The woman held out a hand to me. "The Raven's Eye Woods, near the borders of the Dwarf Domain. Come with us. There's a few people who would like to see you."

I raised my hand. "And how do I know you aren't leading me somewhere dangerous?"

"Listen to your intuition, Lady Megan," the woman said, still holding her hand out. "You know that we are not a threat to you."

Slowly, I lowered my hand, willing the magic away. I took the woman's hand and she led me across the river and into the woods.

After a few minutes of walking, the two led me to a small camp. There were tents pitched up and everyone was wearing armor. There weren't just humans here, but centaurs, satyrs, goblins, and a few dwarves. There was a long wooden table a few yards away with weapons laying on top. Some stopped whatever they were doing or saying and stared at me as we entered.

A man inside a tent threw the curtain aside—a man I recognized. I immediately stopped in my tracks and stared. My heart stopped. By the look on the man's face, so had his. Lord Angus of the Human Domain was staring back at me. He hadn't changed much; he still had olive skin, green eyes, and black messy hair and a goatee. Well, yes, there was a bit of gray in there, but my own red hair wasn't much better.

He looked just as I had remembered him.

Angus stepped towards me, not blinking even once. He stopped a few inches from me and looked me over. I did my best to not turn away.

"Megan…" he said my name like it was almost forbidden. "You…you're really here…"

I gave him a small smile. "Yes, I…I suppose I am."

Angus reached out like he wanted to touch my shoulder but immediately thought better of it and pulled his hand back.

"How did you survive all these years?" Angus asked in almost a whisper. "I thought you were—"

"Auntie!" two little voices screamed.

I looked past Angus to see Nora and Alison racing out from one of the other tents before slamming into me. I held each one of them in a hug, not caring about what anyone else thought as I cried. I held the girls close and tight in each arm before looking back at Angus who was smiling the whole time.

"We found them wandering alone in the forest," a satyr said, nodding politely. "They were a bit frightened, but I promise, no harm came to either of them."

I smiled in return to the satyr. "Thank you." I looked back at Angus. "You, too."

Angus raised a hand to stop me. "It matters not. However, it does seem as though we have a lot to discuss."

I kept the girls close as Angus led me back into his tent. It was large and spacious with a bedroll in one corner and a few swords in the other. Adjacent to that was a dummy, presumably where he puts his armor.

"Thank you for returning my nieces safely to me," I said, "but you should know that there are three more out there somewhere."

Angus's brows went up. "Lord Garrett and Ladies Caitlin and Brigit are here as well?"

"Somewhere, yes," I said. "Today was Garrett and Caitlin's eighteenth birthday. They blew out their candles and then all of a sudden, a storm rolled in and now here we are."

"You were all separated, then?"

"It seems."

"If I may ask, where have you been this whole time, Megan?"

I rubbed the heads of the girls before answering. "We were sent to this different dimension, the Other Realm. To this day, I still don't know how. I don't even know how we got back."

"Obviously with magic," Angus said, more to himself than me. "But who could have sent you all away and brought you back? That sort of power is strong…"

"And forbidden," I added.

Angus crossed his arms and nodded. "You weren't harmed, were you?"

I shook my head. "No. There were no brigands where I was. But even if there were, they wouldn't have—"

"I don't mean brigands," Angus interrupted. "I mean Shadow Knights." I cocked my head to the side and stared at him.

"Shadow Knights…Scathe's men…" Angus tried to clarify.

I sighed before giving him a small shrug. "I have no idea who any of those are."

Angus's jaw tightened as he nodded thoughtfully. "Then, indeed, we have *much* to discuss."

Chapter 3

Garrett

Sir Charles led me to a house with Bruce right behind him after we all separated. I still couldn't wrap my head around any of this. There was a whole *dimension* at war...a world my family and I are from. So why didn't any of us remember? Did my aunt know? *Does* she know? I still have a hard time believing I'm a witch lord.

I should have known better. I have no memories prior to Alison's birth. I can't remember who I am...who I was…

If Aunt Megan always knew, why didn't she tell us? Why lie? Why the hell did I just go along with it this whole time? I never questioned my life-—My parents are dead and I'm the man in this family. That's all I knew and apparently that's all I needed to know.

But is there really more to me? Everyone so far has been calling me a noble, a witch, and stuff like that, but is this who I'm really supposed to be? A witch? A savior? I *can't* be any of that! I barely passed algebra! How am I supposed to help stop a war between evil sorcerers?

It was supposed to be simple. Caitlin and I were going to be starting college soon. She'd be getting her degree in archaeology and I'd be going for an art degree. Caitlin has always wanted to see the world. She's always been obsessed with the History channel and Nat Geo. Her idol in middle school was Rick Steves; Cait always wanted to be like him: to travel, learn languages, discover new things. For as long as I can remember, which isn't very much apparently, she would drag me out of bed and downstairs to watch *The Mummy* movies with Brandon Frasier. (Though it could have also been because she had a crush on Evelyn. I mean, who didn't have a crush on her?)

I have just always loved art and its history. My head has constantly been in the clouds—which never did me any favors with certain teachers. I'd get caught doodling on my scrap paper during classes, but that's mostly because it helped me think.

Caitlin and I were never popular in school. Just the opposite, actually. I had some friends, but we had different lunch periods, so I usually sat alone. So did Caitlin. No one liked her, apparently. Not many kids liked any of us because they thought we were weird. Turns out they were right.

I know Cait and the girls are alright. I know Aunt Megan's alive, too. If I can just figure out where they are—

"Milord," Sir Charles said, snapping me out of my thoughts. "Welcome to our quarters."

It was a one-bedroom home—large enough for a small family—with a table a few feet from the door with a bench on either side. There were a few bedrolls on different sections of the house and a map pinned to the walls on the left.

I smiled. "Thank you, Sir."

Bruce huffed. "Not to your liking, boy?"

I glared at him. "I *do* like it!"

"I am so sorry not everyone has the privilege to live in a magical castle—"

"I never said—!"

Sir Charies put a hand between us, cutting the tension. "Bruce, do not put words in his mouth. You know he said nothing of the sort." Seriously! What is Bruce's deal?

"I'll be right back," I said, heading for the door.

"And where are you going?" Bruce demanded.

"Out for some air," I answered curtly.

"Would you like an escort?" Sir Charles asked.

"You better go," Bruce answered before I could. "He may be trying to escape."

I spun around to scowl at Bruce. "Oh, come on!"

"Gentlemen? Is everything alright?"

Outside my new house was the beautiful woman from before. She looked at us cautiously as Sir Charles answered with, "Yes, Lady Katrina, just a misunderstanding."

So that's her name. Katrina. *Katrina.* Oddly enough, her name did sound familiar, like a song sung to me as a child.

"Would you mind escorting Lord Garrett to the fire pit?" Sir Charles asked. "Anya should be cooking still."

"Of course." Katrina nodded politely.

I gulped. I followed Katrina back to the fire pit where I was given a bowl of rabbit stew and water. I never had rabbit stew before.

Katrina led me to a stump where I sat and ate. The stew was pretty good. She took the stump next to me and watched me curiously. A few times it was like she wanted to say something, but never did. She tucked a few strands of hair behind her ear. She really is beautiful. I finished my stew and sipped my water before clearing my throat awkwardly.

"So...Katrina, huh?"

Katrina's eyes met mine and she smiled. "Yes. I'm Katrina Wilde from the Human Domain."

I smiled back at her. "Yeah?"

"Yes."

A moment of silence came upon us. God, I'm bad at this. This is probably why I never had a girlfriend. Come on, Gare! Say something to her!

"So, do you have any family back home?" I asked.

Not that, you idiot!

Katrina's face fell and she laced her fingers together. She stared at the ground. "No. I have no family."

God, I'm an idiot.

"I'm sorry," I said.

Katrina shook her head before looking back at me. "Not your fault. My mother died in childbirth, her and my brother. His name was meant to be Noah. I was seven when we lost them."

"We?"

"My father and myself. He was an animal healer. My mother was a farmer. The two met when they were my age when one of her cows fell pregnant. They eventually married and had me."

I nodded along, listening intently the whole time. Her whole family was gone. I can't even imagine what that pain must feel like.

"Katrina, if I may ask, how did your father die?" I asked. "If you don't feel comfortable answering, though, you don't have to."

Katrina fiddled with the end of her ponytail. "He was killed during the siege of the Witch Domain."

My eyes widened. "But I thought you said you're from the Human Domain?"

"I am. Months after we buried my mother and brother, we were brought to the Witch Domain. Your horse fell ill and we were summoned. That's how I met you."

I tore my eyes away. She and her father came to my home because my horse got sick. I know she said I'm not at fault, but I can't help but feel that I am.

I took a swig of my water. "Hey, how about we play a game?"

Katrina cocked her head to the side. "A game?"

"Well, I mean, it's more like an ice breaker."

"I'm afraid the winter is not for a few more months…"

I laughed. "No, uh…from my world—my other world—it's a means of getting to know someone else."

Katrina's eyes lit up with realization and curiosity. "Okay."

I smiled. "Okay. This one is called Two Truths and a Lie. The game is pretty much how the name sounds. We tell each other two things about ourselves that are true and one thing that is made up."

Katrina perked up. "Sounds easy."

She looked like a golden retriever puppy. I ducked my head before she could see me blush. "Would you like to go first?"

"How about you go first?" Katrina suggested. "Just so I have an example."

"Sure thing. Let's see…" Don't freak her out, Sullivan. "My favorite color is magenta. I once went on a boat as part of a school field trip. My favorite animal is a wolf."

Katrina pressed her lips together. I could almost see the wheels in her head turning. "The second one is a lie."

"Correct!" I beamed. "I did go on a boat once, but it wasn't part of a field trip. My aunt had an old boss with a boat and he invited us out to sail and have dinner with his family. He was always really good with us."

"That sounds nice."

"It was. Now, it's your turn."

Katrina thought for a moment. She looked like the embodiment of sunshine itself. How she's been through so much trauma and still chooses to be nice to me just tells me even more about her.

"My favorite fruit is cherries," she said after a minute. "I'm afraid of the dark and I know how to play the violin."

I took a minute to consider each option. It would make sense if she was afraid of the dark, especially with all the evil I've heard about. Who doesn't have a fear of the dark? And I don't doubt for even a second that she knows how to play the violin, so…

The first one. She hates cherries. They were her mother's favorite.

"You're not fond of cherries," I say at last. "They remind you of your mom."

A small 'o' of surprise formed on Katrina's lips. "You remember that?"

I stared. "Remember what?"

She shook her head, smiling sadly. "Nothing."

I was just going with what my intuition was telling me. "I didn't mean to upset you, Katrina. I'm sorry."

"I'm not upset with you, Lord Garrett."

"Oh, uh, you can just call me Garrett," I said quickly. "The whole 'Lord' thing just doesn't sit well with me."

It never has.

I snapped my head to the side. There was no one near us. The cook and everyone else had gone into their houses for the night. But I heard a voice, one that I didn't recognize. It sounded like it was *right* next to me!

"Garrett?" Katrina asked. "Are you alright?"

I can't tell her that I thought I heard a voice. She'd either laugh at me or look at me like I was a psycho.

"Yeah, sorry."

Katrina stared thoughtfully for a second before getting to her feet. "Well, come on. I'm going to show you the perimeter."

"Perimeter?"

"So you don't get lost again. Besides, with the war between Jotnar and Scathe, the woods are not safe."

"So how have you guys not been found yet?"

"We're being cloaked by Elven magic."

"Oh...noted."

I set my dishes by the fire pit and followed Katrina around the village. She pointed out the houses and where hers was before having me follow her back towards the waterfall. "Any questions?"

"No, I think I've got it."

"And remember: Don't leave the village without Sir Bruce, Sir Charles, or myself. It's dangerous, especially for you."

"But why?"

"Because you are one of the last witches alive in the kingdom. As long as you have air in your lungs and power inside of you, you will be seen as a threat by Jotnar and Scathe."

I wanted to ask her more questions, but by the time we got back to the village, I was exhausted. I walked her back to her house and started for mine.

"Garrett?"

"Yes?"

"Happy birthday."

"...Thank you. Goodnight, Katrina."

"Goodnight."

As I walked into my home, I noticed Sir Bruce and Sir Charles were already preparing for bed. They acknowledged me.

"Milord, tomorrow you and I will begin training," Sir Charles said as he put on a night shirt. "It's best if you know how to use a sword."

I pressed my lips together. "Fair enough. Goodnight."

"Goodnight, Milord."

"..."

I crawled on to my bedroll and before I knew it, I was asleep. Only this time, something was different. My eyes shot open at the sound of an explosion. I stumbled and fell as the ground beneath me trembled violently. A flock of blackbirds rocketed from the trees behind me, cawing in sync as they flew away. I forced myself to run, ignoring the burning in my lungs. I swallowed the bile that rose in my throat as a castle came into view below the dark gray clouds. It was on fire.

Then I was in the cobblestone streets. People were screaming and running past me in a panic. I bumped into someone's shoulder but pushed on. What I saw next scared me to the core:

There was a man in black armor. Only half his face was exposed.

His eyes...

His dark eyes narrowed at me from across the road. He was wearing a long black cape, too, that swished in the wind. He was wearing an iron face mask and held a long double-bladed axe in his gloved hands and his shoulder-length brown hair was matted in dirt and ash.

I struggled to get away as he started marching towards me. My feet felt heavy and I couldn't breathe. The man in armor knelt on one knee and raised his ax over his head before throwing it at mine. The last thing I saw before I woke up was the darkness in his eyes.

Brigit

My eyelids felt heavy as I forced them open. Great. I passed out. Fucking great. Up until today that never happened.

I smelled something before I was able to actually wake up. Wet grass? My head spun as I sat up.

Blinking, I took in my new surroundings. I was lying on a gold-framed bed with a forest green comforter and sky blue pillows. There were vines crawling up the mint green walls. I looked up at the ceiling, noticing that it was different shades of green swirling around like a hurricane. It looked like someone dunked a paintbrush in different paint canisters and blended them together. It was actually really pretty. Across the room from me was a balcony with golden doors. From where I was lying, I could see that it was lighter than it had been before.

How long have I been asleep?

I rubbed my forehead, brushing away the few strands of hair that tickled my face just as someone knocked on the door.

"Are you awake, miss?" a voice asked.

I straightened my back. That was a guy's voice, and if I'm right, that voice belongs to the elf that Tarzaned our asses out of danger. But I still don't know who this is. I need to be careful.

"Come in," I say.

The door opened. I was right. The elf from before was standing a few feet away from me, respectfully stopping near the end of the bed. I watched him carefully. He doesn't look like he's a threat, but if I'm going to escape and find my family, I need to find out where I am and what is even fucking going on.

"Rest well?" the elf asked.

I nodded. "How long was I out?"

"Almost a full day."

Almost a day? Even for me, that's a record. "Where am I?"

"One of the spare rooms in my castle."

My jaw fell open. "Your *castle?* So, wait. Are you…?"

The elf bowed his head, his hands folded neatly behind him. "Ah, yes. I was told of your condition. I am Prince Salem of the Elf Domain in Sanctuarium."

I gaped at him. "A prince? You're a prince?"

The elf–Salem–nodded his head.

I threw my legs over the side of the bed and stood up. We still had some distance between each other, but I bowed to my waist. "Your Highness."

I never met royalty before. Hopefully, I was bowing right.

"Rise, Lady Brigit," Salem said. "There is no need for formalities."

I did as I was told and stared awkwardly at Salem. Then, if I wasn't already feeling self-conscious enough, my stomach chose that time to growl. Salem smiled politely.

"Come," he said. "You must be hungry."

I followed Salem out of the room. "Yeah. I am. I haven't eaten since...yesterday. Even then, it wasn't a lot."

Salem stopped in his tracks, causing me to almost bump into him. I watched as he offered me his arm. My heart started beating so fast, I thought it was going to burst. No guy has *ever* been this nice to me. I did have some friends back in Prospect, mostly guys, but no one ever showed me...ever treated me this way. After a few seconds of staring at his arm, I took it. We were fairly close at this point.

We started walking. Salem was nice enough to walk at a steady pace for me as he led us down the hallway. The walls were not even bare. Most had windows as long as me or paintings of other elves. There were potted plants outside every door and tall candelabra lit every few feet from the other.

"So, you said that this place is called Sanctuarium?" I asked.

Salem smiled. "Yes. We used to be the closest allies to Clover Talamh. We are neighbors, actually."

"Clover Tal...what?"

"Talamh."

"Tal...ham?"

Salem chuckled. "Talamh. Tal-om."

"Tal-om. Talahm."

"Very good, Lady Brigit."

I hid a smile. "How come you know my name? I never told it to you back in the forest. What even happened back there, anyway?"

We started descending down a long flight of stairs–marble, by the way–as Salem suddenly became solemn.

"My mother has been having visions," Salem started. "She has seen you each time on the top of the Emerald Mountain. It is miles from this castle. Or it was. It crumbled."

"I noticed. How is that even possible?"

"Is there no magic from where you are from, Lady Brigit?"

"No."

Salem continued on with his story. "Magic courses through this world. It is all around us. But the war between Scathe and Jotnar, two evil sorcerers, has been draining it from this world. Magic is what fuels this world. Without it, all will perish." He turned to me. "You are from Clover Talamh."

I snapped my head towards him. "What?"

"It is true," Salem said. "My family was once part of Clover Talamh. There had once been an Elf Domain in your kingdom...before King Arne stole the crown from its then ruler. The elves wanted nothing to do with this new king and so we migrated to this land and built our own kingdom. The capital of Clover Talamh is the Witch Domain, your home." I stumbled, almost falling down the stairs before Salem caught me.

"Are you alright?" he asked.

"Yeah, I'm great," I said as I steadied myself. "Say that again? Did you say I'm from the Witch Domain?"

"You are correct," Salem said. He watched me closely as we continued down the stairs, making sure I wasn't going to trip again. "You have lived there since you were born. That makes you a witch."

Salem took me down another hallway, passing servants on the way. I took all this in. I should be surprised, but for some reason, I'm not. I don't know how, but I feel like I've known for a while.

"So how do I not remember?" I asked.

"That, I do not know," Salem said. "All I know is that five years ago, the Capital was attacked. You and your family then disappeared."

"How?"

"I wish I knew, Milady."

Salem and I walked into the dining area. There was a huge balcony with a staircase heading down. I didn't get a close enough look with my fear of heights and all, but my guess is that we had to be twenty stories up. We had a forest view with mountains out in the distance. The sky was completely white— no sign of the sun anywhere. The table was long and oval-shaped with mahogany dining chairs all around. There was a massive chandelier above the table, hanging not too low from the ceiling. Salem pulled out a chair for me.

Seriously, why is he being so nice to me? I didn't even know that anyone could be this nice.

Or maybe he is just being princely, Brigit!

I sat myself down just as a servant came into the dining room. He placed salad on a plate for Salem and myself and offered us small bowls of nuts and fruits. The servant poured us each a glass of water before bowing and dismissing himself.

Not that I'm not grateful, 'cause I am, but I'm starving. Where's the meat?

I stabbed some lettuce and plucked it into my mouth and the two of us ate in comfortable silence.

When we finished, Salem took me out into the courtyard and showed me three separate archery targets. Besides us and a few elves practicing themselves, there was no one.

"Tomorrow we shall begin training," Salem said. "Learning how to fight is essential in this world. It has been for generations."

"Okay, well, I've always wanted to try archery," I said. That's not all I wanted to say, so, "Thank you for helping me and giving me food."

Salem smiled at me. "You are welcome, Lady Brigit. However, I do believe that you have something else you would like to add."

How does he know me like a book already? "For years, it has just been my Aunt Megan, my brother, my sisters, and me. If the Capital was attacked and we managed to escape, does that mean we have more family out there somewhere?"

Salem's face changed. He went from looking poised to...mournful? "I do not know if any others survived. Many were lost that day, Milady, and not just in the Capital. Though, I wouldn't rule it out."

So maybe there is more family out there somewhere! Maybe I can find them once I find my aunt and siblings. "One more thing. What kind of witch am I?"

Salem's smile reappeared as he led me back inside. "You are a green witch."

"A green witch?" I asked.

"Yes. You know much about plants, herbs, and poisons. Your element is Earth itself. We can teach you how to harness your powers once again and you can bend it to your will. Right now, your gifts seem to be dormant."

A green witch, huh? Alright. "I hope I can do it."

Salem turned to me. "So do we."

Chapter 4

Caitlin

Captain Raina led me across the deck and into another room. My guess was that it was her cabin. There wasn't a bed, but there was a bay window with red cushions and a blanket. In the middle of the room was a round wooden table covered with maps and ink bottles. There were lanterns hanging on the walls and a globe model sitting next to the door and a hammock hanging adjacent to the table. I noticed underneath the table was a wooden door with a latch.

I wonder what's underneath?

Captain Raina untied my hands. "Have a seat."

Cautiously, I took a couple steps past her and planted myself in one of the seats. I glanced at the map as the captain moved by me and reached for one of the cushions on her bay window bench. It lifted up like a latch. The captain reached in and pulled out a book. She took quick strides back towards me and set the book in front of me. "I-I'm sorry," I stuttered. "I don't understand what—"

"Read the book," Captain Raina said firmly.

I stared at the book, sliding my hand across the cover. It was a beautiful book. The title was written in calligraphy and said *Book of Rituals and Magic*. It was a heavy book made with brown leather and the pages were slightly worn. Realization dawned on me.

"You think I have magic…" I said slowly.

"You *do* have magic, Treasure," Captain Raina said, smiling like a Cheshire. "And what luck, me finding you of all witches, of all places!"

I stared at the captain. "I think you have the wrong woman, Captain."

Captain Raina jammed her finger on the cover. "I don't make careless mistakes. You are Caitlin Sullivan of the Witch Domain. You can do magic."

My heart skipped a beat. "Witch? I'm not—"

"If you want to make it out alive, you will do magic," she threatened.

Glaring, I pushed the seat back and stood tall. "Quit interrupting me! You may be a pirate captain and that's great and all, but the least you can do is tell me what the hell is going on!"

Captain Raina stared hard at me for a few seconds before the smile returned on her lips.

"There's a fighter in you, after all. That's good."

My eyes fell to the ground before looking back into hers. "I am not a witch. I think that I would remember that detail."

"Well, clearly you don't," Captain Raina stated, crossing her arms. "As for why I need you, you have very special powers."

"What powers?" I asked in exasperation.

"You're a sea witch," Captain Raina said simply. "You can control water, though, not just salt water. It is the strongest force on earth. You *will* help me get to Asmund Rock." Will. *Not* can. *Not* may.

"I don't even have powers," I repeated in frustration.

"Yes, you do. You just need to remember how to use them."

"I can't!"

"You know what else you can't do? Escape. You won't be able to leave without doing what you must."

It doesn't matter what I tell Captain Raina. She'll just keep arguing. God, she's stubborn!

Suddenly, the ship jerked violently on the waves. The water became rocky as objects in the room began to slip and slide. I stumbled to the wall and slammed my palms flat against them.

The windows blew open, letting in the heavy rain.

Captain Raina clumsily pushed herself towards the door and out onto the ship's deck. Struggling to stay upright, I followed her out. The sky was darker than it had been seconds ago and the waves were rising higher and higher. Water splashed over the side of the ship as the crew ran all over, pulling on ropes to the sails. Captain Raina was nowhere in sight. I grabbed hold of the railing and climbed up the stairs. I was halfway up when a massive wave slammed into me, knocking me over. I spat out the salty water, coughing in the process, and made the rest of the way up. Captain Raina was at the wheel trying to get us out of the storm.

"Where did this storm come from?" I shouted over it. "It was fine minutes ago!"

"I'll get us out of this!" Captain Raina shouted back. "Just stay in my chambers and out of my way!"

"But—!"

Suddenly, I heard music—vocalizing. Everything else stopped. Something so soft and beautiful rose over the cacophony of the storm and the panic. It was mesmerizing...Who was singing...? So beautiful...

Hear my voice just below.

And let me tell you tales from long ago.

Follow me under the sea.

And be with me.

More vocalizing followed after that. It was the most beautiful singing I've ever heard in my life. It was haunting, but beautiful. I walked down the steps, following the singing. I didn't even care about the storm anymore.

Come with me to the ocean floor.

As all sailors have before.

Nothing else can be compared.

Leave all behind; don't be scared.

Let the waves carry you away.

Come now, we mustn't delay.

Have no fear; nothing's wrong.

Come to where all sailors have gone.

Humming. Long, beautiful humming echoed in my ears as I got closer to the side of the ship.

Hear my voice just below.

And let me tell you tales from long ago.

Follow me under the sea. And be with me.

Stay with me for eternity.

Together we shall be free.

Let me take you down,

Down to where men have drowned.

Another step closer. Then another. My memories became fuzzy. Why was I here again?

Who *was* I?

Forever we shall venture into the deep.

Your heart and soul I shall keep.

Leave all who you were astray. As the sun sets on this day.

I hear your call, my dear.

Let me whisper words of forever in your ear.

We shall be together forevermore. As you sink to the deep blue floor.

I reached the side of the boat and looked down over the side. There was a woman who had climbed up from...something...rope...? Maybe the waves raised her up...? She was beautiful. Her skin was as pale as moonlight and her eyes were doe-shaped and blue. Her brown hair was long and slicked back from the water. Her breasts were exposed and her tail was long and shimmered. There were hues of blue and purple on her tail and the moonlight danced off it.

Hear my voice just below.

And let me tell you tales from long ago.

Follow me under the sea. And be with me.

The woman caressed the side of my face, taking my chin between her thumb and forefinger. She pulled my face closer to hers and just as we were about to kiss—

A loud *BANG* went off! A gunshot! The woman screeched before recoiling. Her grip on the boat almost slipped, but she managed to hold on just a bit longer. I snapped out of the trance and stepped backwards. Captain Raina had pulled out her long sword. The beautiful woman who put me in the trance had a tail! A siren! A real life siren! And turns out, she wasn't so beautiful. Her entire face changed. Scales of gray and blue etched across her face and her teeth became long—at least a few inches long—and pointy.

"Oh, my God!" I gasped.

Raina swung her arm back and then aimed for the siren's neck. She scratched a line across her throat with her sword. I was expecting red blood to ooze from her neck, but instead, it was...clear... The siren's eyes fluttered shut before her grip loosened from the ship and she fell. I ran to the edge and watched as the siren's body turned into water and foam before even making contact with the ocean.

I looked back to Captain Raina. I almost died... She saved me...

Captain Raina threw her head up and shouted as loud as she could over the storm to those who were still alive. "The sirens are sinking the ship! Pull her out!"

Captain Raina gave me one last look before hurrying back up to the wheel. The crew pulled on the ropes, doing what they could to keep the sails secure. The singing continued, but they weren't going to get me this time. I ran to the bow and looked ahead. There was nothing.

The sirens were going to kill us all if the storm didn't do that first. My heart sank. I'll never be with my aunt or my brother and sisters again. I'll never find them.

Something came over me, but this time it wasn't a spell. It was anger. These monsters were not keeping me from the people I love! I will see my family again! And I am not going down this way!

My hands began to tingle. It was a sensation, kind of like when your hand falls asleep. It felt cool, too. Not chilly, but cool. Now...don't ask me how, because I don't know, but something happened. I don't even know how I did this, but I did...I stared deep into the water and held a hand out. The water stilled and the ship began to sail normally. The rain subsided and the lightning vanished. Everything was calm.

I relaxed, realizing that the sirens had vanished and that the crew was staring at me. I looked at each member, spotting Sheila staring at me in wonder. Finally, my gaze met Captain Raina's who had made her way over to me.

She smiled. "I knew you had it in you, Treasure."

Brigit

The next day, I woke up to find a long-sleeved lime green shirt hanging over a chair by my brand new desk along with a pair of black pants and brown boots. I got dressed and went straight to the staircase. Waiting for me was Salem. Our eyes met and I fought my hardest to not avert my gaze (which is hard when I suck at eye contact and find it extremely awkward.) Not to mention Salem's not...ugly...and nice...

He offered me his arm just like yesterday and I took it. (I mean, if he's offering, right?) We went downstairs and ate a quick breakfast that consisted of tea, eggs with cheese and peppers, bread, and strawberries. As we made our way out to the courtyard, I overheard a few of the servants talking about pirates near one of the neighboring kingdoms.

Pirates? As if I didn't already have enough to freak out about, I have to worry about possible pirate attacks?

"Keep your feet shoulder width apart," Salem instructed as I gripped the front of the bow—the stabilizer rod—with one hand with an arrow pulling back the string. I kept the arrow aimed for the grass as I adjusted my stance. If this is going to protect me, I'm going to get this right.

"Flatten your back, Lady Brigit," Salem instructed as he pressed his hand on the small of my back.

I obeyed, feeling warmth creep up my neck. Oh, God. Oh, God. Oh, God. Oh, God! I don't know how to handle this! This has never happened to me before!

Fucking relax, Bridge! He's just trying to help you. He's your teacher right now...and *way* out of your league.

Salem took a step back. "Good. Now, take aim..."

I raised the bow, hoping to God that Salem couldn't see the new shade to my cheeks. I stared hard at the target and firmly pulled the arrow back. The target wasn't that far away, but I was still positive I wasn't going to make it on the first try.

"Let go."

I released the arrow and—bull's-eye?!

Salem laughed, patting my shoulder. "Wonderful, Lady Brigit! Truly, what a prodigy!"

I laughed in disbelief. "Thanks... I, uh...nothin' to it."

Salem chuckled. "Again."

Somehow, archery was like riding a bike. I never did this in Connecticut. Maybe I did this in my old life and that's how I'm a pro? Or maybe I'm just getting cocky with beginner's luck. Regardless, I pulled another arrow out of my quiver (and totally did not almost drop a few others) and pulled it back on my string. I took aim.

Bull's-eye.

Holy fuck!

"Again."

Bull's-eye.

"Again."

Bull's-eye."

"Again."

Bull's-eye.

For ten minutes.

"You've done well, Lady Brigit," Salem said as he yanked the arrows out of the target and handed them back to me. "You truly have a gift."

I smiled at him. "I'm okay."

"Give yourself more credit. You're a natural."

"Indeed she is."

The two of us look back in the direction of the castle. A tall beautiful elf approached us. She had tan skin and long silky black hair and brown eyes. She was wearing a long lime green dress trailing behind her and wore several gold and silver bracelets around each wrist. There was a brown satchel dangling by her side. She was wearing a crown on her head. It was made from silver in the shape of a V, which pointed down right between the elf's eyes. A tear-shaped emerald hung from the tip. She smiled regally at me.

"Lady Brigit," Salem said, "you may not remember, but this is my mother, Queen Valentina."

His *mother?* Are you shitting me! She doesn't look any older than the twins!

I curtsied. "Your Majesty."

The queen bowed her head in turn. "Lady Brigit." She reached into the satchel and handed me a scroll.

I took it. "Thank you, but what is it?"

"This is a scroll of earth magic," Queen Valentina explained. "With this, you can study and practice your magic."

"This is great! Thanks!"

The queen chuckled. "Don't mention it."

She's charming. Her son is charming. I feel out of place.

"My son, please take Lady Brigit out into the forest and show her the hideaway," the queen said.

Salem bowed his head. "Of course, Mother." The what now?

Salem led me out a good way from the castle. I had no idea what he was talking about when he said he was going to show me his hideaway. I mean, fuck, think about it. In the movies, this is how the stupid white bitch dies: going into the forest with a man she just met. (Under different circumstances, I mean.) But I could tell Salem was being genuine when he said he wanted to show me.

"This is in case we are ever under attack," Salem stated as he helped me down a path. "You go here and hide. There is food, water, and blankets."

"Good to know."

Silence fell over us. Until Salem said, "Mother and I discussed this a bit before you woke this morning, but we agreed it would be best if you knew."

I gave Salem a quizzical look. "Best if I knew what?"

"About the prophecy."

I stopped in my tracks. "What prophecy?"

Salem stared at me. "The prophecy of the star."

"The...star?"

"It was said centuries ago that a great evil would plague our world," Salem explained. "The only ones that could relieve us of this evil would be the different parts of a star. Water, the healer. Air, the wise. Earth, the strong. Fire, the creator. And Spirit, the bridge. You and your siblings are the ones from the prophecy."

I let out a long breath that I didn't even realize I was holding in. My legs felt like pudding. "What elements exactly? I know I'm earth, but what about my brother and sisters?"

"Your brother, Garrett, is a death witch. He helps the dying pass on and speaks to the dead. His element is Spirit. Lady Caitlin is a sea witch, though she can also create storms. Her element is water. Nora is a cosmic witch, meaning she knows of the sky and works with planets and celestial magic. Her element is wind. And for little Alison, she is a draconian witch. As you can imagine, her element is fire."

"...Oh...is that all?"

Salem took my hand, keeping me from tripping over a root. "I know it is a lot to take in."

"You really have no idea."

Salem stopped. He let go of my hand and crouched down. He lifted up a wooden latch, revealing a whole room underground. I felt like we were on an episode of *M.A.S.H.*

"Now remember, go here and lock this if you are ever in danger in this part of the woods," Salem repeated. "Never venture further than this point."

I nodded. "Okay." Salem closed the latch and brushed moss and dirt over the latch, hiding it from plain sight. He brushed the dirt off his hands and looked back at me. "Are you okay?"

I shrugged. "Sort of. It's just that all of a sudden I'm thrown back into a life I don't remember and I'm one of the ones whose destiny it is to save a magical world. Sounds like something out of a YA fantasy novel."

It was Salem's turn to give me a quizzical look. "A...what?"

"Nothing."

Salem shrugged before taking my hand. "Come. Let's go home."

Home. I smiled at him and gave his hand a light squeeze. "Yeah. Let's go."

Chapter 5

Garrett

Days went by after my arrival and I still hadn't been able to use magic. Maybe after being away from this world for so long it affected my powers. Or that's what I thought at first.

I began training with Sir Charles every day after breakfast for at least two hours. He wanted to teach me how to use a sword. He said that once my powers return, I'd be doubly prepared for a fight (if there's ever the need.) I didn't see much of Katrina during the day.

According to Bruce, her life and tasks were not my concern and I should leave her alone.

Another day passed and as soon as breakfast was over, I grabbed my sword and met Sir Charles behind our house.

"On time again, Milord," he praised as he drew his sword. "Ready?"

I drew my own sword. "Ready."

The two of us raised our swords, pressing the ends of our blades against each other's. I didn't realize when we first started training just how heavy swords were. I don't understand how some knights can fight one-handed.

Sir Charles raised his sword, much like how he did yesterday. Immediately, I blocked his attack. Turns out those drills helped. Sir Charles pulled back.

"Good. Now, we're going to do this again. This time, push me off."

"Got it."

Once again, Sir Charles raised his sword back and swung towards me. I blocked his blade with my own. He was applying some pressure to force me to back down. I planted my feet and gripped the hilt of my sword. I struggled, but managed to push Sir Charles off me.

"Excellent," he said. "And remember, you must keep your target in sight. You can sidestep your opponent's attack while figuring out your next move. You won't be able to miss since your sword is part of you." He tapped his arm. "You won't miss it if your aim is true. However, if you really want to come out victorious, defense is the best offense rather than waiting for the perfect opportunity. You will have to take on the role of defense at some point, though, no matter how skilled you are on offense."

"Okay. Gotcha."

Sir Charles stared at me for a few seconds. "Have you had that nightmare again?"

"Last night? No, I didn't."

"I just wanted to be sure you weren't putting on a brave face," Sir Charles said. "Your first night here, you woke up screaming."

I rubbed the back of my neck. "I said I was sorry."

"You have nothing to be sorry for, Lord Garrett, despite what Bruce claims. We all understand that you don't wish to talk about what your nightmare was about, but do know that we will all listen. There are nights where we have nightmares, too. Especially about the siege."

I gave him a sad, knowing smile. "You do, don't you?"

Sir Charles gave me a half-hearted snicker. "I do. I was there when the siege happened. I was there on business. I expected nothing. I will make sure I am not unprepared for battle again since…" He let out a shuddered breath. "I had a daughter named Muriel. She wasn't much older than you when the Capital was attacked. We lived in the Human Domain before it all happened. I tried searching for her, but when I arrived home…"

He stopped, pinching the bridge of his nose. He was a father. I can't even imagine what it's like to lose a child. Losing a friend is one thing, so is a parent or a sibling, but a child? "Anyway," Sir Charles sighed, "we should keep practicing. Hold up your sword." I raised my sword and we continued training.

After a few hours of blocking, lunging, parrying, and countering, Sir Charles and I shook hands and parted ways. Scathe and Jotnar's war destroyed the lives of so many people. I've only been here a few days, and so far, I haven't heard of or seen anything good come from this war.

Everyone is suffering and they don't even care.

I told the truth when I said I hadn't dreamt of that man in dark armor last night. That nightmare felt so real the first time…

I wasn't even paying attention as I turned the corner and almost bumped into somebody: a tall man with dirty blonde hair, blue eyes, and a goatee.

"Ugh! I'm sorry!" I said, holding my hands up.

"I should be apologizing," the man said. "I wasn't paying attention."

"No, really. It's my fault."

The man laughed. "If we keep going about like this, we'll be here all day."

"Yeah, you've got a point." I held out a hand. "I'm Garrett Sullivan."

The man smiled and shook my hand. "I'm Graham." His hand felt cold. Weird. It's like a hundred degrees out.

"What were you doing back here, sir?" Graham asked.

I showed him my sheathed sword. "Training."

"Ah, a great skill to have. When I was a lad, I used to help my grandfather in his shop. He was a blacksmith."

"Cool."

"No, actually, it was quite warm there."

I shook my head. "No, I mean that it sounds amazing."

"Ah," Graham said, getting it, "I see. That is language from the Other Realm, yes?"

"Yeah. I lived in a state called Connecticut. It's the Constitution State and—"

"Garrett?" Sir Bruce asked behind Graham. His brows were knit together in what was most likely a mix of confusion and annoyance. "What are you doing?"

I shifted to the side so that I could see him better. I gestured to Graham. "I'm talking to someone. See?"

Bruce's brows went up. "Well, boy, you should get your eyes examined. There's no one there."

I'm sorry. What?

"What are you talking about?" I asked. "This is—"

I tore my eyes away from Graham...who was right in front of me...for a few seconds.

Neither of us moved...but when I turned back...Graham was gone.

Garrett

Katrina and I decided to check the perimeter on horseback. I had never ridden on horseback before, so I was a bit nervous. Thankfully, Katrina was nice enough to help me. She showed me how to put on the saddle and how to use the reins. Katrina led the way into the forest heading north on her horse. Her horse was cream-colored with a sandy brown mane. Mine was completely black, even his mane and tail.

"What's your horse's name?" I asked.

"Heaven."

"Neat. Uh, what's his name?"

"Pluto."

Pluto. Suits him.

I didn't pick the name, of course.

My head snapped to the left and then to the right. There was no one around. I looked behind me. Just trees.

"Katrina, did you hear something?" I asked.

She shook her head. "Not a thing, Milord."

Try looking down, Red.

I stared at the back of Pluto's head. "It...it...you can talk?" I whispered.

Telepathically with you, yeah.

A horse. I'm talking to a horse.

"Yeah, Red. We can talk."

"B-but how can no one else hear you? How come Katrina can't hear you?"

'Cause she's not a witch, fairy, or Deity. Only if you have magical or mystical powers can you understand animals.

"Huh...well...huh."

Wow...You're just full of big vocab words, huh?

I rolled my eyes. "Sorry. Just horses talking or 'talking' isn't the norm from where I lived for the past five years."

Well, get used to it, Red. If not, the voices—all of them—in your head are going to drive you mad.

"Voices?" I whisper-shouted. "What voices?" Pluto stayed silent after that.

Katrina and I were crouched near the bank of a river, gathering water into canteens. "When the winter sets in, I will teach you how to track animals. Sir Bruce will teach you how to skin them."

"Sir Bruce?" I say unenthusiastically.

Katrina grinned. "Is he not your favorite person?"

I shrugged as I cupped water into my hands. "I just don't think he's fond of me, if anything."

Katrina took out her braid, letting her golden hair flow on either side of her face. She was beautiful before, but now...I gulped down the water and wiped my mouth with the back of my hand.

"Don't be too offended, Garrett," Katrina said softly as she smoothed her hair down. "Sir

Bruce has lost so much, just as we have. After the siege, the Domain that was invaded after the Human Domain was the Dwarf Domain. He and his wife and father were traveling through beforehand on the run when the attack began. His father was old and fragile, but Scathe's men forced themselves on his wife before killing her and beat his father to death. The only reason Sir Bruce is still alive is because Sir Charles saved him."

My heart started to hurt for Bruce. He was forced to watch his loved ones die before his eyes. That's why he's so angry.

"But why does he hate me?" I couldn't help but ask.

Katrina gave me a sympathetic look. "Not that any of us agree with him, but Sir Bruce feels that you were the son of Queen Amelia of the Witch

Domain. You went missing for five years when everyone here has been forced to survive under horrible conditions."

"So he blames me for not being here? For not being able to do anything?"

Katrina nodded once, eyes pressed shut. "Yes."

I turned on my heel and climbed on my horse. Katrina stared at me from the riverbank in surprise. "Garrett?"

"I'm going to find a way to bring my powers back," I stated firmly. "I wasn't able to do anything before. Now I won't stop until Scathe and Jotnar's war ends."

Katrina gave me a wide, blinding smile. "Of course, Milord."

We got back to the village and Katrina insisted she take care of Pluto for me while I figured out a way to regain my powers. I passed some villagers and made my way into my house. No one was there. I sat myself down on the floor, straightening my back and crossing my legs. I closed my eyes and focused on my breathing. It took a lot of effort to empty my mind. My brain apparently was against me trying to focus, just as it's always been. I breathed in. Then out. In. Out.

In. Out.

I was trying so hard to focus, but...my back was starting to ache. My nose became itchy. I needed to pee.

I was about to call it a day when images started flashing in my mind. *A man was standing over me; he was about six feet tall with pale skin and shaggy red hair and blue eyes. He looked just like me, only...there was something dark in him, something cold and sinister. He looked angry beyond understanding.*

The man with red hair looked away from me and straight ahead. Then the image changed. There was a dark castle sitting alone far away in the mountains. Snow was falling from the midnight blue night sky. It was dark inside. Then the image changed to...something horrifying. There was a...beast...sitting on a throne. His skin was green...his eyes were black...completely black... He wore a black torn shirt and cape...armored boots... He had long, sharp claws at the tips of his fingers... They were each at least eight-inches long... There were long, swirling black horns on his head... The image changed back to the man from before—to the man who looked like me. The man who had turned away from me to look straight ahead snapped his attention back to me, only this time, he didn't look like, well, an angry, older version of me. His face changed to the monster's that was sitting on the throne. The monster growled low and deep.

It was telling me its name.

Scathe.

I gasped, my eyes shooting open. Sir Charles, Sir Bruce, and Katrina were on either side of me shaking me.

"Garrett! Are you alright?" Katrina asked, her voice cracking. She got down on her knees and took me by my shoulders. "What happened?"

They were all staring at me in worry, even Bruce. Sweat trickled down my forehead. My shirt was soaked.

Panting, I asked, "What...what happened?"

"Milord, you were screaming," Sir Charles said. "We heard you."

I stared at each of them. "I was screaming?"

I hadn't even heard myself scream. I didn't even know that I was doing it! Something—a feeling—weighed upon my mind. I suddenly felt the urge to throw up, but I had to know. I stared up at Sir Charles, realizing and trying to ignore the fact that I was shaking.

"I had a vision of Scathe," I croaked. "He was...he looked like *me*. Why?"

I already knew the answer, but I had to ask anyway. Sir Charles and Bruce looked at each other and then back to me.

"He's my father isn't he?"

The room went silent for a moment, but then, Sir Charles looked me in the eye and said, "Yes. You're Scathe's son."

Chapter 6

Megan

"Is there a way for you to locate the rest of your family?" Angus asked a few days later.

The two of us were walking and talking, passing people by in our hideaway. Nora and Alison were playing with the fellow children elsewhere. They've adapted quickly. They miss their siblings, just as I do, but so far, they seem to be doing just fine.

"I have tried," I admitted, "but much of this land has been cloaked by Queen Valentina, making finding them impossible. But hopefully, they're all safe. That's what matters. And I won't give up until I find them again."

Angus smiled at my words. "I know you enough to know that that is very much true."

"We're family. We won't stop searching until we're together again."

Angus and I walked to one of the tents and stopped in front of a table. There was a long piece of paper with scribbles and notes for plans. Only a select few were allowed to get in and out of the camp and into the territories of Scathe and Jotnar.

"There may be a way to reach them without using a tracking spell or having to leave,"

Angus said to me. "Astral projection?"

I took a seat. "I could try it, I've never really been much of an expert with that."

Angus took a seat across from me and crossed his arms. "I remember you saying you wanted to learn years ago. You were sixteen, I believe."

"You remember that?"

"I remember a lot," Angus replied. "Like how you wore a sleeveless turquoise dress when we first met. Your hair was up in a braid and you wore a white scarf around your neck. You were studying with your tutor under the willow tree by your home, the Dark Castle. You were summoned by your parents, who you did not have a good relationship with at the time. You were all lined up in the middle to greet my father and I in the order of your births. First it was your brother, Varian, Felicia, yourself, Vivian, and...Amelia."

Tears pricked at my eyes. "Amelia and I...we are not close. We haven't been in years... Especially now."

Angus gave me a knowing look. "Then you're aware of what's become of her?"

I clenched my hands into fists on my lap. "She is the wife of Jotnar, Nimh, the Insidious

Sorceress."

When I crossed into this world, I saw visions of Amelia, who once looked so much like Brigit and Alison. But growing up, Amelia was spoiled and vain. She became judgmental and narcissistic...much like our own mother. Both of them...they are carbon copies of one another. When Amelia married Eluf, it progressively got worse. She became emotionally and verbally abusive towards her children. *He* certainly didn't help matters. I was there to witness some of it; other times I had visions and nightmares. Even the children told me some of it. Only he was physically abusive towards them. Of course, whenever allies or ambassadors visited, they both put on masks. Even then, they weren't completely convincing.

I saw what became of my little sister. Her skin turned ashy gray and cracked. Her hair was still long and black as a raven's feather. Her eyes were no longer brown from what I could tell. They were sewn shut. Her lips were blood red along with her nails, as long and sharp as a butcher knife. She used to be, well, not thin, but now, she was so skeleton-like, you could see the slow beating of her heart. I had no idea she had one. Last but not least, she wore a crown wreath on top of her head: one made from thorns and needles.

My sister became just as ugly on the outside as she was inside.

"Girls!" I called from outside of the tent. "Nora! Alison!"

The girls came running to me, giggling and smiling. Their hair bounced off their shoulders before they came to a complete stop.

"Auntie, the centaur boys played knights with us!" Nora shouted in excitement.

"Yeah!" Alison said. "We didn't want to be princesses! We wanted to be heroes!"

Hearing those words come from their mouths really says a lot more than they realize. I took their hands and we started walking towards our tent. "How would you two like to practice magic? You both can be like real heroes."

The girls squealed and pulled me long, excited to get started. Guess I got my answer. We laughed the rest of the way there until—*Traitorous whore!*

That voice sounded familiar. I looked around, trying to find out where that voice was coming from, debating whether or not to warn Angus, take the girls, and flee, but the girls weren't fazed in the slightest. They continued playing and laughing joyfully. They hadn't heard the voice, thank the Gods.

It was Nimh's voice.

I waved my hand past the side of my head, energy coming to life. Light blue magic shimmered through my fingertips. I thought of a shield, a barrier to protect my mind and the girls' from the true traitor whore. I felt a change. The energy in the atmosphere changed. We were safe. I walked towards Nora and Alison, ready to begin our lesson, ignoring the slight feeling of someone angrily and frantically clawing at my mind, failing to get in.

Caitlin

We escaped the storm. I got us out of danger. Me. *Me.* I still don't really understand how I did it. It was instinct...I guess. Second nature.

I really have done magic before and there really is power inside of me! Sirens are real!

Magic is real! I *am* magic!

Captain Raina snapped her fingers just inches away from my face. "Focus, Caitlin. This is very important. You need to learn this."

I sighed. "I don't know anything about reading maps."

"Which is why I'm trying to teach you. The other night you saved our asses and that was magnificent, but I need you to know more than just that. Reading maps is essential. What would happen if you were left alone, lost, afraid? You need to know how to read a map. We're starting with the basics." She pointed to the compass. "I trust you know what this is."

I glared at the captain. "There's no need to be condescending. I know what it is; it's the compass rose."

Captain Raina looked back to the map. "Very good. You do know your stuff." She pointed to the words at the very top. "And, uh, this?"

Again, I glared up at her. "The title. Right now, we're in the Raven Ocean in Clover Talamh, heading towards Asmund Rock, west of Fenrir-Himinn, one of Clover Talamh's neighbors."

"And this?"

I looked at the part of the map where there was a drawing of a small island. It said in calligraphy, *Isle of Shadows*. It was at the near bottom of the map, southeast of Fenrir-Himinn.

"What's over on the Isle?" I asked.

Captain Raina waited a minute before answering. "Supposedly, there's a beast who inhabits the island."

"A beast?" I gasped.

"Aye," Captain Raina answered. "I don't know just how true the stories are, but I do know this: Anyone who steps foot on the Isle never comes back."

A chill went down my spine. Someone knocked on the door, interrupting our session.

"Enter," Captain Raina said.

The door opened up to reveal Sheila and a few other members of the crew carrying trays of food and pitchers and goblets.

"Dinner, Captain," Sheila said.

Captain Raina and I removed the maps and let the crew set the table up with food. Different smells filled the air: ones of different spices and meats and vegetables. Sheila set down a tray and lifted the lid, revealing a delicious golden turkey. I could see the steam evaporating into the air.

I didn't look at the captain, but still I asked, "Where did you get all this food from?"

"We do trade things for food, Treasure," Captain Raina said from behind me. "We don't always steal. Some of us happen to be good negotiators."

Sheila and the others dismissed themselves, closing the door behind them. Captain Raina pulled out a chair for me. I stared at it and then her and then back at the chair. She gave me an amused look.

"I haven't set a bomb on your chair, Treasure. You may sit."

I eyed the captain suspiciously. "And you're being nice to me all of a sudden...why?"

The captain raised a brow. "I'm not the scoundrel you think I am, Caity Cat."

That's debatable. Sighing, I sat down and Captain Raina gently slid me closer to the table before putting food on two plates.

"You don't have to do that for me," I said.

"Why not? I am the captain of this ship. You're a passenger, a guest. What kind of person would I be?"

She handed me my plate. "The kind that plans to use me as a pawn in her revenge plot." Captain Raina laughed as she poured herself a glass of wine. She sat down.

"You never told me what you're getting revenge for," I said, taking a bite of my food.

Captain Raina sipped her wine before answering. "Well, what use is it for you to know? You are, as you say, a pawn."

"I'm just saying, you seemed very adamant about me triggering my powers."

I reached over to grab a roll, not realizing that Captain Raina had the same idea in mind. Our hands collided and our eyes met. She looked slightly surprised. The captain didn't look offended that I touched her or annoyed. If anything, she looked slightly pleased.

I pulled my hand away. "I'm sorry."

The captain shook her head. "I'm not going to shoot your head off or stab you in the eye, Treasure. Relax." She poured a second glass of wine and handed it to me.

I stared at the glass.

Captain Raina gave me a mischievous crooked smile. "First time?"

I continued staring at the wine. "I'm not of age."

"My dear, I don't know how things worked in this *world* of yours, but here, you're legal to drink as of thirteen. Besides, you're among pirates. We don't give a damn about rules."

She had a point, but it still didn't feel right. "What about...some of the crew members?"

Captain Raina gave me a look. "What about them?"

"Well, some...most...are men, and...I just...I've heard stories of what can happen if a woman drinks—"

"I will not allow that," the captain stated firmly. "Those types of 'people' aren't allowed on my ship. If I had any suspicion that anybody on my ship was a monster, then trust me, dear,

I'd blow their brains out and leave them for the sharks."

Something changed in her eyes. She meant every word of it. Maybe it's because she needs me for whatever she has planned and maybe not, but I can tell that Captain Raina just wants to protect me. She won't let anyone lay a hand on me.

"Thank you."

"You're welcome."

The two of us stared a little longer at each other before returning to our meals. Her eyes were dark and beautiful. If I wanted to, I could probably get lost in them.

"By tomorrow morning, we'll be on Darby Island," Captain Raina stated after clearing her throat. She looked up at me and smiled. "Tell me, Treasure; you say you've never had a drink in your life. How would you feel about stopping at a tavern?"

Chapter 7

Brigit

The next morning was just like the last. I woke up, got dressed, had breakfast with Salem, and went outside to practice more archery. The only difference was that the targets were farther away, which made seeing hard. Did that stop me from hitting each one smack-dab in the middle?

Nope.

After a few hours of practice (and yes, I was exhausted), Queen Valentina showed up. She wasn't alone this time, though. There was another elf next to her, a man. He was taller than the Queen, too. He also had tan skin, brown eyes, and short black hair. Just like the queen and Salem, he wore different shades of green clothing with brown leather straps.

Salem's posture changed. "Mother."

The Queen smiled at the two of us before gesturing to the elf next to her. "Salem. Lady

Brigit, I would like to reintroduce you to my eldest son, Akoni, heir to Sanctuarium."

"Hi—er, hello."

Akoni's hands were folded behind him as he stared at me. He didn't look very happy to see me. If anything, he looked unimpressed and, well, stuffy. He kind of reminds me of Mr. Darcy from *Pride and Prejudice*, except I don't have the feeling that he's got a heart of gold. I think he sees me as inferior. No, not because I'm a lady and he's a prince; more like he sees me as inferior simply because he thinks himself better. Glancing at Salem in the corner of my eye, my guess is that Salem views his older brother the same way.

"Akoni has been to the Dwarf Domain in our kingdom," Salem told me without looking away from his brother. "You'll have to excuse his absence."

"Yes, indeed," Akoni said. (Wow. His voice is deep.) "You'll soon come to realize that I have several matters to attend to in order to show the kingdom what kind of ruler I intend to be."

"If there is a kingdom to rule at all," Salem argued. "If this war doesn't end soon, who's to say that their feud won't escalate and come to our land?"

"Mind your tongue, Salem," Queen Valentina warned. "You know that Jotnar and Scathe's powers are harmless here. I made sure of that myself years ago."

I looked from Salem to Akoni. How old is Akoni, anyway? Twenty-one? That's usually the age people are when they ascend the throne in the fantasy movies I've seen. Salem's probably a little older than me, but he acts *a lot* older. The brothers don't look happy to see each other. I've gotten in fist fights and arguments with Garrett and the girls before, but mostly because that's just how we've always been. We annoy each other and piss each other off, but we always get along in the end. This, right here, is different. The two look like they wanted to be anywhere else but here with each other and the only thing keeping them from getting into a fist fight was their mother.

The queen took the crook of my arm. "Come, Lady Brigit. You and I are to start training you in magic."

Salem took my quiver of arrows and bow as the queen led me across the courtyard. The whole time, I could feel Akoni's eyes on me and I didn't like it.

• • • • •

"Let's begin," Queen Valentina said. "Your element is earth, as you know. You are a green witch. Magic has been in your blood since the dawn of time. You are in sync with earth." The Queen took my hand and extended my arm towards the treeline. "The earth will bend for you at your beck and call. Magic is powered by energy and emotion. You must keep your focus.

If you're not careful, you could drain yourself or hurt someone else."

Queen Valentina stepped away, giving me space. What was I doing exactly? How was I supposed to summon my powers if I had no clue how to do that?

"Breathe, Lady Brigit," Queen Valentina instructed. "Remember, you and the world are one and the same."

I closed my eyes and focused on my breathing. This was weird, posing like this and having someone watch. I blocked the queen out of my thoughts and flexed my fingers. I thought back to when I did hiking club in middle school. I can't remember which trail it was, but I remember it being a beautiful, cloudless spring day. The snow was melting and we hiked through trails of mud and wet sand. Along the trail, I brushed my fingers against bushes and shrubs.

There were birds chirping above and there was absolutely no wind.

Suddenly, my fingers began to tingle. I slowly opened my eyes to find that my hands were glowing. *Glowing.* Magic encompassed my hands completely in mint green light. I laughed silently to myself in disbelief before turning to the treeline. I imagined the white birch trees in the very front growing taller and taller. I raised my hands up over my head and towards the sky, still focusing on the trees. Sure enough, the trees did start to grow. They grew longer and higher, obeying my command. The only thing that snapped me out of my concentration was the sound of a doe coming out of the woods. I pulled my hands down and the magic vanished. The trees remained where they had grown as the doe dared to step closer. I've never seen something like this before. The doe eventually stopped, at least three or four yards away from me. She didn't blink once, not even as she crouched on one leg and bowed her head.

Holy fucking shit…

Garrett

I sat next to Katrina during dinner, my back leaning against a tree as Sir Charles came over and handed me a bowl. Today's dinner was deer soup, or venison, according to everyone else.

"Did Sir Charles tell you how he came to lead the Defyers?" Katrina asked.

I shook my head before turning to our leader. "No, he didn't. Sir Charles?"

Sir Charles smiled, giving Katrina a knowing look before sitting across from us with his own bowl. "A few days after the siege, after bringing in Sir Bruce and other survivors, we found sanctuary within the Elf Domain of Sanctuarium. I asked the king and queen what we were to do, but they only said it was not our fight."

I nodded, urging him to continue.

"Queen Valentina and King Ardon have visions," Sir Chalres clarified. "They said they would offer us sanctuary for as long as we needed, but I knew that this war would not be ending soon. I didn't believe them when they said this wasn't our fight after everything we've lost. I asked the Elven monarchy to cloak us from the wrath of Jotnar and..."

I averted my eyes. I still couldn't believe that I was the son of one of these monsters. Scathe is my father, once known as Jonathon Sullivan, a nobleman from the Witch Domain as well as a chaos witch with a power to manipulate light and shadows. And my mom, once known as Queen Amelia O'Dwyer, became the Insidious Sorceress, Nimh. After she left my father, she married King Eluf Helvig, who became Jotnar, the Hellfire Tyrant.

"Well, we all know the rest," Sir Charles said, after clearing his throat. "And now, we have hope. One of the saviors is here with us. There is still a chance."

My stomach churned. Right. I am one of the Chosen Ones and I have to save an entire world from my parents and stepfather, whom I have no memories of, and look like the stuff of nightmares. No pressure or anything.

• • • • •

Once dinner ended, I followed Katrina to the horses on the other side of the camp. Their saddles had been removed and they were already at work eating. I cautiously approached Pluto and gently placed a hand on the middle of his back.

"Hey, Pluto," I said.

Hey, Red.

"You know it's Garrett, right?"

Duh. I've been calling you 'Red' since you were ten.

"What?"

Katrina threw her head over her shoulder to look at me. "What's the matter?"

Will she think I'm crazy if I tell her? "Uh...just...talking to Pluto. You know...I can apparently...do...that..."

Katrina looked at me like it was totally normal. "Well, you are a witch, Garrett. Animals are drawn to you naturally. Of course you would be able to understand them." So it is normal here. Okay. Great.

Would you calm down?

Katrina handed me a brush and set her eyes on her horse, Heaven, with a brush of her own. She placed one hand on the side of Heaven's neck and started grooming. I mimicked what she was doing with Pluto.

"This is called a curry brush," she said to me. "I've already cleaned their hooves, but I'll show you how to do that tomorrow morning. This removes dirt and filth from their coat. Not only does this keep your horse clean and healthy, but it builds a bond between them and their rider."

I continued grooming Pluto, avoiding his mane and tail. This was easy.

Oi! Watch how much pressure you're applying!

"Sorry, Pluto!"

· · · · ·

I was escorting Katrina to her home when I heard rustling from the woods. The two of us stopped and jerked our heads to the sound. It was too dark to see anything, but we could hear movements. Then a bush farther ahead moved. Someone was spying on us.

My fingertips tingled. It felt like I was controlling lightning. I don't even know how I was doing this...I slowed my breathing, not once averting my gaze from the bushes. Control your emotions, Gare. Don't be scared. You lose control, someone could get hurt. With my other hand, I drew my sword and aimed it in the direction of the forest.

"Garrett—!"

"Show yourself!" I commanded. "Don't hide from me!"

There was more rustling until...a very *massive* black wolf with yellow eyes jumped forward! I let out a startled yelp, freezing in place as the wolf's front paws landed on my shoulders and knocked me over. I didn't even realize that my sword had fallen out of my grasp. I was too busy staring in fear at the wolf pinning me down.

"Don't eat me!" I cried out.

Then the wolf *recoiled*. It stared down at me in confusion, blinked, and tilted its head to the side.

Lord Garrett? Why are you screaming?

I breathed, "...huh...?"

The wolf pushed itself off of me, allowing me to scoot away. Katrina crouched on one knee and held her hand out to the black wolf.

"Katrina, don't!" I exclaimed. "It'll hurt you!"

"Nonsense!" Katrina giggled. "Look."

The wolf sniffed her hand before setting its golden eyes on me again. *Lord Garrett, I knew you would return!*

I should be used to stuff like this at this point, and yet I'm still surprised. "How...how do

you know me?"

Don't you recognize me?

I slowly, stiffly, shook my head once, the beating of my heart slowing to a normal pace.

The wolf bowed its head. He looked sad, in a way.

I am Orion, your faithful companion.

"Faithful companion?" I asked. "But you're a wolf." Did he smile at me?

And? In the days of the first moon, your kind have accompanied themselves with wolves and dragons. Times may have changed, but certain things have not.

I clumsily got to my feet and brushed myself off.

I didn't mean to frighten you, Spirit Witch. It's just that I have been searching for you for so long. When I found you here, I just got a bit carried away.

"No, it's fine. I just wasn't expecting it. You say we know each other?"

Before the fall of the Witch Domain, you and I were hunting companions. We were friends, you and I. It seems your time away has affected your recollections.

I opened my mouth to answer when a horn sounded in the distance. Everyone opened their doors and piled out in a panic. I darted out of the way just in time for a knight to run by.

This wasn't good, I knew.

"What's that mean?" I asked Katrina.

"The barrier," Katrina said in terror. "It's been compromised! Someone's found us!"

Chapter 8

Caitlin

Sleeping was easier that night and not just because the seas were calm. I guess I'm much more resilient than I thought, for, you know, getting snatched up by a pirate. The lanterns had been snuffed out and Captain Raina slept soundly on her bay window while I took the hammock. The Captain even gave me a nightgown. It was beautiful. It was dark blue with spaghetti straps and went down to my kneecaps. Thing is, Captain Raina wore dress shirts or tunics to bed. She's a beautiful woman, no questions asked, but dresses and nightgowns aren't her thing. I even brought it up before bed, asking if she sometimes liked to wear girlier outfits, adding that she would look prettier in the gown than me, but she only snuffed out the lanterns and went to sleep without so much as saying goodnight.

Morning came and still no sun. Gulls flew overhead and I knew we were getting closer to land, Darby Island, to be exact. I was awake alongside whoever was now steering the ship. I didn't have a way to tell what time it was, but I knew it was early. The wind was particularly cold this morning, so when it picked up, I immediately wrapped my arms around myself. It was a lot warmer in the captain's quarters. (Not to mention the nightgown was literally all I was wearing.) I made my way back into Captain Raina's room, ready to look around for a coat or something, only to find the Captain facing the window, her bare back towards me, pulling a brand new tunic over her head. Her dark dreads swung as she looked over her shoulder towards me. I quickly looked away.

"I'm sorry," I said quickly. "I only came in for a coat."

I looked up in time to see Captain Raina's eyes travel down and back up to meet my eyes before giving me a sly grin. "We'll be at Darby Island soon, Treasure. Best not to wear that gown in the tavern, though."

Of course, Aunt Megan was the first person who came to mind when she said that. I never went out much, it wasn't my thing, but whenever I wanted to go with Garrett or Brigit to see a movie or go grocery shopping, I was constantly told to dress appropriately. This world isn't so different, it seems. It's not fair.

Captain Raina grabbed her coat and pulled it on before reaching into the cupboard under the bay window. She pulled out a soft deep blue dress with long sleeves, a black leather belt with a silver buckle, long black pants, and knee-high black suede boots. She piled them all on the table and looked at me. "Make it quick. I don't like to be kept waiting. I have to get to—"

"Asmund Rock," I interrupted. "I know."

The captain crossed her arms, her hip tilted to the side.

I glared. "Do you mind leaving? If you're in such a hurry to get off this ship, the least you can do is let me get dressed in private!"

Captain Raina laughed. "You sure you don't need help getting that gown off?"

My cheeks warmed, which only made Captain Raina laugh harder before exiting the room. God, she is frustrating! I threw my new clothes on and neatly folded the nightgown before leaving the room. I was surprised Captain Raina wasn't on the other side waiting for me, or peering through the keyhole. Everyone was on deck running about and starting the day. I looked straight ahead. In the distance was a small island with long bamboo trees as far as the eye could see.

"Land ho, Captain!" a pirate said from above.

"Aye, we're making port!" Captain Raina shouted for us all to hear. "Get ready to throw anchor!"

Watching Captain Raina switch from being an intense, laidback flirt to an intense, all business pirate was something else. Yes, she's the captain, that's obvious. I just mean that I've been in her quarters most of the time and haven't really seen her in action. She looked like she was in her element.

We walked down the ramp, making it to the island at last, but before I was even a few feet from the ship, Captain Raina stopped me.

"Take this," she said as she handed me a sword.

I shook my head. "I don't even know how to use it."

"I'll teach you when we get to the inn."

I took the sword and followed the captain. "I thought you said we were going to a tavern.

Don't know why, considering it's still morning."

Captain Raina stopped walking and immediately turned around to face me. Startled, I stopped in my tracks, nearly bumping into her. I could see the crew was walking farther away from us and out of sight into the jungle ahead, but I kept my focus on Captain Raina. She was only a little taller than me, taller than I thought. Her captivating eyes pinned me to the sandy terrain, like a cat getting ready to go for the kill.

"Are you questioning me?" Captain Raina asked, her voice low.

Suddenly breathless, I shook my head. Why was I shaking?

Captain Raina let out a long sigh before cocking her head to the direction of the jungle.

"The inn is right above the tavern. I know the owners. Let's move."

Captain Raina turned on her heel and followed her crew into the jungle. I stood there a little bit longer, staring at her back. What just happened?

The tavern was not that far from the ocean. It was maybe only half a mile away. I wasn't really sure what to expect from the inn, but when we came across it, boy, did I underestimate its size. It had to be about the size of a Victorian House with dark brown walls and black roofs. The windows were made from ebony metal with intersecting frames.

"Sailors usually pass through this territory," Captain Raina explained, "many of which are just looking for a place to hide."

"From Scathe and Jotnar?" I asked.

"To name a few."

Captain Raina pushed the door open and we made our way inside. Music filled the air; melodic notes of violins and flutes played loudly from a far corner. A chandelier hung from the ceiling with a ring of lit candles. There was a spiral staircase leading up to another floor to the right and two long banquet tables in the center. People ignored us, laughing loudly amongst themselves and with each other. Many had beer mugs in their hands and women with their breasts exposed sitting on their laps.

The crew and I made our way to the bar where a tall man with dark skin and eyes stood cleaning a glass. If I had to judge the man's age, he'd probably be in his late twenties. He wore a gray tunic, the first few buttons undone, overalls, black leather boots, and had a snake tattooed on his wrist.

"Martin!" Captain Raina called out to the bartender.

The bartender looked up, his eyes finding Captain Raina's. "Raina!"

Captain Raina offered him a wide smile before taking a seat. The two shook hands and laughed as the rest of us took seats on either side of our captain. Well, I did, most of the crew just tossed whoever was already sitting at the bar on the floor.

"Been a while," Martin said. "At least seven months, right?"

"Aye, almost eight," Captain Raina said. "Where's Jaq?"

"He's downstairs in the wine cellar. Just got a new shipment about a day ago."

"Ah. Now tell me, is this your fifth year being together?"

"Try four, Captain."

The two smiled as Martin began pouring drinks. It was sweet; they're old friends. As Martin slid a mug towards me, he raised a brow. "Are you new to Captain Raina's crew?"

I glanced at Captain Raina before returning my attention to Martin. "Yes. I come from a land far away from here. I agreed to be a part of Captain Raina's crew in exchange for passage across the world."

Captain Raina gave me a subtle look of approval before taking a swing of her drink. She wouldn't stop telling me last night during dinner how important it is that I keep my real identity a secret. If people knew I was back and alive, I could be in serious trouble, and because dying isn't in my five-year plan, I agreed to go along with it.

"And your name?" Martin asked.

"Cassidy," I said. "Cassidy Buckley."

"Nice to meet you, Cassidy," Martin said.

I smiled, accepting the drink. I sniffed it. Rum? I lifted the mug to my lips and took a small sip. Wow! That is sweet! Oof! Not used to that!

"What are you doing?" Captain Raina whispered as she leaned in. "You want to blend in, right? Drink the bloody rum."

I was about to argue with her when I stopped myself. She's right. I can't let people know who I really am or else I'll get caught. I need to stay alive so I can get back to my family. Without holding back, I took a huge swig of the rum.

• • • • •

The crew was given keys to the inn upstairs. Some even had either men or women with them that they met in the tavern. Not wanting to let me out of her sight, Captain Raina said we were to share a room. Only problem?

There was one bed.

Captain Raina locked the door behind us and removed her hat. I removed the sword from my belt and placed it on the table. The captain went to work pulling out a map from her coat pocket and took a seat.

"You still haven't told me, Captain," I pointed out.

Without looking up from the map, she asked, "Haven't told you what?"

"Why do you need me," I said. "You need me for revenge, but revenge for what?"

Captain Raian ignored me. I wasn't about to let her out of this, though. Not this time.

"If I'm going to die, I'd at least like to know what for," I pushed. "What did Jotnar and

Scathe do to you?"

"Drop it."

"Tell me what happened."

"As your captain, I'm telling you. Drop. It."

"You're really not my captain. You're holding me against my will!"

The chair she was sitting on screeched against the hardwood floor as Captain Raina pushed herself out. She was on her feet and in front of me in an instant. I stood my ground.

"I told you to drop it!"

"And I told you you're not my captain! Why is it so hard for you to listen? You expect everyone else to listen to you, meanwhile, you refuse to listen to others! Why!"

"Just listen to me for once, Margaret!"

The air went still. It was so quiet, you could hear a pin drop. The two of us were breathing heavily at this point. I wasn't sure how thin the walls of this place were, but I think the other guests could hear us arguing.

"Who's Margaret?" I asked softly.

Captain Raina's eyes were wide, unshed tears ready to burst.

"Captain, who is Margaret?" I asked.

After taking a few uneasy breaths, Captain Raina replied, "She was my little sister. We lived in the Witch Domain of Clover Talamh. Our home was destroyed...our mother...during the siege, she was killed under the rubble that was our home. Margaret and I tried to run, but there was a monster in the streets. His eyes were as black as night. Jotnar. He saw us. Using magic, the monster was able to levitate a carriage meant for one of noble birth. He threw it at us. I told Margaret to get out of the bloody way, but—"

Captain Raina stopped, barely holding back a sob. My heart tightened. I had no idea. I went to take her hand, but Captain Raina quickly turned on her heel and disappeared out into the hallway. She slammed the door behind her hard enough for the whole building to shake.

Brigit

"I can't believe what I did!" I exclaimed to Salem as we walked side by side down the corridor to his room. "Just...holy crap! I made trees grow! *Grow!*"

I was smiling ear to ear like an idiot, but Salem wasn't bothered by it. He was smiling at my enthusiasm. It was getting easier to talk to him. Before coming to Sanctuarium, I never would have been comfortable like this around anyone outside my family. Don't get me wrong, I have always been close to the twins, but those two are joined at the hip. Not only that, but Nora and Alison are way too young at this point to confide in or understand anything I tell them. I'm the middle child of five kids and sometimes, it kind of sucks. I love my family, okay? I just want someone, a best friend, to talk to like they do.

"I knew you could do it, Lady Brigit," Salem said. "I am very happy for you."

My hair slid down the side of my face, thankfully hiding the blush that crept across.

"Thanks."

Salem stopped in front of the door to his room and opened it. But instead of going right in, he held the door open for me.

"You don't have to do that," I said. "It's fine, really."

"But you are my guest."

This guy is not going to give up, is he? I'm not complaining. I'm just not used to it.

Instead of arguing further, I stepped inside. Salem's room was beautiful! All his walls were painted an aquamarine color with hues of forest green at every corner. His bed sat far from the side of the room and closer to the balcony outside. The light green curtains gently blew on the balcony and there were vines winding up and over the walls. His bed had a gold frame and was covered in a large silk quilt that was different shades of green. His whole room just reminded me of summer itself.

"Does this mean that I'm going to get stronger the more I practice?" I asked.

Salem placed his bow against the side of his bed, alongside his quiver and smiled at me. "Yes. Whenever you choose, I can accompany you and you can practice."

"I'd really like that."

But something kept bothering me. I know that I can't be alone just because the queen doesn't want to be too careful, even with her magic, but Salem seems really adamant about not leaving me alone with Akoni. I don't have a problem with it, honestly, because Akoni gives me the fucking creeps, but at the same time, I want to know why.

So I asked.

"Why don't you want me to be alone with Akoni?" I asked.

Salem, who was looking through some papers, stopped. He lifted his head, staring straight ahead at the wall. I immediately became suspicious.

"Your mom doesn't seem to mind me being around him, but you do," I went on. "I don't blame you, okay? I just have this feeling about him. I know he's your brother, but I don't completely trust him. I don't know what it is."

Suddenly, Salem's head tilted back and he gasped. His eyes began to glow—they were completely white. The papers in his hands fell and he threw his arms back. He sounded like he was being choked. I was at his side in an instant and grabbed his shoulders.

"Salem?" I cried. "Salem!"

He wasn't answering me. He couldn't.

"Salem! Salem, come on! Wake up!"

His breathing got worse. It sounded like he was wheezing. His eyes began to glow brighter and black veins beneath his eyes faded in and out of sight. I shook him harder.

"Salem!"

The castle began to shake. An earthquake! I was causing the earthquake! My *panicking* was causing the earthquake! Tears spilled down my cheeks as I shook him harder.

"Salem! Please! Please, Salem! Come back!" I cried.

Salem's eyes squeezed shut and when he opened them again, they were back to normal. His eyes weren't glowing anymore, there weren't any veins ready to pop, none of that. Letting out a breath, Salem fell backwards, his legs limp. I quickly caught him, reaching underneath his arms, and carefully set him down. He was heavier than I was, but I didn't care. With what just happened, there was enough adrenaline in me to fuel the magic in this world, replacing it with what's been lost so far. Salem coughed, trying to catch his breath.

"Are you okay?" I asked, staring tearfully down at him.

Salem looked up at me, now looking exhausted. "I am fine. Just a vision."

"A *vision?* You looked like you were dying! You were losing breath and—!"

Salem sat on his knees and cupped my face. I stopped crying and stared at him in shock.

He smiled kindly at me. "I am fine, Brigit. This is normal for me when I have visions. I am fine, I promise you."

He wiped my tears away with his thumbs and pressed our foreheads together. This was something I *definitely* didn't sign up for. My friend was telling me that what looked like suffering was actually him having a vision. Salem, my friend, was telling me that this was normal and fine. Well, not to me. He looked like he was dying! He looked like he was in so much pain and I couldn't stop it. All I did was cause an earthquake and—

Oh, no. No, no, no... Salem and Queen Valentina have been telling me to control my emotions because of how it can affect my magic... I pulled away.

"I caused the Emerald Mountain's destruction," I said, "didn't I?"

Salem's face fell and he reached for me. I pulled my face away. "It was me, wasn't it? Scathe and Jotnar's war may be affecting the magic that runs this world, they may be stealing it, but I caused that mountain to fall, didn't I?"

Salem took my hands and squeezed them lightly, looking me in the eye. "It was not your fault."

I squeezed my eyes together as more tears rolled down my cheeks. God, I hate crying in front of people! Hell, I hate crying, period!

Salem gently pulled me closer to him and wrapped his arms around me. He rested his chin on top of my head and just held me. I pressed my face into his shoulder and let myself cry. Thirty minutes ago, I felt powerful and unstoppable. I finally felt special...but what can I do if I'm not careful enough? I could've *killed* someone! As I cried, held in Salem's arms, I wished to whatever God or Gods that could hear me, if there were any at all, that they could take my powers away. For good this time.

Chapter 9

Garrett

With my sword in my hand, I ran to the waterfall leading into our camp. Everyone was screaming and trying to get away as Sir Charles, Bruce, myself, and a few others readied ourselves. Who found us? How did they find us?

But I still wasn't ready. I've only had a few days of sword training and getting used to my magic again. I wasn't sure what to expect. I did see some men dressed in dark armor carrying axes and gripping whips. These men in particular actually didn't look human at all. First of all, they had massive bat-like wings on their backs stretched out and at least eight feet long.

Second…they looked mutilated; patches of flesh were missing from their faces. Some were rotting off, exposing muscle and—is that part of a skull?

I swallowed the bile that was rising in the back of my throat. Now was not the time to be sick! In the corner of my eye, I saw someone move. My head spun in the direction of the movement and I realized it was Graham. He was standing calmly behind a crate. Is he crazy?

He's exposed! He needs to get out of here!

But no one paid him any attention. I clenched the hilt of my sword, not wanting to die—not wanting to die this way. I was going to fight. I can take a few men with wings. I can do this. I can do this!

Katrina unsheathed her own sword and stood by my side, keeping her eyes glued to our intruders.

"Who are these guys?" I asked.

"The Shadow Knights," Katrina answered. "They work for Scathe."

Someone was making their way through the group of winged men. At first, I wasn't sure who...not until he made his way to the front of the group. I froze. It was *him*. The knight I saw in my nightmares. He was taller, but that was it. He wore the same dark suit of armor, the same dark cape, and had the same dark brown hair and face mask of iron. In one hand, he held a double-edged ax and in the other, a long stainless steel sword. My blood ran cold. It wasn't a nightmare! It was a memory! This man had tried to kill me before and he was going to try to kill me now!

Sir Charles took a step closer to the man in dark armor. "How did you find us?" The man in dark armor didn't answer, didn't move.

Sir Charles raised his sword. "Answer me, demon!"

The man in dark armor swiftly raised his own sword, clashing the two together. He pushed Sir Charles's sword away and went to elbow him in the face. Luckily, Sir Charles ducked out of the way and jumped back just before the man in dark armor swung his ax down, right where Sir Charles was standing. A fight broke loose. The Shadow Knights screeched, taking off into the air and lunging for our army. I ran forward, raising my sword, and swung at the man from my nightmares. Somehow, he knew what I was up to, before I even took a single step. The knight blocked my attack and threw me off.

I staggered back, trying to find my footing. I drowned out everyone and everything else, focusing only on the knight. He took deliberate steps towards me, swinging his sword and ax. What was he going to use first? My heart was beating so fast, I thought it was going to explode.

The knight raised his sword and swung, aiming for my abdomen. I jerked my body out of the way, seconds before it could do any damage. Not giving me time to take a breath, the knight then swung his ax. I ducked, rolling to the side. I didn't stop to wait for his next move. I jumped away again, just before he could give his ax a second go.

Images flashed in my mind—images that I know I've seen before. We were back on the cobblestone streets of the Witch Domain. He was my opponent then, just like he is now. The knight took a step toward me, matching the one in my vision. Another step, again mirroring the memory. Another step. Only this time, I saw four kids playing together in a field by a river on a sunny summer day. There were two boys and two girls. The littlest girl had short black curly hair, slightly chubby, and wore a light green dress with ballet slippers. She tripped, falling forward. The older girl took her hands and pulled her up. The older girl had long red hair and wore a periwinkle sleeveless dress. The younger boy also had red hair and wore a purple tunic, dark blue pants, and dark blue boots. The older boy had short, messy dark brown hair and wore a black tunic with black pants and black boots. They were all laughing, but it sounded so far away. They looked happy.

With a start, I realized who these children were. The two girls were Caitlin and Brigit and the two boys were *us*! Me! Myself and...

His name...Thomas...

I was snapped back into the present, just in time to block the next attack. Thomas swung again with his ax. I somersaulted away, just in time.

Thomas.

Thomas. Thomas.

Thomas swung his sword, but this time, I had a different idea. I felt Spirit's element tingle at the tips of my fingers. My powers were going crazy, itching to bust out and start fighting. But I had to try something...I just had to try at least once... "Thomas, wait!" I screamed.

Thomas halted, his sword raised over his shoulder, ready to strike. I could see the flicker of fear in his eyes. Fear. I didn't see that there before. Before there was just coldness and maybe...just maybe...pity? Regret? Those images I saw...we were all having fun, just the four of us as kids... Why was he attacking me? Who is he?

But that apparently didn't matter. Thomas swung his sword forward, ready to strike. I didn't hold back. I threw my hand in front of me, like I was going to block the sword. I felt Spirit's energy come to life in my palm. Dark purple energy erupted from my hand, shooting straight for Thomas. Spirit hit him, sending him flying across the camp and into the wall of one of the houses. He fell to the ground, dropping his weapons. I quickly got up and threw my arms forward again, aiming for Thomas. Spirit flew from my hands again and...

He *caught* it. Just as he managed to get up on one leg, Thomas caught Spirit right before it could make contact with him. My blood ran cold. The element danced between his fingers menacingly right before he thrust his arm in my direction, sending Spirit right back at me. Spirit slammed right into my chest and I went flying backwards into the rocky wall that was the waterfall. The impact left me breathless as I hit the ground. Hopefully, nothing was broken, but...

Get up.

Get up.

GET UP!

"*NO!*"

My head immediately snapped up at the sound of her voice. Thomas was staring directly at me, along with Katrina, who he had in a chokehold. In his other hand, aimed only inches from her face, was a small sword made purely and simply out of fire. My heart leapt into my throat.

"*NO, DON'T!*"

"Your move, brother."

I felt sick again. "Wh-what did you call me?"

His grip on Katrina tightened. She squeezed her eyes shut and gasped for air. Thomas kept his eyes on me.

"So it is true, you have forgotten me," Thomas said, his voice raspy. "And it seems you have forgotten that *I* am the one who taught you how to use Spirit in the first place."

Brother? He's the one who taught me magic? Too much was happening! Too much was happening and if I didn't do something, he was going to snap Katrina's neck!

I climbed to my feet, reaching for Katrina. "Don't do this. Please, don't do this. She's got nothing to do with this!"

"I realize that..." Thomas replied, pulling Katrina closer to him. "Listen carefully, Garrett. I am going to give you a choice: stay here and fight. You'll die and the prophecy will remain unfulfilled. Or you can take your friends and go. Leave. Run."

My brows furrowed. "What are you talking about?"

The flames at the tip of his sword went crazy, barely kissing Katrina's cheek. She hissed, struggling and failing to pull herself free.

"Leave!"

And with that, Thomas shoved Katrina towards me. I caught her in my arms before she could hit the ground and we both watched in terror as Thomas extended his arm—the one with the flaming sword—at the tip of one of the houses. The fire crawled up and over to the roof, crawling to another house and then another and then another. More screams were heard.

My brother had set our camp on fire.

Caitlin

I sat on the edge of the bed after Captain Raina stormed away. She had a little sister. She was killed by Jotnar. A child! Captain Raina wasn't much older than me and she had to watch her sister die. I can't even imagine that pain. If something were to happen to my brother or any of my sisters, I don't even know what I would do.

After a few minutes, I decided to go downstairs and see if Captain Raina was in the tavern. I had to apologize.

As I suspected, Captain Raina was sitting at the bar, nursing a drink. She was talking to Martin, but her head was down. They looked like they were having a serious conversation, but I couldn't hear them. Mustering up my courage, I took a breath, and walked to the bar. Martin saw me, nodded, and went back to serving other people.

"Here to press me for more?" Captain Raina asked.

I wrapped an arm around myself, shifting uncomfortably. "I shouldn't have pressured you. You're in charge, not me. I'm sorry."

Captain Raina took a sip of her drink before shifting herself on her seat to get a better look at me.

"Luckily, I won't be making you walk the plank," she said with a lazy grin. "And don't look so uncomfortable. You're a pirate who takes shit from no one, remember?"

I smiled at her as she tapped the seat beside her. I gladly obliged. Captain Raina slid her mug in my direction. I took a sip. Rum.

Joy.

I fought the need to shiver and make a disgusted noise as I swallowed the rum. I'm not a rum kind of pirate, apparently. Captain Raina laughed at my disgust before taking her drink back.

"I don't know how you like that," I groaned.

The captain laughed again at me.

"Hello, darlin'."

On the other side of the captain, a man made himself comfortable, leaning against the bar. He was tall and lean, head full of hair, and pale as a ghost. From where I was sitting, however, I could smell the beer in his breath. The man leaned in closer to Captain Raina. Too close.

"Piss off," was all she said before returning to her drink. The man didn't move. "I feel like I've seen you here before, lass." Captain Raina didn't answer.

"How many girls have you taken to bed, sweetheart? Three? Four?" Pervert.

"Was one of them your wife, sir? I've lost count of how many wives I've taken," Captain Raina said.

I bit the inside of my cheek to keep myself from laughing.

The man's face changed. "I'm sure you've taken many. You must have shown them a good time, but I doubt anyone has had as much fun with you as they've had with me." This guy loves to hear himself talk, huh?

Captain Raina chuckled. "Sir, you couldn't take an unmarried woman to bed, much less a married one. You see, women like men and, well, from what I've witnessed, you are anything but. As for why women prefer me, well, my blade is bigger than whatever you have in between your legs."

I turned my head away so that neither of them could see me starting to laugh. She showed him! When I got control of myself, I turned back, only to see that the man was now looking at me. He walked behind Captain Raina and stood in front of me.

"Maybe we'll let Sunshine over here decide that," the man said, stepping even closer into my personal space. "What do you think, darlin'?"

"I think you need to wake up, 'cause you're dreaming if you think I'd go with you," I said confidently.

But the man didn't think I was funny. He wrapped his long, meaty fingers around my arm and squeezed hard enough to cause pain.

"Hey—!" I started.

Captain Raina swung her mug over, hitting the man in the side of the head. I was free from his grasp. The man stumbled sideways and before I could fully register what was even happening, Captain Raina pulled out her pistol and shot the man in the head. I gasped, watching in terror as the man went limp. His head made contact with the wooden floor and blood spilled from his head. The music stopped, the talking stopped. Everyone was staring at us.

What did she just do?

"Captain Raina," Martin sighed, "this is the sixth time that you've done this. I can't afford to keep cleaning up blood."

Captain Raina stared down at the man a few seconds longer before squatting beside his body. She began searching his clothes for something. She pulled aside his vest and came back up with a small black pouch. She tossed it in the air toward Martin.

"For your troubles," she said. "Come along, Treasure."

My legs took a while to move. They were stiff. Eventually, I managed to tear my eyes away from the body and began following Captain Raina up the stairs.

"What's wrong?" she asked as we made it to our door. "Don't tell me you don't think he deserved it."

"You...you *shot* him!"

Captain Raina opened the door and smiled at me. "Pirate, Caity cat."

· · · · ·

At nightfall, we were served soup and bread. Besides that, no one came to bother us. One of the innkeepers came in and took the dishes away when we were done, however, leaving the captain and I alone once more.

"She was a sweet girl, you know," Captain Raina said out of nowhere.

"Who?" I asked.

"Margaret."

Oh…

Captain Raina removed her hat and set it down on one of the chairs. "She was very sweet and very smart; too smart for her own good at times."

I nodded. That's how I feel about my sisters, too. "So, you two were from the Witch

Domain?"

"Yes," Captain Raina said. "Our mother, Leonna, was a witch—a kitchen witch. I wanted to be like her. You see, her dishes were famous in our Domain. She was even offered a job at your castle as head chef, but she declined. You know the rest."

That's horrible. "What about your father?"

"What about him?"

"Where was he?"

"Don't know. He left after my mother told him she was pregnant with Margaret."

That damned pig! Her father left them all alone when they needed him! Fathers are supposed to be there! They're supposed to love and care and protect their children! He wasn't even there!

"I took a job as a seamstress," Captain Raina went on. "I was pretty good at it, but what I really wanted to do was make food for people. Everyone in all the kingdoms would come and tell others. Everyone would be welcome. Then Margaret died…" She let out a shuddered breath. "I wanted to die more than anything. My father was gone, as was my mother, and then my sister. But I soon realized I had something to live for. Vengeance. I wanted to kill Jotnar. I want him, Scathe, and Nimh dead. But I knew I couldn't do it alone, no matter how much I told myself that I could. So I went out to sea in search of my cousin. She was a pirate—captain of the Crimson Kraken, like I am now. She taught me everything I know about pirating: swordplay, mapping and charting, sailing. One night, we found ourselves on the run from other pirates. The cannonfire woke me up. I went to find my cousin, but when I did, she was on the verge of death. In her last breath, she made me captain. We managed to escape, but at a great cost. We then threw my cousin's body, along with many friends', into the ocean."

Captain Raina and I were facing each other now. Her fists were clenched and her shoulders had slumped. I've never seen her so defeated. I didn't know what else to do except... I got up, took a few steps forward, closing the distance between us, and wrapped her in a hug. I expected her to go stiff and rigid but she didn't. Instead, she wrapped her arms around me and hugged back. I can't imagine her pain. I can't remember my parents or my past, but she does. She's had to live with this alone, shouldering the responsibility of leading her crew and keeping them alive.

After a while, we pulled away. The captain smiled at me. "Thanks, Treasure. I needed that."

"I could tell."

"Come on. We leave tomorrow."

"Already?"

"We need to keep moving. And I got what I came for."

Something tells me that she's going to keep that certain detail to herself.

Chapter 10

Caitlin

The next morning, Captain Raina and I had breakfast in our room. It was pretty simple: warm porridge and tea. I thought sleeping next to her would be awkward, but it was anything but. We slept as far from each other as we could on our own sides of the bed, our backs facing each other. I was respectful of her space and she was respectful of mine.

"Go on," Captain Raina said, wiping her mouth with her napkin. "Out with it. You want to know why we came here of all places."

I sipped my tea. "You know me too well already. Can you blame me for being a little curious?"

Captain Raina gave me a lopsided grin and reached into her coat pocket. Her eyes stayed glued on me as she pulled out a necklace and showed it to me. The chain itself was gold; as for the actual necklace, it was gold like the chain, but the emblem was shaped like an octopus. Its eyes were sapphire blue; it looked like the octopus was staring into my soul.

"It's beautiful," I said to her.

Captain Raina smiled, pocketing the medallion. "It was my mother's. I thought I lost it when she died but I heard that scavengers raided my home after the siege and stole it. I don't know how it managed to survive."

"How did it get here?" I asked.

Captain Raina pushed her chair out, stood up, and stretched.

"Jaq, Martin's husband, managed to slip it away from one of the thieves and kept it safe for me. Martin has lived on this island all his life, but Jaq and I were friends. He lived in the Human Domain in Clover Talamh. He came with me to find my cousin."

"Really?"

"The pirate's life is not a life for him. He's found himself a future. He and Martin love each other. I understood his reason for leaving."

Captain Raina and I grabbed our weapons and met the crew downstairs. There were drunken individuals sleeping in chairs either at the bar or at a few of the tables, even some of the musicians. Martin was behind the counter cleaning along with another man. This man had tan skin, bright green eyes, long black hair, and had a trident tattooed on his bare shoulder. "Morning, Martin," Captain Raina said. "Jaq."

"Indeed it is, Captain," Martin said.

The man—Jaq—smiled at Captain Raina and then to me. "So, this is Cassidy?"

Captain Raina glanced at me. "Yes, my new recruit. Cassidy, meet Jaq."

"I've heard about you," I said politely. "Captain Raina has told me about you."

Jaq raised a brow and laughed. "Has she?"

Captain Raina rolled her eyes. "Shut up, Jaq."

"Or what? You'll have me walk the plank?"

"Don't tempt me."

I could tell she wasn't serious. They were just two old friends teasing each other and having fun.

"We'll be carrying on now," Captain Raina stated. "Until we meet again."

"Bye, Captain," Martin said.

"Goodbye," Jaq said. "Oh, and, Cassidy, don't let the Captain get your goat. She can act like a big blubbering baby half the time."

Captain Raina scowled at Jaq's joke. "Listen, you bilge-sucking—"

I quickly took Captain Raina's shoulders. "Okay, we're leaving! Bye, everybody!"

We boarded the ship and lifted the anchor. Captain Raina immediately ascended the steps and took the wheel.

"Raise the flag higher!" she shouted. "We must make haste, mates!"

I stood beside her. "To Asmund Rock?"

Captain Raina nodded, staring at something far away, something I couldn't see. "To Asmund Rock."

After a while of sailing, Captain Raina found me leaning against the railing. I had been staring off into the sea. It was the most beautiful thing I've ever seen.

"Liking the view?" Captain Raina asked, leaning next to me.

"I never thought I'd see the ocean like this," I admitted. "I've always wanted to. I mean, I did once, but that didn't count. I always wanted to see the world and discover new things."

"Maybe you were meant to be a pirate, then."

I snickered. "Hardly. I don't have it in me."

Suddenly, we heard something behind us. We turned around to find some of the crew jumping around, skipping, and dancing. One of the crew was sitting on a barrel playing an accordion. They were laughing. Some danced with arms locked together, others danced with daggers clenched in their teeth.

Captain Raina took my hand and led me toward the dancing crewmembers. "Dance with me, Caity cat."

I tried to pull away. "I can't dance!"

"None of us can! That's what makes it more fun!"

Holding hands, Captain Raina and I spun around in a circle with the crew cheering us on and cackling. We spun faster and faster until Captain Raina placed her hands on my hips and lifted me into the air. I couldn't help laughing as I looked down at her. She was laughing, really laughing. I had no idea how strong she was, either. She gently set me down, linking our arms together. We skipped around in a circle and for a moment, just a moment, it felt real. There wasn't anyone else on this ship except the two of us. I had no worries or fears. There was no war going on. It was just us.

Then…"Captain!" Everyone stopped laughing and dancing. One of the crew, who had taken over steering the ship, leaned over the balcony, panic as plain as day on his face. "There's a ship behind us, Captain! They're gaining on us!"

Captain Raina and her crew dispersed, running to their posts. I leaned over the side of the ship to get a better look at the ship coming after us. The ship itself was completely black, from the hull, to the bow, to the stern, to the masts. The sails were also black, but there was something embroidered on one of them. It looked like a compass, but the arrowheads were shaped to look like runes.

"Who's coming for us?" I cried up to Captain Raina.

Teeth clenched, a deep fury came to life in her eyes, one that I hadn't seen up until now. Captain Raina replied, "Jotnar's men."

Megan

Nightmares have filled my mind for the last few nights. Each time it was the same thing: Nimh. They all started off the same: I was playing with Amelia and our other siblings as children. We were playing by Robin's Creek, just south of our home. Our parents, Lord Liam and Lady Emer O'Dwyer, were back at our palace home, tending to papers. They were never good parents. Our mother was neglectful and was known for drowning her sorrows in ale and wine. Our father just could never be bothered with us. He always had an excuse: I need to work, children should be seen and not heard, I have no time to play.

Our older brother, Varian, was the first-born. He looked just like our father. Both had dark brown hair and sea green eyes. Our father was Lord of the Witch Domain (obviously) and was an eclectic witch—a witch who uses multiple practices in his craft—with Spirit as his element. As such, he always wore purple. Our mother looked like Amelia the most, though Amelia's hair was always long, unlike our mother's. She was a hearth witch with wind as her affinity.

Varian never wanted to be Lord of the Witch Domain. All he ever wanted was to leave that palace and start a family of his own. Unlike our father, Varian was a chaos witch with fire as his element. And unlike the rest of us, Varian hated his powers. He hated the fact that he was a witch at all. He ignored our parents' threats to come to the rituals and be involved in spellwork, much to their anger.

Let's just say it never ended well for him.

However, Varian, when he was of age, left our palace, pushing his powers down. One day, in the marketplace, he came across a woman—a human woman—with olive skin, gray eyes, and shoulder-length, almond-colored hair. Eve was her name. She was a bookkeeper at one of the inns looking to make her way into the world. The two fell in love and married. They had two daughters, Kaylee, who was two years younger than Caitlin and Garrett, and Shauna, only a year older than Brigit.

Felicia, the firstborn daughter, my oldest sister, was an eclectic witch like our father with Spirit as her element. She was always very bright, but never one to be part of a team. She faced our mother's wrath more than any of us, other than Varian. Because of that, once she was old enough to leave, she never spoke to either of our parents. She left, not wanting to be a noblewoman, either. She joined a brothel where a man planted a seed inside her. She gave birth to a boy—the first grandson—Aiden. He was six years old by the time the twins were born. He had sandy blonde hair, like Felicia, though hers was always long and curly. His was not. Felicia had brown eyes, but Aiden had blue eyes, no doubt like his father's. However, Felicia was never around to take care of him. She sent him away with my parents, where they raised him while she worked. As he got older, they became more estranged. And once again, four years after Brigit's birth, Felicia fell pregnant again with another child. A boy, once more. Finn. This time, we did know who the father was. He was a nobleman from the Human Domain of a neighboring kingdom, but he was spoiled, entitled, and selfish. He raised their son to be the same way.

Because of that, Finn was never the favorite grandchild.

I am a sea witch with water as my element, the middle child. I acted more like a boy, according to my parents; I played more with the boys and spoke more with them. I had several sisters growing up and even then, I never felt like I was one of them. Unlike either of our parents, I had red hair, just like my grandmother, Fiona O'Dwyer, my father's mother. She was a noblewoman from the Witch Domain who married a half-witch from town. Aside from that, my life changed when Angus and his father arrived at our castle. He was the first man I ever loved. He was smart, brave and kind. I knew that maybe if I married him, he could take me away from all this.

That never happened.

But Vivian, a green witch with earth as her element, was the kindest of us all. She had long dark brown hair and eyes, and accepted the fact that she would have to marry a noble. To this day, I still never understood how she remained so kind and thoughtful when we were forced to live through all kinds of hell. She married a few times, the first two never worked out well. Her third and final husband was a nobleman, an Elf from Sanctuarium. The first two were nobles, I should clarify, but they never treated my sister right... I may or may not have made them pay for how they treated her... Vivian was my best friend in the family, much like how Nora was Alison's. As if the abuse and mistreatment wasn't enough, Vivian always wanted children, but after being seen by a nurse, it was revealed that she was infertile. Her third husband did have children of his own, but they were in their early teens at that point. She always treated them with respect and showed them love, the love we were never shown.

Amelia was always spoiled. She never cared about anyone but herself. Whenever we had company, she would put on a mask and pretend to be sweet, but even then, it wasn't a very good mask. Whenever a servant "stepped out of line" she became ruthless, insulting them or making a mess for them to clean. Amelia was a cosmic witch with air as her element... If someone crossed her, it didn't matter how, she would create a storm which would destroy their homes. She had suitors lined up for her, regardless. How? I know not. She was cold and ruthless, but our mother still saw her as pure and incapable of causing harm.

Eventually, Amelia married Jonathon Sullivan. They had the twins and Brigit together. Then Jonathon became unfaithful and Amelia left him. She went crying to an old flame, Eluf, the first born and heir to our Domain—our kingdom. He had broken her heart when they were young, leading to Amelia wishing for death. We all tried being there for her, even when she didn't deserve it. She didn't care. She didn't even think about her children. She only thought of *her* future, what would happen to *her*, what would become of *her*.

Soon, only a year after leaving Jonathon, Eluf married Amelia while she was pregnant with Nora. Two years after Nora's birth, she had Alison. Now here we are...Amelia was the Insidious Sorceress, Nimh, and married to Jotnar. Together, they ruled the kingdom in fear—with Scathe, who was once Jonathon, constantly trying to rip the throne away from them. My siblings are dead.

Varian and Eve were killed in their house during the siege when magic caused their house to crumble. They were crushed. Whether or not Kaylee and Shauna escaped still remains a mystery. Felicia was killed with Finn, trying to get away from the Shadow Knights. Their bodies were found in the streets. The two had been stabbed and left to bleed out. Vivian and her husband were paralyzed by Shadow Knights in their home and were unable to do anything as these monsters slit their throats.

I don't know how I got away. I don't know. I don't know. I don't know! I don't know! I don't know! But I am one of the last of the O'Dwyers. My family was killed and somehow, for some reason, I was spared.

"Thank you for breakfast, Angus," I said, setting my empty bowl down.

"Thank you," Nora said.

"Thank you," Alison repeated.

"You're welcome," Angus chuckled. "I'm happy to help."

Nora turned to me. "When's our next magic lesson?"

"In a little bit, okay?" I said, fixing her hair. "I need to talk with Lord Angus first."

Alison stared at me with her lily pad green eyes. "Where's Gary and Caity? And what about Brigit?"

I bit my lip and took Alison's hands. "We're going to find them. Don't worry. We'll see them again. Just remember, they're safe. We're safe. That's all that matters right now."

"How do you know they're safe?" Nora asked.

I took her hand and looked from her to Alison. "I just know. Now go play and have fun."

Nora took Alison's hand and the two ran out of the tent. I looked up at Angus. "Any word on where they could be?"

"Not yet," Angus answered. "I'm waiting to hear back from a raven."

He took a seat next to me. "How did you get a cloaking spell to work, anyway?"

Angus looked away, suddenly unable to meet my gaze. "I had some help."

"I can tell. But who cast the spell?"

Angus hesitated before answering me. "The Lady of the Fairies, Freya."

My eyes widened. I was immediately on my feet. The stool I had been sitting on fell over on its side, but I didn't care. "Did you just say Lady Freya of the Fairy Domain?"

"Megan—"

I started pacing. "You know that the fae are enemies to witches!"

"I had no choice!"

Angus was on his feet now, blocking my path. "Almost all witches in this land were wiped out. We needed a place to hide and there were enemies hunting us down like wild animals. Time was running out, as were our options!"

"So you accept help from the fae?"

"Megan, it was the only way."

I took a breath and rubbed my temples. "Fine. It was the only way. Does that make her an ally?"

"It's possible. It may also be possible that she knows where the rest of your family is."

I clenched my teeth. "I am *not* asking the fae for help."

"I know your rivalry has been alive since the days of yesterday," Angus said, holding my shoulders, "but please. Consider this. If we don't hear back from the raven, we will have to look to other sources. This may be the only way to find your family."

I was about to rebut when Angus leaned down and kissed me. He *kissed* me, something he hadn't done in years. Whatever I was about to say was completely forgotten about as I stood taller and kissed Angus back.

Chapter 11

Thomas

I haven't had a restful night in a long time. Sleeping has been hard for me. When I was younger, I suffered from night terrors; I'd wake up screaming in the dead of night, which caused my mother to rush in to check on me. I can't remember what I'd see in my dreams. When I woke, it was all just memories of darkness.

My mother loved my father, though I never knew who he was for a while. She'd tell me stories of their time together and how he was always a good man.

My mother always said she loved me, but she never was good at showing it. There were days where I was so cold and hungry. I tried telling her, but my mother never acknowledged me. It was like she was in another time; while her physical body was right in front of me, mentally, she was elsewhere, most likely thinking about my father and wanting him so badly to come back.

Eventually, my mother couldn't take it anymore and threw herself over a cliff. I can't remember her name. I do remember she had sun-kissed skin, brown eyes, and long, wavy dark brown hair. She was a fortune teller—a very skilled one. Ask her any kind of question. She knew the answer, whether it be about a past life, the future, relationships, it mattered not. She just always knew.

To this day, I can still smell her perfume: jasmine.

I didn't know my mother killed herself until the news spread to my village three days later. I had no one to feed or take care of me other than myself, which was nothing new. I just figured she finally left me for a better life with my absent father. The Captain of the Guard found her body, which others in the village identified. I was found, six years old and all alone. I have always been alone.

I woke up with a start, taking a moment to remember where I was. I sat up in bed and stared at my two callused hands. What these hands have done—the horrendous things—the monstrous things…

My room was small, only big enough for a bed and my wardrobe. I had a window, but the view wasn't spectacular: only the courtyard and shed.

As usual, I was the first to wake. I rubbed my temples before climbing out of bed and preparing for the day. I dressed in my usual fashion: a long-sleeved pullover black shirt, black leather pants, long black suede boots, and my black trench coat. I crept down the hallways. It was dark; no candles were lit. Not ever. Not even during the winter was there ever a fire. Magic fueled this castle. We had no need for lumber, sunlight, or any other miscellaneous things. That's what my father told me growing up, anyway.

I made my way downstairs, through the dining area (grabbing some bread and fruit and then stuffing them inside my satchel), and into another corridor. There were guards posted just outside the door to the dungeon. I paid them no mind and went on. Flicking my wrist, I summoned a ball of fire in my hand. I sprinted down the rest of the way and turned to where the cells were. Inside one of them was *her*.

Muriel. Hearing my footsteps, her eyes slowly fluttered open. Her long black hair fell past her bare shoulders. Her skin was dark, as were her eyes. Her gray dress was long and covered in dirt. When she realized it was me, Muriel's eyes lit up and she quickly sat up on her knees, taking the bars in her hands.

"Thomas!" she beamed.

I grabbed a nearby torch and used the fire in my hand to light it. I placed the torch back on the hook above Muriel's cell and extinguished the flame in my hand before crouching on my side of her cell.

"I came as soon as I could," I said, reaching for my satchel. I pulled out the bread and the fruit, slipping them through the bars and into her hands. "Here, eat this."

Muriel gladly took the food, setting it in her lap. "Thank you."

I took her hand. "It was all I could grab in the moment—"

"Thomas, I appreciate it, really."

I pressed my head against the bars. "I want you back in my arms."

"I know. I want you to be in mine, too. You and Petra."

My heart tightened at the sound of her name. "I will find her, Muriel. I promise."

"I know. Are you sure you can't just ask my father for help?"

I chuckled humorlessly. "My dear, your father would not listen to me, not with everything I've done."

"You had no choice, Thomas."

"I know that, you know that, but no one else does."

Not even my own siblings. I haven't even told my father that they have returned to Clover Talamh...or that their memories were completely wiped of this world. Of him. Me.

"I need to go," I said. "But I'll come back to check on you when I've finished my patrol."

"I look forward to that." Muriel smiled, blinking away tears. "Seeing you is the only good thing about being stuck here."

I stroked her cheek with my thumb. "I will stop him. I'll find a way to free you. Now eat." I stood up, making my way to the stairs.

"I love you, Thomas," Muriel said gently.

"I love you, too," I said back to her. I smiled once before taking the stairs back up. I keep my promises. No one will hurt the people I care about again. I don't have much to go on as a plan, but what I do know is this: Once I kill my father, I am going to kill Nimh and Jotnar. Not just for what they did to Muriel, to me, but what they all did to my family.

Garrett

"Run, Katrina!" I yelled.

I could hear screams echoing in the distance as Katrina and I ran hand-in-hand. The camp had been lit ablaze. I felt like I was running in the pits of

Hell. I ignored the pain in my chest as we ran past more houses and...bodies. There were bodies scattered across the camp. Some had huge scratch marks across their backs. Others were bruised and beaten. Many were dead, but I didn't stop to count them.

Suddenly, Katrina was yanked out of my grasp. She screamed as a Shadow Knight lifted her up into the air and began flying away. I ran after them, summoning my magic.

"Spirits, I need you!" I cried. "End this beast!"

I stretched my hand toward the sky—toward the monster. Spirit slammed into the Shadow Knight, turning it into dust. Katrina screamed as she fell. I stopped in time to catch her, only I wasn't prepared. We both fell with a hard thud to the ground. It took a second to get my bearings...and to see that Katrina was sitting directly on top of me.

Oh...

"Come on! Get up!" Katrina said, pulling me up. "We have to run! Go!"

"The horses!" I shouted.

The two of us ran to Pluto and Heaven, taking them by their reins. They were in a panic.

What's happening, Red?

"I'll explain later! Get us out of here!"

Katrina and I mounted the horses and started running in the direction of the woods.

"The cloaking spell only goes so far!" Katrina explained. "Once we cross the border, we'll be out in the open! We'll have to find another place to hide!"

"Sounds like a plan!"

We rode faster and faster, trying to put as much distance between ourselves and the burning camp. I dared myself to look over my shoulder. Every house at this point was burning. Smoke was licking the sky followed by flying silhouettes of the Shadow Knights. I turned back to see a Shadow Knight screeching like a banshee, claws out, and lunging for me. I was just about to summon Spirit when Orion jumped on the monster's back. He threw his head back, snarling and baring his fangs, before slamming his head into the Shadow Knight's neck. The creature screeched louder, trying to get Orion off him.

However, Orion was the one with the high ground. Orion threw himself forward, swinging the Shadow Knight over his shoulder and sending it into a large fire. The thing shrieked as it burned, and a smell I hope to never smell again filled the air as we took off.

We crossed the barrier, exposing ourselves to whatever darkness awaited. We all met at a river nearby, the same one Katrina took me to. There were survivors, but no one looked happy. Some were bleeding, some were passed out, some were crying.

Katrina and I climbed off our horses and stared at the sight. This is what happens when you rebel against Scathe and Jotnar?

"I'm going to go find Sir Charles," Katrina said quietly. "He'll know what to do next."

"You think he's okay?"

"He's probably not happy, but besides that, yes. He's a warrior, the strongest of us all." Katrina was about to turn when she pressed her hand on my shoulder and pecked my cheek.

"Thanks for helping me, by the way."

All I could do as she walked away was stare.

Chapter 12

Caitlin

Members of the crew began to climb the riggings to get to the crow's nests. The seas became rocky and the wind started picking up. I spotted some of the crew loading the canons and went to help.

"No, Caitlin!" Captain Raina exclaimed. "Control the water!"

I nodded and ran to the bow. Leaning over, I held my hand out to the sea as the crew prepared for battle. We were suddenly lifted up on a wave before being slammed back down. The sea was out of control! I turned to the side and imagined a massive wall appearing between us and the ship behind us. A few seconds later, there was an explosion behind us. Everyone gasped and spun their heads. Water had rocketed miles up into the air before flowing into a long, clear wall as tall as a mountain. It looked almost like a beacon on the water. I held my hands up to the wall, my feet shoulder-width apart.

Sheila ran to my side. "That won't hold them back, Caitlin. They'll find a way across! There are still openings on either side they can come across! Not to mention sailing through the wall won't do them any harm!"

"It may not stop them, but at least we'll get a head start!" I said with a grunt. "Tell the captain I won't be able to hold the wall for long. We need to hurry! Keep loading the cannons just in case!"

Sheila ran in the direction of the captain to tell her the news. Muscles strained as I struggled to keep the wall up.

We just need a head start… We just need a head start…

I looked over my shoulder. It was all just sea. There were no caves or islands we could head to and hide in. Sweat dripped down the side of my head and my muscles were screaming. The ship suddenly shot up on another wave and slammed back down. I tripped, losing my focus. The wall faltered—only a little—but it was enough for Jotnar's crew. Their ship sailed through the watery veil, faster than they had been going beforehand.

We were running out of time.

Panicking, I ran to find Captain Raina who was still steering the ship.

"It was a good effort," she said.

"Just not enough. They're right behind us!" Unless… "Captain, let them catch up to us!"

Captain Raina (rightfully so) looked at me like I was nuts. "*Let* them? You want to be lost to Davy Jones?"

"If they get close enough, I can sink their ship!" I explained. "Right now this is the best chance we've got at stopping them!"

Captain Raina considered it before turning the wheel all the way to the side. "Alright. Off with you."

I ran down the steps and back on to the deck. Jotnar's ship was coming in close.

"Ready!" Captain Raina shouted over the sounds of the waves. "Aim!"

The hull of their ship was closing in…and…

"Fire!"

Cannonfire sounded and shook the ship. We made some hits, but the enemy had cannons of their own. I had to act fast before they sank us first. I climbed up on the side of the ship, taking position. I thought of a hot spring. I imagined the streams of water rocketing up towards the sky, much like my wall had minutes before. If I do this right, they'll be blown sky high! "Now, Captain!" I shouted over my shoulder. "Turn the ship away!"

I felt the ship spin as Captain Raina released the wheel. I raised my hands, flicking both my wrists. The water beneath Jotnar's ship exploded, sending the ship flying into splinters and slivers of wood miles above us. I jumped back and ducked to avoid getting hit. When I dared to look up after a few seconds, the enemy's ship was gone. The crew cheered at our victory.

I did it! I saved us! I made my way to Captain Raina, excited to share our win, when I saw she was lying on the ground, holding her bleeding arm.

"Oh, no!" I exclaimed. "Your arm!"

"I nicked it!" she said through clenched teeth. She cocked her head to the ground to reveal a long iron hook. "One of Jotnar's men shot it at me with a bow before their ship went up."

I pushed her hand away to get a better look at the bleeding. It was a long, deep cut that went straight across her upper arm.

"Hang on," I said, "I've got this."

Placing my hand over her cut, I only thought of healing her. I thought of taking away her pain with the healing properties water has. Tendrils of water poured from my palm, trailing across Captain Raina's injury. The bleeding stopped and the cut melted away, like it had never even been there to begin with. There wasn't even so much as a scar.

Captain Raina looked up at me, her breathing still heavy. "Thank you."

"It was nothing."

"Nothing?" Captain Raina got to her feet and took my hand before pulling me up. "You just saved my crew. You saved me. You call that nothing?"

Captain Raina led me to the top of the stairs and raised our linked hands up into the sky.

"Listen up, mates! For saving our skins from Jotnar, for showing bravery and boldness, Caitlin Sullivan shall be rewarded as being my first mate! First Mate Caitlin of the Crimson Kraken!"

The crew cheered and whistled their congratulations. Hearing this news, I couldn't help but stare in astonishment at the captain. She smiled at me. "You are now officially one of us."

Thomas

I rode back to my men on my horse once our patrol of the castle had ended. Nothing was out of the ordinary. No one was out, despite it being later in the morning. Not even ravens could be heard in the forest. We rode back to the castle, the one that had been home to Garrett, Caitlin, Brigit, and myself.

That was before everything fell apart.

As I sharpened my sword in the courtyard, knights passed, carrying helmets and talking quietly amongst themselves. Others practiced with swords and archery. The Shadow Knights were out either hunting or interrogating prisoners. To think they had all once been dead before my father resurrected them to take out Jotnar and Nimh. They were constantly blood hungry and ruthless, always looking for something to kill. If it weren't for me keeping them in line with the spell I cast on them to serve only me, there would be no one in the kingdom for my father to terrorize.

I've learned never to trust anyone. First my mother, then my father, and eventually, I learned not to trust Queen Amelia and King Eluf. As a child, I was allowed to visit my brother and sisters, but even then I knew Amelia was not fond of me. To keep her reputation untarnished, she spread a rumor that my father had been unfaithful to her their first few years of marriage when in actuality, I was born before he had asked for her hand. In Amelia's eyes, I was only a worthless pest—a roadblock in her marriage and in her life. Life with my father was not what my mother talked about when she was alive. He fed me when he remembered, and whenever I angered him, he'd whip me and lock me in one of the towers. I'd bang on the door and scream until my voice was hoarse before falling asleep alone in the cold room.

The only thing that kept me alive were my brother and sisters. Until Muriel came along.

• • • • •

When dinner had ended, I placed some chicken, salad, and a corn muffin on a plate.

Carrying that in one hand and a goblet of water in another, I made my way to the dungeon. Muriel was sitting on the floor, her head down with her hands folded neatly in her lap.

"Muriel?" I called.

Muriel lifted her head at the sound of my voice and smiled. "Hello, Thomas."

I placed the goblet down next to the plate on the floor and waved my hand over them. A black mist enveloped the meal, teleporting it into Muriel's cell. "Thank you."

"You don't have to thank me, dear."

"But I do. Scathe is keeping me here locked up all hours of every day. It may not be a great life I'm living right now, but I thank the Gods every morning that I'm still even alive and that I have you."

She stood up and wrapped her fingers around the bars of her cell. I covered her hands and stared into her eyes.

"How can you still be so full of light after being trapped in here for over a year?" I asked.

Muriel smiled. "Because I have hope. I have to hope that I'll get out, that I'll be with you and our family again and that you will all bring back the light."

I gave her hand a light squeeze. "If I find my siblings, how will I know they won't regain their memories and hate me?"

"If they truly are your family, then they will understand."

"Family doesn't have to forgive each other."

"I know. You still haven't forgiven your mother."

"Do you think I should?"

"No."

I reached through the bars with one hand and cupped Muriel's face. "Do you think Petra will forgive me?"

Muriel smiled, covering my hand that rested on her cheek. "There is nothing to forgive, Thomas. She was taken from us. You tried to protect her, as a father should."

"As a parent should, my love."

Suddenly, we heard footsteps near the door. The dungeon went completely dark. The room suddenly became colder than it should have been. Father was summoning me.

"I have to go," I said.

Muriel's lip trembled. "I hate hearing you say that."

"I hate saying it," I said as I brushed a few strands of her hair past her ear, "but this is the only way right now to ensure your safety. I'll be back in the morning."

"Same time?"

I smiled. "Always."

Even though I didn't want to, even though it killed me as it always did, even though I'd give anything to stay with Muriel, I released her from my touch. But before I went upstairs to meet with my father, I flicked my wrists, setting all the torches on fire, offering Muriel some light in the darkness.

Chapter 13

Muriel

I listened to Thomas's footsteps getting further and further away. It worried me every time he had to go. I would have nightmares of Thomas dying by the hands of Scathe. Every nightmare of him dying was different. I'd be forced to watch him drown, bleed to death, hang, burn alive, and sit in a tub of his own blood, staring at me with cold, lifeless eyes. I'd wake up calling his name desperately with tears streaming down my face. He'd be there at once, always knowing when I was having nightmares. He couldn't hold me, but just his company was enough.

That's a lie. It's not enough to not be with each other, to be out of reach. I want to hold him and Petra. I want to be out of this cell. I want our home back, our freedom, I want this war to end.

Every day I pray to the Gods for my father's safety as well as the safety and health of my own family. I pray that we see each other again and that we make it out alive.

I never knew my mother, but my father was always good to me. When he wasn't with the knights, he was playing with me and tutoring me. For the longest time, my father had been my best friend, my only friend.

Until I met Thomas.

One day, I was in the marketplace buying items for dinner when I spotted a boy, just a few years older than me, buying herbs from a nearby shop. I didn't see his face at first, only the back of his head. Something drew me to him and I dared to step closer, trying to look discreet.

When the boy turned, I finally saw his face. He looked older than he appeared, a solemn look on his face.

Though he was quite handsome.

I turned away, continuing on in the marketplace. But something was wrong. Something had happened to spook a horse-drawn carriage, one of King Eluf's. It sped towards me in the street, showing no sign of turning, slowing down, or stopping. I froze, unable to move. Mere inches away from the spooked horses, I was pulled into the air and out of the way. When the stranger set me down on my feet, I started to thank them, realizing it was the boy from the nearby shop.

"Are you okay?" the boy asked.

"I am," I said shyly. "Thank you."

The boy smiled, cocking his head toward the disappearing carriage. "You should be more careful. I hear the king is a temperamental bastard."

"Shh!" I giggled. "You can't say that! It's treason!"

"Only if he hears me say it himself," the boy said smugly. "Until then, he would have to take the word of another. Even then, he'd still need proof before he flogs me."

I chuckled. This boy was fearless—possibly mad—but fearless. "I'm Muriel."

"Thomas."

The two of us walked along through the marketplace talking about our hobbies and dreams. I told him how I loved reading and longed to open my own shop; that my father was Captain of the Guard.

"Charles Morgan, eh?" Thomas asked. "I've met him. He's a great warrior."

"He is, but if you don't mind, how do you know my father?"

Thomas averted his eyes downward, suddenly shy. "My siblings are the Sullivans."

My eyes widened. "The King's wards?"

"I wouldn't say wards, but yes. I am their older brother." He paused. "Go ahead. Say it."

"Say what?"

"That I'm a bastard. It's true, so it is not an insult."

I shook my head, my brows knit together. "Thomas, you are no less a man just because you are their half-brother. You deserve love and respect just as much as anyone."

Thomas snickered in disbelief. "That is kind of you to say, Muriel."

"I only speak the truth."

"Thomas!" a boy cried.

A young boy ran over, one with red hair and a purple cloak. "Thomas, come! Mother is going into labor!"

The boy with red hair pulled Thomas along, but Thomas turned to look at me one more time. "Meet me here again tomorrow, Muriel. I wish to see you again."

My heart skipped a beat and I couldn't help but smile. "I wish to see you again, too, sir."

Thomas flashed me a smile before letting his brother pull him the rest of the way to their home.

Brigit

For the next few days, I kept practicing archery and working on my magic. Salem was by my side supporting me and helping me at every turn. I still felt awkward about my breakdown, but Salem was nice enough to not bring it up. Something tells me, though, that my breakdown is the main reason why he's been at my side.

One morning after breakfast, Queen Valentina sent me out to find herbs and bring them back. She gave me a list of their names along with descriptions—the poisonous kind and the non-poisonous kind. When she said that Akoni would be accompanying me, however, Salem insisted that he go in his place, saying that Akoni needs to focus more on preparing for his coronation in the next month.

But I knew better.

Salem walked side by side with me into the woods, his quiver and bow at the ready. Apparently, a hidden group of rebels—the Defyers—had their camp compromised, even with a cloaking spell, so Queen Valentina doesn't want to take any chances, but since I'm a green witch, she says I need to know more about plants and herbs.

"I don't mean to pry, Lady Brigit," Salem said, holding his hand out for me, "but have you had any recollections of the past?"

I took his hand and let him help me over a fallen tree before answering. "No, can't say I have."

"I'm sorry to hear that," he said as we continued on. "No one deserves to lose memories of who they were."

We stopped in front of a tree that went as high as the eye could see. It was covered in long green leaves about the size of my arm with long green blossoms sitting together. I looked at the list and back at the blossoms. "Salem, these are cloves, right?"

I showed him the list with the drawings. He nodded. "Indeed they are, but do you know their magical properties?"

I was tempted to look back down at the list, but the urge to impress Salem with my own knowledge suppressed that feeling.

"Protection, money, love, and power, to name a few," I said.

Salem smiled at me. "Very good."

He reached up and plucked a few of the blossoms from the tree, handing them to me. "When we get back to the castle, we will have to put them in jars. My mother has a lair where she does magic, but we'll be sure to have one built for you soon."

I placed the cloves in my satchel, trying to hide the smile stretching across my face. "My own lair?"

Is that a blush I saw on Salem's cheeks? "Well, you are a guest in our home. It makes sense that you have your own space."

I bit the inside of my cheek, stopping myself from breaking out into a fit of laughter. "Sounds good. This is my new home, so...yeah. I agree. I'd love to have a place of my own to practice magic."

Salem's face lit up when I said the word 'home' and he took my hand. "Let us continue with your learning, Milady."

. . . . .

Later on, I was alone in my room lying on my bed, smiling to myself. I like Salem. A lot.

I think he likes me, too.

I thought it was weird how girls in school would get so worked up over a crush. I mean, technically a crush is just your brain releasing a hormone, which is why you feel so excited.

That's all it is.

And yet, here I am, smiling like an idiot and thinking about Salem constantly. I get super excited when meals come around because I know Salem is always outside my room waiting for me. He accompanies me everywhere. It can't just be because he's being a good host, right?

I was always afraid of getting into relationships. Not just because I was afraid of rejection and humiliation, but because I've seen and heard about all the bad things—the toxic traits. I've seen some couples get in and out of relationships, someone would cheat, someone would manipulate and gaslight another, sometimes someone would show up in class wearing clothes that would cover up their skin in 90 degree weather. I didn't want anything like that to happen to me, so I kept to myself, never taking a chance.

I sat up in bed, throwing my legs over the side. I'm going to tell Salem I like him. I'm going to tell him! I've just got this feeling that we're supposed to be together, that he likes me back!

I sprinted to my bedroom door, ready to yank it open and run throughout the castle until I found him, when I heard two people quietly talking a few feet from my room.

"Mother, you know that this isn't appropriate." Akoni? "You know as well as I that this is completely unacceptable."

"Akoni, Salem is not courting her," Queen Valentina said. "He is simply trying to keep her safe and help her regain her powers."

"And what of her memories, Mother? Has he been trying at all to help her regain those, too?"

"Mind your tongue, Akoni."

105

"Forgive me, Mother. I didn't mean it in that way. I just can't help but feel that maybe

Salem does not want her to regain her memories at all."

Why wouldn't Salem want me to remember? What's even going on?

"No one knows that she is here, my son," Queen Valentina said silently. "She is still your betrothed, you don't have to worry."

I covered my mouth, stifling a gasp, and backed away from the door. Legs shaking, I threw myself in my chair and pressed my hand flat against my chest. My heart was racing so fast, I may as well have just run a marathon. *Betrothed? I'm fucking engaged? To Akoni?*

I let out a shuddering breath before letting the tears fall rapidly down my face. This can't be happening. This can't be real.

How can this be happening?

Chapter 14

Thomas

"Let me out!" I cried in the darkness. My fists banged on the door of the tower. I was in the highest one—the one Father always threw me in whenever I displeased him. He didn't whip me this time, which was surprising, but I silently thanked the Gods for it, if they could hear me. The only thing in that room besides me was a stone bed against the wall, but there were no blankets, not even a pillow. The only light I had was the light of the moon shining through the teardrop-shaped window. I had thought about escaping on many counts, but the drop was too far down. Sometimes I would imagine sprouting wings as dark as a raven's and flying far away from here. I'd take my brother and sisters with me and we'd fly to the moon and stars together. The daydreaming would help when I wanted to drown out the sounds of my growling stomach and the pains that would follow.

Fat tears wetted my cheeks as I slowly stooped to the stone floor. "Please let me out…!"

The image changed and suddenly I was storming across the throne room towards my father. This was after his transformation to a horned beast. He stared at me incredulously, putting his hand up to keep his Shadow Knights from lunging at me. Panting—blood boiling—I raised my voice, storming closer and closing the distance between us.

"Where are they?" I demanded.

Father gave me a small, lazy shrug. "Who?"

I clenched my fists, fire igniting the candles in the room. Even the fireplace that was always out came to life with a roaring fire.

"You know exactly of whom I speak!" I growled. "What have you done to them!"

I gasped, shooting up in bed and covered in sweat. Breathe, I reminded myself. Just breathe.

Every night I had a nightmare and every night I've been forced to relive every horrible thing that I've had to endure. When I was with Muriel, I still had nightmares, but she was always there to remind me that those days had passed, that I was safe.

How I long to feel that way again.

Breakfast was the same as always. I ate on one side of the table next to where Father used to sit. Other knights, the mortals, would join me, but we never conversed. We ate our biscuits and sausages, not having to acknowledge each other. The knights spoke with each other, but never conversed with me. They all feared me too much as Scathe's son and lieutenant. That was fine.

As I ate, I thought back to when Muriel, Petra, and I would eat together. I helped Muriel cook on more than one occasion. The first time we did so, I had confessed that I had been cooking for myself before I even learned how to read. It was a small kitchen in her home, hardly enough room for two people, but we never complained. I did try to respect her space, however.

Muriel cooked bacon and eggs while I assisted her with the toast and seasoning. When she prepared our plates, I poured each of us a glass of milk and brought out the silverware. We made conversation as we ate, talking about our families. She was the first one I ever confided in about them: about my parents, my brother, and my sisters. I didn't break down, not even once. I never shed a single tear telling Muriel my story.

But she did. She placed her hands over mine and looked me in the eyes, her cheeks stained with tears. She told me two words that surprised me, two words I never heard anyone say to me in my fifteen years of life.

"I'm sorry."

When Petra was born, I was the one making breakfast while helping Muriel care for our daughter. Petra was a newborn at the time we found ourselves a new home. She had my dark brown hair and her mother's beautiful brown eyes. I never had a good parental figure in my life, but I knew I wanted to be better. I wanted to take care of my family, to show them love and protect them.

Then I realized my father had sent his soldiers to our home. He found me. I failed my family. He took them away from me. He took Muriel and kept her locked away in his dungeon. As for Petra, neither of us knew. Father promised that no harm would come to her, but only if I obeyed every one of his commands. If I stepped out of line, he'd kill Muriel and Petra. His first command that I was forced to follow: kill my brother and sisters.

In the throne room, I had tied up a man in rags. A Defyer. His hair was matted and he was covered in bruises. The knights had found and captured him after I set their camp on fire. He put up a fight, which is impressive. Usually prisoners are too afraid to breathe in the presence of one of us.

"Where have the Defyers gone?" I asked calmly.

No answer.

I lifted my hand and squeezed my fingers into a fist. The man began to suffocate, his veins starting to pop in his head. I released him from my hold, allowing him to gasp for breath.

"I will...never...tell...you..." the man coughed.

I cocked my head to the side and the man screamed in pain, screaming like he was on fire. Well, in a way, he was. His blood right now burned through his skin, setting him ablaze, including his heart. I straightened my head and the man started to wheeze, tears pooling from his eyes.

"They're...heading...towards...the...Dwarf Domain..." the man panted. "Please...please don't do this. Please stop...make it stop. Please."

So I did. I flicked my hand upward. By doing so, the man's head twisted and the life left his eyes.

I took the body out back and watched it burn for a few minutes. I had the information I needed, but I had to torture it out of an innocent man, a survivor. At the end of the day, he and I were not so different. Perhaps in another life, we could have been friends. Perhaps in another life, we would not have lost so much.

But such things were not in our control.

Inside the study, I was surrounded by knights. I had set a map of the kingdom over the table. I stood in the very center while the knights stood on either side studying the map.

"The Defyers are heading towards the Dwarf Domain," I said, tapping a gloved finger on the map. "That's where most men who are part of Jotnar's army are stationed. Up until today, they had a cloaking spell to protect them. If they keep going in that direction, through the Dwarf Domain unharmed, they may reach the borders of Sanctuarium."

"How long would that take them?" asked a knight.

"With horses, about a week," I said simply.

And my brother would be among them.

"What is the plan?" asked another knight.

"We'll have to follow them," I explained.

"Going into a territory full of Jotnar's soldiers is suicide!"

"Which is why we will not be going to the Dwarf Domain," I said, pointing to the Human Domain on the map. "The Defyers were hiding here. The Elf Queen of Sanctuarium cast the cloaking spell in the first place, one I was able to penetrate. I can also get in undetected."

"You'll be going after them alone?" a knight asked in disbelief.

"I don't intend to kill the Defyers. There are many, yes, but we have more in numbers. Besides, it's not them I have to kill."

"Lord Garrett."

I swallowed. "Yes. All I have to do is find him first."

"And if Scathe demands to know why none of us are with you?"

"You will all go out on patrol to secure our territory," I explained, pointing from the Human Domain to the Centaur Domain to the Goblin Domain. "I will place a cloaking spell on myself to stay hidden from his visions, as well as Nimh's. Stay within our borders and stay hidden. No harm will come to you. If, for whatever reason, you find yourselves back here, tell Scathe I sent you back to avoid Jotnar and Nimh."

A slight pain shot through my arm. I balled my hands into fists at my side and held back a groan. "You are all dismissed. Meet outside within the hour. Scathe is summoning me."

Without any more words, the knights filed out of the study and made their way down the corridor. I folded up the map and tucked it on the inside of my coat before the burning sensation returned, this time stronger, like someone had taken a hot iron skillet and pressed it against my skin.

Scathe was not in a patient mood. Locking the door behind me, I walked in the direction of Scathe's quarters. I only ascended the first flight of stairs before I raised my arms up on either side of my head. My body tingled for a moment before my surroundings changed. I was standing in a dark room with a four-poster bed that had been broken in half. The windows were covered with curtains that had been blanketed in layers of dust. There were some candles scattered on the floor, but they had not been lit in half a decade. In the center of the room, slouched in an armchair covered in velvet cushions, was Scathe. Carelessly slamming my arms against my sides, I glowered at him.

"I was nearly done with my meeting when you summoned me the first time," I said, hardly suppressing a growl. "You didn't need to do so a second."

"This is important, Thomas," Scathe said airily. "I have no time to sit here and wait."

"Clearly."

"What was your meeting about?"

"The knights and I will be patrolling the borders for the next few days looking for anyone who might have some information on the whereabouts of the Sullivans."

"Is that so? What of Nora and Alison Helvig? Megan O'Dwyer?"

"Can *you* not find them?"

Scathe's eyes shot up and stared hard at me, threatening. "My powers are weak the longer I am away from my talisman, yet one of them is closing in on it. You, my *son*, have to find out which one, take back my talisman, and kill the others."

"You think one of them is nearing the location of your talisman?" I asked, hardly believing a word he said.

"MY TALISMAN IS THE ONLY THING KEEPING ME ALIVE BE-SIDES THE THIRST I CRAVE FROM SEEING NIMH AND JOTNAR DEAD!"

The words echoed off the wall, much like a batcave. I didn't flinch.

"Return my talisman to me, kill those bloody, sniveling parasites," Scathe hissed, "or I will kill Muriel and your child and force you to watch."

The amount of strength it took for me to not summon my powers and kill him myself was unbearable. I wanted to. I wanted to end his life desperately, but with the hex Scathe placed on me, it kept me from doing so. And he is the only one who knows where Petra is. An invisible force pushed my powers back as if someone was pushing my head underwater.

I gave Scathe a low bow, keeping my eyes glued on his, not hiding the hatred I felt for him.

"Yes, *Father.*"

Chapter 15

Megan

Angus and I managed to pull away from each other after our kiss right before one of his recruits arrived. I left the two to talk as I went to find the girls. On the other side of camp, they were playing tag with a few of the centaur and satyr children. I called them over and we began our lesson. I am a water witch, so I know nothing about air or fire magic. Varian was supposed to teach Alison as she got older while Nora would have learned from, well, her mother. I only taught Caitlin how to use her water magic, but perhaps, I could give the girls some idea on how to control their powers in general.

"Let's begin," I say as the girls sit on a few nearby stumps. "Anyone with magic can cast a spell because they seek out something: clarity and purpose. We use magic for a reason: to protect ourselves and others. But magic can take energy, time, effort, and most of all, focus and belief. Sometimes those last two are hard to come by, especially because we were in a place where magic didn't exist."

"There's magic here, though," Nora pointed out.

I smiled. "Exactly. It's everywhere. Magic is energy that flows through every living thing, including you."

"It's a super power, then?" Alison asked.

I clapped my hands together gently. "Power, my little spitfire, is what we use to channel our magic. We must build it up if we are to use it, which is what we're doing right now. With power, you can manipulate any magic and influence it to do whatever you desire. Actually, that's essentially what spells are. They are fueled by emotion and are another way we can use magic."

"So are we good witches," Nora started, "like Glinda?"

I shrugged. "Well, that's the thing, sweetheart. Magic isn't good or evil, it's only the heart of the witch that matters. As I've said, we use our power to keep ourselves and each other safe. To keep you two safe, sometimes Auntie Megan has to hurt people, bad people. Not everything is black and white. Does that make sense?" The girls nodded.

"Now, just like with normal, everyday life, words have an impact," I continued. "In spellwork, words have power. Writing your thoughts and feelings in a diary, for example, or wishes, helps manifest results. In fact, sometimes, a journal can be more than that. You can use that to create a grimoire."

"Grim—what?" Alison asked, her eyebrows scrunched together.

I chuckled. "A book of spells, Ali. You don't need one, of course, but it helps. Spells are mostly used to bring balance when needed. When magic doesn't flow both ways, things could go wrong. If you create a spell yourself, that's when they are even more impactful."

"Is that what we're gonna do today, Auntie Megan?" Nora asked excitedly.

"Are we gonna cast a spell?" Alison eagerly asked.

I put my hands up. "Not quite yet. First, we must channel your powers, so stand up."

The girls obliged and stood on either side of me. "You each were born with an element to help you in your craft. Garrett is a spirit witch, meaning he can see and speak with the dead."

Alison grabbed my skirt and hid her face in it. "That sounds scary. I don't like that power."

I stooped down and patted her head. "Power isn't something you should fear, my sweet. You must embrace it. Caitlin's element is water and Brigit's element is earth. Together, they can do just about anything they wish." I turned to Nora and caressed her cheek. "You, Nora, have wind as your element."

Nora's shoulders slumped in disappointment. "Wind? That's lame."

I bit the inside of my cheek to keep from laughing. "Wind is a very strong element, honey." I pressed my forefinger and middle finger against her forehead gently, barely tapping her. "Air represents the mind, communication, memory, wisdom, and divination. It can be tricky, especially if or when you don't know how to use it. Let me tell you what I know of it, okay?"

"Okay," Nora huffed.

I'd be a bit more disappointed in her lack of enthusiasm if she wasn't so cute. "Okay. Air is an element that represents east. Think of it like this: You represent the east and Caitlin, whose element is water, represents the west. Are you with me so far?"

"I think so."

"Great. Air represents the season of spring, a time of rebirth, new life. It is all around us, which makes your use of it even stronger. It's what we breathe and keeps us alive. Here's how we're going to access your powers. Clear your mind and pay no attention to the distractions around you. You must be relaxed."

I picked Alison up and stepped away. Nora stayed standing, hands relaxed at her sides and closed her eyes. Her chest slowly rose and fell, almost like she was asleep. I looked at Alison and put my finger to my lips.

"Now, Nora, listen to my voice," I said. "You must center yourself. Imagine your magic, your energy, harnessing. You should be able to feel it. Focus on your own energy. Mind your breathing, in through your nose and out through your mouth slowly."

Nora stood completely still, doing exactly as I told her. Standing there with Alison in my arms, there was no wind. Not at first.

"Imagine a yellow glowing light," I told Nora, "as bright and yellow as the Sun. That is your power."

Nora remained unchanged, still standing tall, her back straight...and then the wind picked up. It started low and soft and then it grew stronger. Leaves floated off the forest floor and elevated around Nora, circling her in a cyclone of sorts. Her feet lifted off the ground and in seconds, Nora was levitating. Her feet dangled as she floated higher, but she didn't seem to notice.

"Whoa!" Alison giggled. "Look at her! Look at her, Auntie!"

Smiling, I called up to Nora, "Nora, open your eyes!"

Nora's eyes fluttered open and she looked down. Her eyes widened and she let out an excited squeal. "I'm doing it! I'm doing it! Look at me!"

The wind grew stronger as did Nora's excitement. The leaves in the trees miles above us were trembling and soaring. I put Alison down and walked to where Nora was floating and held out my hands. Nora bent down and took them, allowing me to pull her back down to earth.

"I flew!" she exclaimed.

"You did great!" I shouted. "Good job! You're a natural!"

"I wanna fly! I wanna fly!" Alison chanted as she ran to my side. "Nora, I wanna fly with you!"

"After we practice a bit more, Alison," I said, touching her shoulder. "It's your turn to harness your power, which is fire."

"Fire?"

"Yes, fire. Now, listen carefully. This one is very, very powerful and even dangerous if we're not careful. Fire represents the south, opposite of Brigit, whose element represents north. There are several aspects of fire: It's powerful, it represents bravery, excitement, and love, but it can also represent action and danger."

Alison gasped, taking a step back. I took her hands and pulled her closer. "Remember, I'm teaching you how to use it. And remember, it isn't bad magic, okay?" Alison slowly shook her head, eyes wide as saucers.

I rubbed her arms. "Fire represents instinct, drive, energy, strength. It is something you shouldn't play with, though. You must be extremely careful with this one."

Alison shifted nervously on her feet. "What if I accidentally burn something while we're here?"

I cupped her face. "I will put out the fire with my own magic. No harm will come to you or any of us. I promise. Now, focus on your breathing. In through your nose and out your mouth, just like Nora. Don't think of anything, don't listen to anything, but the sound of my voice. Think of bright red magic flowing through you like Christmas lights."

I took Nora's hand and walked us a few steps backwards to give Alison some space. She closed her eyes and tried accessing her powers. Though, Alison was different from Nora and younger. Her breathing wasn't relaxed and she kept flexing her fingers. Nothing was happening.

After a few moments, Alison sighed. "This isn't working," she complained.

"You just have to keep trying," I said.

"I can't do it!" Alison argued, stomping her foot. "I fucking suck!"

"Whoa!" I yelled. "Watch your language, Alison Helvig!"

I assume I have Brigit to "thank" for teaching her that word. "We just have to keep trying.

You'll get it."

"No!" Alison screamed. "I can't do it!"

"Alison…"

"I want Gary and my sisters here!" Alison screamed at the top of her lungs. "I want my brother and sisters back! I don't want you to teach me! I want them! I want my brother and sisters back!"

Alison turned around fast and ran back in the direction of the camp with Nora running after her and calling her by her name, leaving me alone with what felt like a knife being driven into my chest.

Thomas

I went straight down the stairs to the cells where I found Muriel sitting in the corner leaning her head against the wall. The torches were still lit, so I could see her face. She stared up at me.

"Thomas?" she said. "What is it?"

I stropped in front of the door, wrapping my fingers around one of the bars. Muriel stood and wrapped her hand over mine. The light of the flame cast shadows on the walls and reflected in her eyes.

"I have to go," I whispered. "I can't say where or why in case Scathe hears of it. I'll be back within a few days."

Muriel's fingers tightened over my hand. "You can't just tell me something like that and expect me not to worry or wonder why."

"Muriel, please," I pleaded quietly. "To protect you and Petra, I have to be discreet."

Muriel's jaw tightened, but she nodded in understanding. "Do whatever it is you have to. Just come back to me."

I reached as far as I could through the bars and gently took the ends of Muriel's hair in between my fingers. She smiled as I twirled it around and played with it. She used to do something similar with me when I had nightmares. I'd wake up panting and covered in sweat and Muriel would pull me into her arms, shushing me, before laying my head on her chest and stroking my hair until I was able to return to sleep.

"I will come back, Muriel," I said. "You have my word."

"Just as I have your heart."

I smiled and stroked her cheek briefly with my forefinger before darting back up the stairs.

• • • • •

The knights and I mounted our horses, weapons at our sides. I pulled out a small vial full of shimmering purple magic and pulled off the cork. The magic poured out and floated into the air before swirling to the ground. It created a trail as far as the eye could see heading deep into the forest, heading towards the Dwarf Domain.

"We have a long ride ahead of us," I said. "Let's move."

I pulled on my horse's reins and we began our journey with the purple magic showing us the way. Just as our last horse stepped past the treeline, I raised my hand over my head and flicked my wrist. I could feel the magic encasing the knights, shielding them. Now they could not be tracked or spied on by Scathe.

We have to be careful. If Scathe doesn't kill us, Jotnar and Nimh will. The only other time I had been in their territory, besides when I visited my siblings, was years ago when I snuck into the castle planning to assassinate them.

I was on guard, even with my cloaking spell. I moved along the shadows in the darkness of the night, putting guards to sleep. I was closing in on their quarters when all of a sudden, someone willed me to stop in my tracks. I couldn't move no matter how much I tried. I was paralyzed, not even a finger could move. I couldn't speak, couldn't cast a spell, even in my mind.

I was the most powerful witch in the Domain and I couldn't undo this spell. "Oh, look, a waste of space," a voice hissed.

Nimh.

I could feel her closing in on me from behind. The room became freezing cold, almost like it was the dead of winter. I felt Nimh's long, claw-like fingernail slide across my shoulders as she passed me before she forcefully grabbed a fistful of my hair and yanked my head back.

"You aren't welcome here, bastard filth," Nimh growled.

There was nothing inside her, no compassion, no soul. Nimh snapped her fingers and a black cloud engulfed me. A sinking feeling appeared in my stomach as I was teleported back to Scathe's castle. I was lying on my stomach in front of his throne, able to move again. I raised my head, expecting to see pure rage and annoyance on his face. No. Scathe stared down at me with more of a disappointed look than an angry one. I had failed. I was useless to him.

"Stupid boy," he growled as I got to my feet. "Sit down."

Scathe threw his arm out, sending an invisible force plummeting into my chest. I was knocked off my feet and sent flying into the stone wall. The air in me escaped when my back slammed violently against the wall before landing hard on the floor. I groaned and forced myself up, even with my weakened arms.

"Father..." I croaked.

Scathe took two quick, deliberate steps forward before raising his arm, his fingers bent. My body levitated into the air out of my control. Once again, I was paralyzed and unable to move. My body was slammed again into the stone wall, forcing a long, deep gasp out of me.

"I am not your father, you worthless imp," Scathe growled. "For failing to kill my enemies, you can stay in the tower for the next twenty-four hours without food."

He flicked his wrist. Everything became dizzy as I was teleported into the cold tower I had spent so much of my life in. The younger version of myself would have pushed himself up, tears wetting his face, banging like a madman on the door, screaming and crying himself hoarse. This time, I didn't. For the first time in my life, I didn't move. I didn't try to get up. I didn't run for the door. I stayed there lying on the floor, unmoving, with tears slowly cascading down my cheeks and nose. I don't know how long I stayed that way, but as I lay there ignoring the cold, a thought crept into my mind. A horrible thought. A dark, irreversible thought.

The next day when Scathe would let me out to fetch things from the market, I was going to end my own life.

Chapter 16

Thomas

"Everyone get some rest," I said as I put the fire out. "We'll be up at dawn and our ride to the Dwarf Domain will continue. I'll take the first watch."

The knights nestled into the ground, some tucked beside trees, others struggling to find comfort on the ground. There were no crickets chirping, no owls hooting, nor the light of fireflies. It was completely secluded except for us and our horses. I was alone with my thoughts.

I thought of Petra. She was being kept alive so that I would go with what Scathe ordered. Her and Muriel. The day I went to the marketplace, the day I planned to take my life...I went in search of poisonous herbs. I hadn't told anyone what I was planning to do, not even Garrett or the girls.

Then I ran into Muriel. When I saw her, time stopped. Everyone else disappeared and nothing else mattered. I find it humorous...I...forgot why I was even at the market in the first place. Muriel was a vision and I mean that in multiple ways. She was the epitome of beauty and grace, compassion and strength. When our eyes met I knew that she would be the one I'd spend the rest of my days with. I didn't see my past anymore. I saw a future with her, one that would be bright and glorious. I saw a home with her, a child. My brother and sisters would visit and we'd talk, drink, and share a few laughs. I imagined Garrett leaving the Witch Domain—leaving the kingdom—and starting a farm with that girl from the stables. Caitlin would leave and explore the world and make new discoveries that would go down in the history books. Brigit would also leave the Witch Domain and join the Lunar Knights in Sanctuarium. She'd become Captain of the Guard and marry a good man, perhaps even have a child. From the very beginning, I had known about her engagement to Prince Akoni; she and his younger brother, Salem, had not yet met. I never liked Akoni, but I did like Salem. He'd be a better suitor.

Years passed and then Scathe found us. He took my family from me. The moment Scathe made me yield, the moment I swore allegiance to him, I also made myself a silent promise. I was going to kill Nimh, Jotnar, and then him. I'd kill all three of them.

"Wake up," I said to my knights after two hours. "Take over."

The knight begrudgingly got to his feet and staggered to the stump as I lay down on a patch of leaves and twigs. I could feel nothing through my armor, but I closed my eyes, crossed my arms, and was soon asleep.

"Thomas," Muriel whispered. "Thomas."

My head rolled to the side and I forced my eyelids open. I was in a warm bed with a large, warm comforter covering me. I looked up to see Muriel looking down at me, the moonlight shining through our window and lighting up her face. Muriel shifted slightly, which in turn, caused the comforter to slip, exposing her breasts.

"You were having a nightmare," Muriel explained in a hushed tone. She brushed my hair out of my face and kissed my temple. "You were shaking."

I rolled over and pressed my ear against her chest. Her heart was beating softly, calmly.

Nothing ever seemed to rattle her. She was always so strong, even with learning my truth.

"Feel better?" she whispered.

I answered her by planting a kiss on her mouth. She cupped my face, deepening the kiss before burying her hands in my hair. The covers fell off us, revealing both our bare bodies as I gently bit Muriel's bottom lip. She let out a soft moan as I kissed her neck. I cupped her breasts as she wrapped her legs around me, urging me closer.

I planted a kiss on her collarbone, breathing in her scent. Muriel leaned back against the pillows letting out a deep moan. Locking eyes with Muriel, I lowered my head, trailing kisses across her chest and on each shoulder right before ducking my head and taking her breasts into my mouth. My tongue flicked against her nipple as I fingered the second. Muriel whimpered, fisting locks of my hair tighter in her hands. I turned my head and sucked on her second breast as my hands slid down her sides and gripped her hips. I pulled her closer. Her hair pooled over the pillows like spilled ink as her back arched. Muriel spread her legs open, silently urging me to continue.

"I want you inside me, Thomas," Muriel said breathlessly. "I want you inside me *now*."

I couldn't stand it anymore. I placed my hands on her inner thighs, kissing her before thrusting myself inside of her. Once. Twice. Again and again. Muriel gasped and cried out in ecstasy. I snarled at the side of her beneath me. Our bodies were connected. I could hardly breathe. Muriel moved her hips in sync with mine and within minutes I climaxed. I growled her name passionately, but I wasn't done. I turned her over so that she was lying on her stomach before grabbing her waist and lifted her up.

"Thomas…" Muriel moaned.

With one hand planted firmly on her hip, I slid my other hand lower until I reached the sensitive part between her thighs. Muriel groaned as she allowed two of my fingers entrance. I curved my fingers, feeling inside of her. "Thomas, please…" she begged.

"Please what?"

"Don't…don't stop."

I pulled my fingers out and slid my hand back towards her waist before thrusting myself deep inside of her once more. Her fingers clenched the sheets as our bodies jerked in sync. Muriel's screams grew louder as she began to climax, this time with me joining her. The only sounds we could hear were our panting breaths.

"Thomas?" Muriel's voice echoed. This time, there was no one there, or no one that I could see. It was pitch black. "Thomas, I have blessed news! I went to the medic today to see why I wasn't feeling well. My love, I'm pregnant."

"Milord? Milord, it is morning," a knight said from above.

I groaned, rubbing my eyes and pinching the bridge of my nose. Getting to my feet, I tried to shake the dream. I want to hold onto those memories, but right now I have to focus on my brother. I just need a lock of his hair for a spell to trick our father. After burning down his camp and threatening his woman, he wouldn't hesitate to fight a second time—the minute he sees me, he'll fight.

"Breakfast is ready, Milord," a second knight said, handing me a bowl.

I raised a hand to stop him. "No. This is the point where I leave you. The borders are just beyond these hills. Stay hidden. After the second sunset, if I am not back, return to Scathe's castle without me. I'll meet you there when I can."

"Yes, Milord."

I mounted my horse and pulled on her reins. Morrigan turned her head and we trotted down the hills.

Scathe will have your family killed if you fail again…and then he will kill you. Make sure to watch your back, even when you return, Tommy boy. "I'll do my best, old girl. Now, on we go."

Muriel

I woke up as the sun rose in the sky to the smell of bacon and warm biscuits. Sitting up, I found a plate of food a few feet away from me. That wasn't here before. I smiled to myself. Thomas must have used magic to send it to me. I ate my breakfast with the crackling torches as the only sound to accompany me.

"Eat up, Petra," I said sweetly as I held my daughter in my arms. "It'll make you strong."

I sat on the chair near the roaring fire with my daughter on my breast. Thomas had just left to work at the blacksmith's shop, leaving the two of us alone. As I sat there feeding Petra, I thought of what I would have for lunch: Tomato soup with basil was nice and simple. It wouldn't take my attention away from Petra too much. When dinner comes around, that's when Thomas should return. He'll clean up as usual and then he'll help me cook our supper. What should we make as our baby rests? Pottage stew with baked bread sounds nice. We have all the ingredients we need here: carrots, parsnips, onions, turnips, mushrooms, green beans, broth, red wine, cabbage, and seasoning. While we prepped the ingredients and cooked, Thomas would take me in his arms and we'd dance until we couldn't dance any further.

The full moon was in a few days—the Cold Moon—which meant that a festival was coming to our village. Perhaps the three of us could go.

My thoughts were interrupted by the front door busting open and slamming down on the floor. Clutching Petra close to my chest, I jumped up. There were mutilated monsters dressed in armor with beastly wings. They snarled and drooled, accompanied with knights in dark armor—more human ones—with swords and long spears.

Petra screamed as the creatures and soldiers barged into our home. I tried to turn and run, but two of them caught my arms and squeezed while a third knight, one of the human ones, went to grab my daughter.

"NO!" I cried, holding onto my screaming child with all my strength. "NO!"

With the two human knights holding me back, the third one at last ripped my child from my arms wailing at the top of her little lungs.

"NO!" I screamed. "DON'T TAKE HER! YOU CAN'T TAKE HER   !"

The knights pulled me out of my home and forced me to their horses. I squirmed and pulled, trying to break free and take my daughter back. I didn't know if I could run fast enough. I could try stealing one of the horses, but how fast could these winged-monstrosities fly?

"Move, woman!" one of my captors barked as we stopped in front of a deep brown horse with a masked rider. He reached down, grabbed my arm, and lifted me onto the front of his horse.

"NO!" I screamed. "NO!"

"Take her to Scathe," a fourth knight said. "He wants her and the baby alive. I'll take the child. Remember, no harm must come to either of them. Scathe wants his son to obey him."

Thomas? "NO!" I screeched. "NO!"

And then we rode off towards Scathe's castle.

Chapter 17

Garrett

Most of us helped in whatever way we could when more of our crew showed up over the next few days. Katrina, Sir Charles, and I helped bandage the wounded and did most of the hunting. Orion tracked down as many survivors as he could, bringing them back to our new hideaway. I noticed there weren't as many of us as there had been when I first arrived. There was less, like, a lot less.

One evening as I changed the bandages off a wounded soldier, Orion returned with a small group of people—Bruce being among them. He looked worse for wear: His face was covered in dirt and dried blood and his hair looked matted and wild. Even his armor had a few cracks in it.

I turned my attention back to the wounded soldier as Sir Charles passed me. "Sir Bruce is alive, Milord!"

I smiled respectfully at him. "I'm glad he's okay. Really. Really, I am. We should see if he needs help, food, water, ya know?"

"Indeed you are correct," Sir Charles said, slapping a hand on my shoulder with enough force to nearly knock me over.

I gently patted the soldier on the back, smiling at him, and urged him to stand up and take off so that I could help aid another soldier.

"You didn't know you had a brother, huh?" a lady centaur asked, holding her bandaged arm.

I shook my head as she sat on the fallen log. I unwrapped her bandage. "No. It wasn't until the two of us were fighting that memories came flooding back—old feelings. Why was he attacking me? Even back then..."

The centaur gave me a sad, knowing grin. "Then you must know that he was the one to lead the siege to your mother's castle in the first place."

I bit the inside of my cheek as I set her old, bloodied bandages aside and grabbed the roll beside me. Wrapping the new bandages around her wounded arm, I said, "Of course. He was working for Scathe this whole time."

"Then that is your answer, Lord Garrett," the centaur replied. "That is why he led a siege to the Witch Domain and wiped out most of your kind and your family. Scathe is a powerful, evil being. He is feared throughout the land alongside Jotnar and Nimh. Thomas followed his orders out of fear."

I pulled out my scissors and cut the bandage when it was long enough before securing it. "That was his choice to make. It was the wrong one. My memories of my childhood—what I can remember—Thomas was a good brother and a good friend. I saw him whenever I could. *That* Thomas was different."

Thomas had to have had a reason for doing this, but...he attacked everyone here. He put us all in danger. He killed the family I had. He threatened Katrina. What if he hurt the girls?

What if he *tries* to? I can't let that happen.

The centaur examined her arm and stood. "Thank you, Milord."

I smiled. "No problem, miss...?"

"Lucille."

"It was no problem helping you, Lucille."

Lucille gave me a small wave before walking away in the opposite direction. No one else needed their bandages changed, so I took a seat on the log and opened my palm. Dark purple energy appeared, floating before my eyes, warm and electrifying. Does Thomas want this, my power? Will he not stop until he catches and kills me?

"You!" Bruce bellowed, pointing a finger at me from the top of the hill.

Everyone stopped whatever they were doing—gathering wood, carving weapons, skinning fish, grooming the horses—and looked at Bruce who forced his way past Sir Charles and stormed towards me. The temple in his head looked two seconds away from bursting.

"You did this!" Bruce growled. "You brought doom upon us all!"

I jumped to my feet, Spirit dissipating, and stared in shock at Bruce. "Me?"

"Bruce, stop this!" Sir Charles ordered.

Bruce ignored him. "You should have just stayed away like the coward you are! Because of you, our home is gone! Because of you, we are vulnerable! We are in Jotnar's territory! We are dead because of you!"

"Now hold on!" Sir Charles barked. "This is not Lord Garrett's fault!"

"Isn't it?" Bruce growled. "When our Domains were infiltrated, when our children were killed or forced into their armies, when our wives, mothers, sisters were violated and killed, where were you? When these tyrants stole our land and started this war of bloodshed and darkness, where were you? When we were all suffering... *Where. Were. You?*"

I didn't speak. How could I? Bruce is right. Things have gotten worse for everyone here because of me. They're in even greater danger now because of me. If anyone here is caught, they'll be tortured and killed. There was only one option: "Then I'll go," I said.

Everyone gasped and looked at me in surprise, even Bruce.

"No," Sir Charles said quickly as he made his way to my side. "You can't! It's dangerous out there!"

"Well, Bruce is right," I argued, "I have brought more suffering and struggle to everyone here. My brother found us and destroyed your camp. Besides, my family is still out there, lost and alone. I have to find them."

"And where will you all go?" Sir Charles asked. "There are not many safe places in the kingdom left to hide."

"I don't know," I said honestly, "but at least we'll all have a better chance of surviving if I'm not here."

Without another word, I marched towards Pluto and mounted him. I grabbed his reins and pulled him in another direction, ignoring the staring faces of the survivors here as we rode off.

Dusk came as I dismounted Pluto and pulled him along. It was getting darker and harder to see, my feet were tired, but I pushed on. I had to put as much distance between myself and the survivors of the camp. It's funny. The dark used to scare me, it always has. I always imagined monsters and demons hiding in the shadows or under the bed waiting to grab me. Now it wasn't so bad. I hear voices a lot more these days and honestly, these voices belonged to people once before. Yes, they're not alive anymore, but they're still the souls of people. It wasn't so different than walking through a crowd in the streets, in school, in the store. Just like this power isn't so different from me having blue eyes or red hair. I didn't choose my hair color, my height, or my powers. It's all just a part of me, something I'll have to live with. And you know what? I'm okay with that.

Lord Garrett!

Leaves crunched behind us and twigs snapped. Pluto and I stopped walking and turned to find Orion hurrying towards us, his golden eyes giving him away in the darkness.

"Orion?" I asked. "What are you doing here?"

I had returned from hunting with Katrina when we heard that you had left!

"Katrina?"

As if on cue, Katrina rode in on her own horse. Her face was a mix of relief and sadness. The closer she rode, the more I could tell that her eyes were wet. She stopped a few feet from us and quickly climbed off her horse.

"Why would you leave?" she asked me, her voice cracking.

"I'm a danger to everyone there, Katrina," I said. "I tried to help the best I could. I thought regaining my powers would help me make things better. I thought if I had them, I could help bring justice and peace, but I only put you all in danger."

Katrina looked at me like I had just slapped her. (As if.) "We have been in danger for years, Garrett!"

"Thomas came and destroyed your camp just like he destroyed the Witch Domain!" I argued. "He led another attack towards you guys! And just like last time, I couldn't do anything to stop him!"

"Neither time was your fault!"

I looked away. "I disappeared when the siege of the Witch Domain happened. How do I know that I didn't make us disappear?"

"You wouldn't do that."

"How do you know?"

"Because I know you, Garrett." Katrina closed the distance between us and took my hands. "You wouldn't have left your loved ones in peril on purpose and you wouldn't have willingly given up your memories of me."

Pluto neighed, nodding his head. *Ooh, girl!*

I gave Pluto a 'knock it off' look before looking into Katrina's eyes.

"Please come back," Katrina said. "We'll all look for your family. It's best if we all stay together."

I squeezed her hands. "Okay, but after we rest."

Katrina and I found a spot by a tree and huddled up against it. Orion lay down beside us as did Pluto. I wrapped my arms over Katrina in order to keep her warm. She did the same and soon we were both fast asleep.

Caitlin

I followed everyone into the mess hall for breakfast. Captain Raina insisted that Sheila would bring us our meals, but honestly, I just wanted to do something nice. It had only been a few days since she made me First Mate and so far, I've been treated with a little more respect. Before no one harassed me or degraded me, mostly because Captain Raina threatened to either 'blow their brains out' or 'walk the plank'. Then no one would even look at me once they saw my powers. Now they all talk to me like I'm one of them.

I smiled to myself. A pirate witch with pirate friends and a pirate witch captain. Sounds like the stuff of legends.

The sous chef handed me two bowls of fish and shrimp soup and I made my way to Captain Raina's quarters. She was drinking from a flask, standing in front of the window, looking at the calm seas. When she saw me, she took a bowl from me and with the other hand pulled out my chair.

"Thank you," I said.

"No thanks needed," Captain Raina said with a smile.

The two of us ate in comfortable silence. I wonder sometimes if she has had to eat alone ever since she had been made captain. Captain Raina preferred privacy, which I completely understand, but she cares a lot about her crew. She may not always say it or show it, but she does. This is her family. But did she spend most of her time alone after her first family died?

"So tell me, Treasure," Captain Raina said, sipping from her glass, "after we eat, what say we do a bit of practice with not just swords but magic?"

I swallowed my soup and smiled at her. "That sounds like a good idea. I always wanted to learn how to use a sword."

"Why didn't you?"

I blushed. "Sword fighting doesn't exactly come in handy where I'm from."

"Ah, yes. Connect-a-kit."

I let out a small laugh, much to Captain Raina's surprise. "Connecticut."

"That's what I said."

I giggled. "Oh, well. Yeah, that's where I'm from, er, where I was sent to."

Captain Raina looked at me curiously. "What's it like?"

"Well, for one, we don't really ride horses," I explained. "It's more of a sport or hobby. We drive these things called cars. They're machines with wheels that can travel far distances at really fast speeds, but that's not really recommended."

Captain Raina rested her chin on her folded hands, urging me to continue.

"There are also these things called movies," I continued. "It's like moving paintings or portraits that tell a story."

"Like a play?"

"Like a play."

A light burned in Captain Raina's eyes. "Fascinating. Your world seems to be very advanced."

"It is, but it isn't all what it's cracked up to be," I said.

"Tell me, what about past relations?"

My eyes widened. Well, that came out of nowhere! "I've...never been in a relationship."

"No?"

"No one really liked me," I explained. "Everyone thought my brother, sisters, and I were strange. We were outcasts."

Captain Raina leaned back in her seat. "Well, then you really are one of us. That's all pirates are, Treasure. We are outcasted from the world, unwanted, and rebellious. We do whatever we please and no one can say anything to us about it."

Captain Raina took her glass in her fingers and raised it towards me. "A pirate's life for all, dear."

I raised my glass and connected it with hers. "A pirate's life for all."

"Shoot for the stars and don't look down." Then we drank.

We were still alone in her quarters when we cleared the table of our dishes. I helped Captain Raina move the table aside and we began. Captain Raina reached down into her shirt and pulled out her medallion.

"This is the medallion my mother wore," Captain Raina said. "She always wanted to leave the Witch Domain and see the ocean. In a way, this feels like she's here with me, getting her wish."

I smiled at her. "Your family will always be with you, Captain. You may not be able to see them, but they're here."

"Always the optimist, huh, Treasure?"

Captain Raina held her hands out on either side of her, palms up and fingers flexed. Immediately, I saw sparks, like electricity shooting through her fingertips. A purple mist floated from beneath her feet, forming into tendrils as they floated up, covering her back. I stared at Captain Raina's eyes, though her attention was focused at looking straight ahead. Her eyes began to glow, turning completely white and cloudy. The energy in the room changed and I suddenly felt like we weren't alone. I could feel some sort of presence here, taking up as much space as possible.

"You're not just a witch, are you?" I said at last.

Captain Raina shook her head. "I come from a family of voodooists."

The room went dark and there were figures beginning to take shape. How crazy is that? I was seeing figures in the *dark*. Captain Raina closed her eyes, breathing in through her nose, and closed her hands into fists. The figures disappeared and the darkness melted away. Captain Raina turned to face me.

"Asmund Rock is where Scathe's talisman is," she said to me. "It is the source of his power. If I can get my hands on it, I can destroy it. He'll die."

"Why are you telling me this?"

Captain Raina looked upon me with sad, pleading eyes. "You really don't know, do you? You still haven't figured it out?"

"Figured out what? You're scaring me."

Captain Raina looked down and gently took my hand. She looked back up at me and stared right into my eyes. "He is your father."

Scathe...H-he...He's my *father?* One of the three tyrants that took this world apart is my father?

I shook my head. "That can't be right. My father died in an accident..."

Captain Raina's hands squeezed mine; her face became softer. "No..."

"He and my mother both died in an accident," I told her quickly. "After Alison was born. We all were there!"

"Do you remember the accident?" Captain Raina countered gently. "Any of you? Can you remember your childhood prior to the last five years?"

Tears stung my eyes and my heartbeat quickened. "No...No...None of this is true...It can't be true...!"

Captain Raina took me in my arms and hugged me. I would have been more surprised if my world hadn't just been turned upside down. If Scathe is my father, then that means Nimh is my mother! They're both evil! They've hurt and tortured people! They took Captain Raina's family away from her!

I pulled away. "I'm so sorry. I'm sorry."

Captain Raina wiped away my tears. "For what?"

"They killed your family. They took your childhood away, your innocence—!"

"They have done the same to you," Captain Raina interrupted. "You had nothing to do with this."

I stopped crying. "I think that's the problem. I was gone for five years, my memories were taken and so was everything else. People suffered and died because I wasn't here." I took Captain Raina's hand. "I will help you end this war."

• • • • •

I blocked Captain Raina's attack. Our swords clashed again and again, faster and faster. She had more experience, but she would give out pointers and tips to correct my form and to better my fighting. Everyone else was below deck, probably just mingling or playing some sort of game.

It was just the two of us on deck. We were supposed to be taking sword fighting seriously, and we really were trying to, but we were also laughing and having a good time.

"Easier when gripping the hilt, Treasure," Captain Raina laughed. "It'll make fighting a hell of a lot easier for you."

I loosened my grip and lunged. Captain Raina blocked and pushed me off. She snapped her fingers and suddenly, long black tendrils lifted me up into the air. I squealed as I dropped my sword and kicked my feet.

"No fair!" I giggled.

Captain Raina looked up at me and laughed. "Pirate, Caity cat." She curved her forefinger and I was dropped.

I landed on my feet and went to grab my sword when Captain Raina thrust her hand towards me. An unseen barrier pushed me up against the door to her quarters, pinning me there.

Captain Raina walked towards me and laughed.

"Nice work, Treasure," she praised. "Good form."

"What do you mean 'good form'?" I giggled. "I lost."

Captain Raina leaned closer, smiling devilishly. "You didn't know how to fight your opponent. You let your guard down."

The invisible barrier lifted and I was suddenly free, but I didn't move. Instead, I placed my palms on either side of the door and locked eyes with the pirate captain.

"I'm not the one who just let her guard down."

Before Captain Raina could say anything, I pushed myself off the door and planted my mouth onto hers. Her lips were soft and gentle against mine. I could feel her smiling through the kiss. I felt her set her hands on my shoulders and pulled me in closer. She was taller, even with the heels. I placed my hands on her hips and opened my mouth to her. One of her hands cupped my chin as she set her tongue inside.

My first kiss was everything I had imagined it to be and then some.

Chapter 18

Thomas

Morrigan and I rode for another day and a half before we came upon the Dark-wood Forest. Only the lowlifes of the kingdom group here and unless you know your way around, you'll never find your way out. Several kinds of creatures found homes here the moment Jotnar's grandfather took the throne: ogres, minotaurs, basilisk, Sui Elves, and golems.

All of them are terrible, fearsome creatures. They're large, tall, sometimes hairier than others, and are always hungry for humans to devour. Some look more human than others, some have human-like ears, others have sharp ears like elves. Some even have cone-shaped horns atop their heads. They are violent and grotesque; Gods help you if you come across one. Minotaurs are beings half-bull, half-human. There are some that are pure of heart, but even that is very rare. They are arguably the strongest creatures to exist, lifting as much as a dead horse above its head. Basilisks are giant serpentine creatures that can kill by just staring at you. It would only take a second and you would be dead. Sui Elves are a type of elf—think like the treacherous ancestors of the elves that live now, the elves that came before—only the Sui never speak. They snarl like animals, have no sense of sight, but have heightened senses. They also don't respect the lives of animals and nature. They aren't peaceful. They're cannibals, feeding on their kin, whether or not they're still breathing. Golems are creatures made from mud or clay, brought to life by magic. Depending on the purpose, golems can actually be loyal protectors, but they have to follow exact orders, meaning the one who creates them has to be very precise.

I don't like this, Tommy boy. I don't like this at all.

"I don't either, but the spell is leading me here," I said, stroking the side of Morrigan's neck. "Garrett is in there somewhere. I have to find him." *Yeah, 'cause last time ended so well.*

"Scathe tracked him down to that camp," I reminded. "He knew that I lied about them being dead."

Yeah, and I'm sure you suffered when he found that out.

I patted her neck again. "I was fine."

No, you weren't. As a matter of fact, I hope that your father drops dead.

"Come on," I said, not bothering to hide my smile. "In we go."

The woods were a lot darker than any other forest that exists. It was about ten in the morning, cloudy as usual, but not gray. There were no signs of a storm. It was like night itself made its home in the forest; there were shadows at every corner, covering every inch of the woods. There were no signs of life—no birds, squirrels, deer. All the leaves on the ground were dead and there were hardly any in the trees.

This just screams horror novel.

"Would you stop?"

After a bit of riding, following the purple trail, I could see that the magic's light was dimming. We were getting closer.

You sure we can't just book it outta here and join a circus?

"Morrigan, my brother is here," I whispered. "He doesn't know what lurks in these woods. It's a miracle *we* haven't been attacked yet."

You've got a point, Tommy boy. Still would rather turn into a pile of horse meat, but you're the rider.

We walked along, still following the magical trail. I could not tell what hour it was, but the further into the woods we got, the dimmer the light. Leaves crunched underneath Morrigan's hooves and I hoped that it would be the only sounds besides our breathing that we'd hear.

I dismounted from Morrigan and gripped the hilt of my sword. I refuse to tie her here of all places. If there are creatures lurking about, she needs to be able to get away as fast as she can.

I waved my hand over the lower half of my face and my mask appeared.

I don't think wearing that is going to be a good idea, Tommy boy.

"I have to," I whispered back. "I need to make it appear as though he is dead. I need him to be scared and angry enough to fight me. All I need from him is a lock of hair and a few drops of blood. I'll be back in ten minutes tops."

Then we can get out of these creepy-ass woods?

"Yes, I swear."

For your sake and that of your girls, you better.

I started on my way through the forest as quietly as I could. The magic's light was getting dimmer and dimmer, meaning I was closing in on Garrett. All I need is his hair and some blood. With that, I can create a copy of him— dead—and present him to Scathe. Once I do that, he'll tell me where Petra is. I can get her back and find his talisman. Once I have the talisman, he'll of course think I'll be giving it to him, but that won't be the case. With the talisman in my grasp, I'll be able to kill him.

Then my family and I will be free.

The purple light went out, much like a candle flame. I ducked down and crouched behind a large dark tree. A few feet from me, sleeping comfortably against a tree were two people, one of which I'd recognize anywhere with his head of hair. Garrett and the lady Katrina. Beside him was his dark horse resting. They must have been separated from the group after my attack.

I carefully and quietly unsheathed my sword and stepped closer. He was going to wake up, which is exactly what I needed.

TRAITOR!

As I figured, Orion growled from behind and lunged for me. I raised my palm, radiating a golden light. Orion whimpered as the light made contact with him and he bounced back, slamming into a tree. I heard the horse snort in confusion.

"Garrett!" Katrina gasped. "Garrett, it's him!"

I turned around just in time to see Garrett climb to his feet and unsheathe his sword. Purple magic radiated off him angrily like a roaring fire.

"You!" he growled.

"Good to see you again, Garrett."

Chapter 19

Megan

I thought over what Alison said over the next few days. I am not her mother. I'm not a parent, I never was. I had no interest in having children, but I was there when each of them came into this world, so they've become my own in a way. For the past five years, the girls were always close to their brother and sisters. We had each other, but they were especially close to Caitlin. She always had a maternal nature. Whenever the girls were hurt or needed help with their homework, they would come to me on occasion, but it was always Caitlin they wanted. She never argued or said no. She loved them and did whatever she could to help them, even when she was busy with her own homework.

I'll never be their mother or their sister. I could never fill that void and I never want to. I just want to feel wanted, to know that they'll need me in their lives for something.

"Lady Megan," a lady dwarf said as she approached me. She handed me a letter. "Lord Angus sent me to give this to you."

"What is it?" I asked as I took the letter. It was somewhat yellowed from passing time, but not on the verge of turning to dust by touching it.

"Your father's letter," the lady dwarf said simply.

Heart skipping a beat, I opened the letter. "He's alive?"

The lady dwarf's face fell with rue. "No, this was from before he died. It was given to Lord Angus before the siege."

My heart fell. "Oh. Okay. Thank you."

The lady dwarf took off in the opposite direction and left me alone with the letter. Satyrs and centaurs and humans passed me, talking amongst themselves and carrying wood and tools as I scanned one of the last things my father ever wrote. Just looking at his handwriting alone made my lips tremble.

Lord Angus,

I have known you and your father for a very long time. I am sorry to hear of his passing; you see, we were very good friends. That tree on our land that you and Megan met at was the first place your father and I met as well. His family came to discuss trade with my parents. My father thought it would be a good change of pace to get to know him and become acquainted. Little did either of us know that it would lead to long-lasting years of friendship and loyalty.

I'd like to think I was a good father to my children, though I know I'd be lying to you and myself. I wasn't always. A father should love and be there for their children, something I never was or had done.

It took me years to get close again to all my children, especially Varian and Megan. Do not mention this or show this letter to any of my children, but I was the most fond of Megan. Whenever I needed assistance with a task, she was the one I always went to—or who came to me.

She has a kind heart, but is thick-headed at times. She doesn't have a temper, in fact, she is quite calm, but is stubborn like a bull. She requires structure, but isn't close-minded when it comes to entertainment.

I tell you this not as a warning, and not because you don't already know this, but to remind you that all she has ever wanted was someone to love. She wants to love someone and be loved in turn—to explore and have adventures, to have someone to grow old with just as her parents have.

Which is why I give you my blessing to ask for her hand in marriage. All I ask is that you treat her well, but don't always let her order you around, either. Also, two invitations to the wedding.

I look forward to calling you my son.

Sincerely,
Lord O'Dwyer

He...Angus was going to ask me to marry him? He wanted to marry me?

Heart pounding all over again, I clutched my father's letter close to my chest and ran for Angus's tent. He had a lot of explaining to do! I reached his tent in no time at all and found him sharpening his sword. Panting, I confronted him.

"You were going to ask for my hand?" I showed him the letter.

Angus looked at the letter and then up at me before sheathing his sword. He stood up and opened up the curtain for me. I picked up my skirts and stepped inside, blinking away the tears that readied to fall.

When he closed the curtain, I hissed, "Start talking."

Angus let out a quiet, shaky breath and averted his eyes to the ground. "I had asked your father for your hand, yes. It was a week before Scathe's attack on the Capital. No one could visit him because he fell ill with the plague, but I had asked him prior to that. In response, he sent a letter by raven. He and your mother accepted."

I did my best to blink away the tears, but it was no use. They poured from my eyes and trailed down my cheeks. My father and I finally put the past behind us when he caught sickness. I at long last forgave him only for him to die. I never knew what took him first, the sickness or the war. I never got to say goodbye to him or my mother, my brother, my sisters. I wasn't here...I didn't get to bury him. I didn't get to say 'I love you' one last time. If he is buried, I don't know where.

Angus crossed the room and pulled me into an embrace. I cried in his arms, weeping for my father, for his father, for what we lost, and what could have been.

•   •   •   •   •

"We can't just get the fairies to release us from our bargain!" a knight exclaimed during a meeting later that evening. "They're the ones protecting us, cloaking us from the magic of these tyrants!"

"Fairies are dangerous!" I argued, stopping myself from slamming my hand on the table. "They are manipulative and vengeful! Whatever you offered them in exchange for their security is not worth it! Don't you know what happens if you insult one of them?"

"Better them than Jotnar, Nimh, or Scathe!" another knight argued.

"No, it isn't!" I argued. "We have to find a way to break this deal!"

"And who will protect us?" a satyr asked.

"She will," Angus said, stepping beside me and placing a firm hand on my shoulder, "as will I."

I covered his hand and smiled. "We all must rely on each other. We can't let fear rule us, especially not now. We need to keep each other safe and not go to someone who threatens us or holds something over us. That's false security as well as tempting fate. I will go to the Fairy

Domain and speak to the Lady of the Fae. I will get us out of this deal."

"You will not be going alone," Angus said. "I will accompany her. Darcy," he jerked his chin in the direction of a satyr, "you will be in charge in my absence. Keep everyone safe."

Darcy nodded. "Yes, Milord."

The meeting ended and we all went our separate ways. After dinner was finished, I bathed the girls and dressed them for bed. I tucked them into their bedrolls and prepared for bed myself. Angus was already there waiting for me. He lifted the covers for me and I slid in beside him, tucking my head against his shoulder.

That night, I dreamed of something I had long forgotten about. I was younger this time, no younger than when I first met Angus. It was snowing outside. The sky was gray and the snow on the ground was soft and piled high. Flakes of several sizes floated down from above and covered my hair. I brushed my fingers against the frosty bushes and walked down the blanketed mountainside. There were houses in the distance with lanterns lit through the windows and everything was quiet.

I walked on, not quite absent-mindedly, but rather...I had someplace to go. Somewhere to be. I was meeting someone somewhere…

Brigit

I packed my things as soon as I heard Akoni and Queen Valentina step away. I can't do this! I can't live my life for someone else! I can't let my life be decided for me! Megan didn't even tell me what really happened to my parents or Nora and Alison's father! I understand that it would have sounded crazy at the time, but still. All these lies and half-truths! I can't take it anymore! I don't want this! I never asked for any of this!

I threw my satchel over my shoulder and walked out onto the balcony. I stretched my arm out, reaching for the tree. A branch began to grow, getting closer and closer to me. I looked over my shoulder one last time to make sure the coast was clear and carefully stepped over the balcony.

Don't look down! Don't look down! Don't look down, bitch!

I planted a foot on the branch and lunged, grabbing hold of the tree for my freaking life.

Don't let go! Don't let go! Don't fucking let go!

I swung my body over, holding tightly onto the branches. I moved my foot aside, planting it on a second branch and started climbing down. As I climbed, I started crying again. I don't even like Akoni! I haven't known him for that long, but already, I can tell that he's not for me! I don't want to spend the rest of my life with someone I can't stand! Someone I don't even get to choose! Salem shouldn't have kept that from me! I had every right to know! Was I supposed to just accept it? Is that how things are done here? Well, I fucking won't accept this or live like this! This is my life and no one is going to tell me how to live it! Someone wants my life, they'll have to kill me because I'm not giving it away!

I reached the bottom of the tree, only inches from the ground. I released my grip and rubbed my hands together. Before leaving, I tucked a map into my satchel. I just need to follow it. I'll head to the hideaway Salem showed me and stay there until I figure out exactly where to go. Someone can help me. Maybe I'll finally be reunited with my family.

"You're not even going to say goodbye?"

Salem approached me from behind. He didn't look disappointed, confused, or betrayed.

He only looked sad.

I tightened my fingers around the strap of my satchel. "I figured it'd be easier this way. I'm not good at saying goodbye to people." I faced him, glaring. "Except for your brother, who you forgot to mention was my 'betrothed'! One I don't even remember or like! Or *chose*!"

Salem averted his eyes and hung his head like a scolded puppy. "I wanted to tell you—"

"But you didn't!" I yelled, stepping closer. "You didn't tell me!"

"I just...wasn't sure how."

"Why? 'Cause it wasn't your place? I had every right to know and you kept this from me!

People can't make my choices for me!"

"I never wanted to do that, Brigit!" Salem argued.

"You lied to me! How do I know you're not lying to me now?"

At that, something inside me changed. I was angry (duh), but something in me snapped like a chain. I gasped, tilting my head back and threw my arms out. Something burst from inside me. A large green energy emerged as big as a storm cloud and morphed into a shape—a magical lime green bear reared back its head and growled loud enough to shake the trees. I stared in awe at the...whatever it was.

"An aura?" Salem gasped in shock.

"Wh-what is that?" I stuttered.

"Auras are spiritual animal protectors that aid your powers," Salem explained in one breath, keeping his eyes glued on the magical green bear. "Everyone with magic is born with them."

The bear looked at me and then at Salem before turning away. It was behaving just like a normal bear. This...this was...something else… "Whoa…" I gasped.

"Indeed." He looked at me and smiled. "It suits you."

"I'm still angry."

The bear vanished in green light as Salem took the remaining steps in my direction and stopped right in front of me. We were only inches apart now. Giving me an apologetic smile, Salem took both my hands and kissed my knuckles, which turned my ears pink. He looked back at me and smiled.

"I know. Please forgive me, Milady."

Whatever anger I had felt for him disappeared. God, why can't I just stay angry at this guy?

"Will you stay?" Salem asked. "I will speak with my parents about releasing you from this betrothal. I will not be making attempts, Milady. Mark my words, I *will* get you out of this."

Chapter 20

Megan

"Have some porridge, Auntie Megan!" Nora insisted as she pushed a bowl in front of me.

I laughed. "Alright, but only if you say 'please.'"

"Pretty please with caramel on top?" Nora said sweetly.

"Caramel?" I asked with a raised brow.

"Caramel's delicious and cherries are overrated."

I cocked my head to the side, sticking out my lower lip. "Fair enough."

I took the spoonful of porridge and took a bite. "Mmm! Nice and warm!"

"It'd be better if there were blueberries," Alison said from the other side of Nora.

"Your wish is my command, little one," Angus said as he took a seat beside me. He reached into his jacket and pulled out a small blue pouch. He undid the drawstrings and reached over to pour blueberries into Alison's bowl. Her eyes and mouth widened.

"Ooh!" she squealed and started mixing the blueberries in.

"What do we say, Alison?" I asked.

Without looking up, Alison said, "Thank you."

"You're most welcome, Princess," Angus smiled.

It was nice eating like this, the four of us together. It reminded me of simpler times. Not so much when I was young because those times were...dark, to say the least...but when the older kids were little, I'd come over and they'd be eating breakfast. Sometimes I'd bring them muffins and bread from the local bakery that was co-owned by a friend of mine, Leonna. I have known her since I first left my parents' home. She had two daughters of her own and always kept busy. I helped her out as much as I could with money, though I was also starting out on my own for the first time. She always had a good heart and a bright, carefree glow about her.

I miss her.

"So when are you getting married?" Nora asked bluntly.

I shot her a look. "Nora!"

Nora pressed her lips together sheepishly before turning her attention back to eating.

Angus chuckled. "We have yet to decide that, Your Majesty, but I promise you two will be the first ones given invitations."

"Will there be cake?" Alison asked.

"Honey, swallow before you talk," I told her.

"And yes, there will be," Angus answered.

"Chocolate?" Nora asked.

"And ice cream?" Alison added.

"Ice cream?" Angus questioned. "What's that?"

I stood up and rotated around the table towards Alison and pulled out a handkerchief. Wiping away the porridge on her face I said, "First we must take care of a few things. Now go play, you two."

The girls jumped out of their seats and ran off to play with the other children while Angus and I finished our breakfast.

I shook my head. "Jeez."

"I've had interrogations that weren't as stress inducing," Angus jokes.

I took a bite of my porridge. "I wonder if I drove my parents that crazy?"

"They are sweet girls," Angus said.

"They are," I said. "I just wish we were all together."

Angus took our empty bowls and set them aside. "We will find Garrett and the girls,

Megan. I swear it."

I sighed. "I know, it's just hard. I've been there since they were born. I worry, especially with all that's going on. What if they're in danger?"

"I understand your frustration, Megan. I do, but we don't know where they are and the younger two need you. You are all they have left."

I nodded. "You're right. I know you're right, I just wish I knew that the others were okay. However, I plan on doing something and I need your help."

Angus offered me his arm, which I gladly took. "Of course, Megan. You name it, I'll give it to you."

I playfully elbowed his side. "I plan on doing a spell to return my family's memories to them. It could be harmful, though."

"Should you perform the spell, then?" Angus asked worryingly.

"They need to know the truth," I answered. "I still don't know how their memories were wiped and mine were left untouched, but I plan on restoring them. They can't go on not knowing who they truly are."

"And what do you need to do?"

I took a breath before answering. "I need to do blood magic."

Brigit

I waited in my room while Salem talked with his parents and Akoni the day after I discovered my aura. It was an incredible feeling! The aura had so much power and so much strength! It felt warm like sitting right next to a fire in the winter and strong, like someone had given me more energy. I never felt anything like it before and the fact that it was a bear, too!

That probably means that Garrett and the girls also have auras. Before all the other witches were wiped out, does that mean they had auras? What a stupid fucking question! Of course they must have!

Animal spiritual protectors.

I'll have to add that to the list of things I need to learn how to use. Something with that much power and strength would probably drain me if I don't know how to properly use it.

My bedroom door opened to reveal Salem. I threw myself off my bed and looked at him hopefully. "So?"

My hopes fell apart as I saw the forlorn look on his face. "My family insists that you keep your engagement to Akoni."

I blinked away the angry tears and crossed my arms. Salem placed his hands on my shoulders and looked into my eyes. "I will not give up on freeing you from this arrangement,

Brigit. This is only a setback. We will just have to keep trying."

I threw my arms against my sides and balled my hands into fists. Don't cry. Don't cry.

Don't cry. Don't cry!

I cleared my throat. "Why won't they let me out of the marriage?"

"Elves have always been tied to the earth," Salem explained. "We all look different. Some are pale, some are not. My family have been rulers for generations. Some have magic, some use weapons, some use both. My mother had a vision of you marrying Akoni before you had even been thought of. When she discovered that you would be given powers of the earth, she considered it a sign."

"It's not fair."

"I know."

I had to marry someone I didn't like just because someone in a vision saw me do it probably decades before I was even born. About a week ago, that would have sounded absolutely insane to me. It is insane now, just not in *that* sense.

"I don't want to marry Akoni," I murmured. "I don't even like him. He's been nothing but distant and horrible. He won't even take my happiness and future into consideration! That's proof he doesn't care about me! He only wants to marry me because he thinks he has to!"

Salem smiled. "You are right, of course."

Salem tucked a finger under my chin and tilted my head to the side before planting a gentle kiss on my cheek. My face instantly warmed—it was warm enough to bake a birthday cake. There's going to be a lot going on: —the war, this 'betrothal', finding my family—which means there's going to be a lot of risks that I'll have to take. I took Salem's wrists and stood on my toes, reaching up to kiss him on the mouth. He didn't recoil or let out a surprised sound. He leaned in and pulled me closer. Besides learning how to use my powers, this was the only worthwhile thing that's happened to me since I woke up in this world.

Chapter 21

Thomas

Garrett pushed Katrina behind him, holding his sword out to me. His eyes narrowed, blazing not with fury, but with warning.

"You have a lot of nerve showing your face in these parts," Garrett said slowly.

"Well, I could say the same for you," I said with a shrug. "These woods are dangerous, though I can't fault you for not knowing."

Garrett gripped his sword tight in his hand. "Stay back!"

I looked at the two of them. Some things never change. Garrett was always protective of Katrina and the girls. I was as well, and protective of Garrett, but he always felt the need to be the father they never had. I paid visits whenever I could, but I could tell their home life—even after their mother married Eluf—was far from perfect. It was dark, cruel, and poisonous and it only seemed to worsen as they grew older. No one ever told me what happened within the palace walls, but I was no fool. I know fear and victims of terrorism and abuse when I see them.

I kept my ax at the ready, but not for them; more for the monsters that threatened to show their faces if they were near.

"I don't wish to harm you, brother," I said.

"I kind of find that hard to believe."

"Fair enough."

"You destroyed the Witch Domain!" Garrett shouted. "You burned down our camp and threatened my friends!"

Orion whined, pushing himself up off the ground with a shake of his head.

"You may want to keep it down, Garrett," I said.

"I don't like saying this, Garrett, but he's right," Katrina said from behind him. "These woods are filled with horrible creatures. It's lucky we haven't been devoured yet."

"Well, we can't just pick up this conversation elsewhere!" Garrett snapped.

I don't have time for this. "Garrett, I'm sorry," I said.

He gave me a confused look. "For what?"

I pulled out my dagger and enchanted it. I aimed it at my brother. Garrett fell to the ground and was pulled towards me. Katrina cried out for him as I took his hand and pricked his finger.

"Ouch!" he yelped.

I flexed my wrist and my dagger disappeared in a cloud of black smoke. Before I could continue on with getting his hair, Garrett pulled his leg back and kicked me in the abdomen as hard as he could. I hit the ground on my side, hearing Garrett push himself away from me. Very well. I needed him to fight anyway. I concentrated on what I wanted to do next; I imagined standing tall right behind him. Electricity surged throughout my whole body and my view changed. Instead of facing the leafy and twig-covered forest floor, I was facing the back of his red hair.

Garrett gasped and turned to face me. I heard Katrina charge. I snapped my fingers and tree branches came to life. Two snatched Katrina by her wrists and lifted her up into the air, higher and higher until she was almost out of sight.

"Let her go!" Garrett ordered as he went for a punch.

I sidestepped his attack and threw a strong gust of wind at him. Garrett went spiraling through the air until he landed a few feet away. Orion growled and lunged for me, but I was ready. I summoned my aura, feeling a surge of new energy bloom in my chest. A dark mist appeared above me and took the form of a large raven. It let out a loud cry and flew towards the wolf, tossing Orion side like a measly pebble.

"Stop!" Garrett shouted as he struggled to his feet. "You're my brother! Why are you doing this?"

"You shouldn't be asking questions, Garrett," I said. "I'll leave as soon as I get what I came for."

"Oh, stop being so damned cryptic for two seconds and talk to me!" Garrett yelled. "I may not remember much, but I remember the brother I once had! He would never attack me or anyone like you have, so what's going on? What's changed?"

I swung my ax. "I take it you know who our father is."

"Did he do this to you?" Garrett asked. "Is he hurting you?"

"He's always hurt me."

"He doesn't have to anymore!" Garrett yelled.

But before he could continue, we could hear screeches coming from the air above us. It was close.

"We can help you!" Garrett said, paying no attention to whatever it was closing in.

"You can't!" I yelled. "It's not just me he'll hurt! It's my wife and our daughter, Petra! Scathe has them! Don't you understand? He'll kill them both if I don't do exactly as I'm told. He wants me to kill you, brother."

Garrett

It hit me like a ton of bricks. He was going to have to kill me. Our father wanted me dead and he was holding Thomas' family over his head to make sure he'd actually go through with it.

Run, Garrett! Orion whimpered.

"I won't run," I vowed. "Thomas, please."

"I don't want to kill you," Thomas said in one breath. "I just have to make it look like you're dead. I only needed your blood and pieces of your hair. With it, I can create a copy of you to present to Scathe. If he thinks you're dead, he'll let my family go."

"You can't trust him, Thomas," I said. "You should know better than anyone what happens if you listen to him."

155

Thomas pointed at me with his ax. "Then you can promise me their free-dom, eh? My child is being kept away from me! I don't even know where she is! Muriel is human! Their lives are in his hands and they'll die if I don't carry out his orders!"

"There has to be another way! It's too risky!"

Another screech from above. It sounded much too close this time. Thomas looked back at me with pleading, frustrated eyes.

"I don't want to hurt you, Garrett, but I need those ingredients. I have no choice!"

I put my hands up and looked my brother in the eye. He has humanity in him, I know it. I just have to appeal to him and get him to listen. "You were the one who taught me how to use my powers in the first place, weren't you?" Thomas' eyes softened.

"You also taught Caitlin and Brigit," I went on. "We were all alone and unloved, abused and neglected. Thomas, I'll never know what you went through, but please...you don't have to be alone. You should never have been left alone. You shouldn't have had to grow up so fast or been hurt the way you have, but killing innocent people won't keep you and your family safe. Please, come with *us*."

Thomas scoffed. "And just go to the people I helped bring terror and loss upon?"

I bit my lip. "If they hear what happened to you, they'll overlook it for a while to help get your family back. You can still fix this."

"You can't trust him!" Katrina called from above. "Scathe is a monster! He'll kill your family regardless of what you'll do!"

I nodded. "Don't you see what he's doing to you? He's twisting you up to be a monster like him, like Jotnar and Nimh. If this keeps going, there will be no kingdom to rule. There will not be a single place for you and your family to run to."

Thomas looked away, considering. He knows I'm right. He has to know that if we work together, we can win. Thomas looked back at me and flicked his wrist. Katrina reappeared beside me in a black mist. I took her by her arms, helping her stand upright.

"Thank you," I said. "Come on. We have to get out of here. Then we can come up with a better plan on how to get your family back."

I held my arm up for Thomas to take. For a minute, he only stared at it, like he wasn't sure if I was being sincere. After a few more seconds, Thomas raised his own arm and we clasped our hands in agreement just as another shriek echoed in the skies. Katrina gasped, squeezing my arm in fright. Orion came to my side and growled at the sky.

"Thomas, what the hell was that?" I asked, trying to control my voice.

Thomas stared at the sky in fright. "The Bananaigh."

I threw my head over my shoulder to stare at him. "The banana? Bandanna—the what?"

"Get on your horse," Thomas ordered. "Both of you, now! We have to leave!"

I pulled Katrina along, meeting Pluto and Heaven halfway. She climbed quickly on top of her horse as I shakily mounted Pluto.

I don't like this at all, Red.

"I know, me neither."

I pulled on the reins of Pluto and we all took off in the opposite direction, back to where the new hideaway was. The screeching was getting louder and closer. I snapped Pluto's reins and we rode faster until we were neck and neck with Thomas and his own horse.

"What is that?" I asked in a panic. "What's coming after us?"

"I told you—the Bananaigh."

"Yeah, but what is it?"

At the sound of another shrilling, blood-curdling scream, my head snapped over my shoulder. I regretted it the second I did. Flying towards us at an inhuman speed was something from my worst nightmares. The Bananaigh had no feet at all, but it was hard to tell because of how translucent its lower half looked. It had the head and shoulders of a goat with long spiraling horns and deep red eyes. Its hands were shriveled and bony looking like they belonged to an old lady, and it wore a long, raggedy, torn brown cloak. It screamed again and rocketed down. Not knowing what else to do, I ducked, barely missing its black claw-like fingernails.

Get us out of here! I silently ordered Pluto.

My stomach was in knots and my breathing was shallow. Sweat dripped down the side of my head and my hands became clammy. I don't want to die this way! I can't!

Katrina was on the opposite side of me with Orion right on her tail. "In case you can't already tell," Katrina said in a panicked breath, "that is an airborne demon."

"Yeah, I figured that," I replied.

Thomas's horse let out a frightened sound as they quickly leapt over a fallen tree without missing a beat. "They haunt battlefields or places where war and bloodshed took place."

"They're drawn by violence," Katrina added.

So does that mean something really bad happened in these woods or had this been a battlefield once before? What other monsters are in these woods then? And for crying out loud, how do we get rid of the one chasing after us right now?

"You ride ahead of me!" Thomas demanded, almost like he had read my thoughts.

"What are you planning?" I asked.

"Just go!"

Katrina, Orion, and I traveled faster, running farther ahead of Thomas. I didn't look back at first, but curiosity got the better of me. I turned my head and watched as Thomas spun around on his horse and summoned fire into his hand before shooting it at the Bananaigh. It let out another screech before darting out of the way. Thomas spun his horse back around and hurried to catch up with us. The Bananaigh is a spirit, right? An entity of sorts? I slowed down enough for Thomas to catch up, until we were riding side by side and ducked to avoid low branches. The creature was still right behind us.

"Thomas, summon Spirit!"

He nodded. The two of us flicked our wrists, summoning purple energy—Spirit—into the palms of our hands. This energy was flickering like fire, urgently, like Spirit was saying, 'Come on! Throw me!'

"Count of three!" I said. "One!"

158

"Two!"

And together the two of us roared, "Three!"

Simultaneously, Thomas and I pulled on the reins of our horses and spun them around. Their hooves skidded to a stop and the two of us tossed Spirit into the air like we were throwing baseballs at the Bananaigh. It shrieked as our elements warped around the Bananaigh, morphing into purple mists that seemed to be pulling on and tackling the air demon. It shrieked again, pulling away and trying to escape.

"Nice work!" Thomas praised. "Now, let's go!"

I know Bruce wasn't going to be happy to see me, but then again, I doubted anyone else would be thrilled to see Thomas. He can pay for his crimes after we set his family free. They shouldn't have to suffer. In a way, I can understand why he followed Scathe's command. He just wanted to keep his family alive. Scathe abused and twisted him for years until he became a killer, but honestly, what lengths would anyone else go to in order to protect their family? No, what he did is messed up and inexcusable, and Thomas knows that, but he wanted to help his loved ones.

We didn't stop until we reached our new hideaway—the one Bruce sent me away from. I was trying to think of some way to get Sir Charles and Bruce to listen when my heart plummeted into my gut. There were bodies everywhere—some piled up—some scattered about. They were all covered in blood and stab wounds. Some lay fallen beside the hill or in the treeline like they had tried making a break for it. Some had spears pierced into their stomachs or chests, pinning them to the ground.

I threw myself off Pluto and looked at the scene. More innocents were dead. Bile rising in my throat, I threw myself to the ground and let myself puke my guts up. I gagged and hacked as more came up and tears stung my eyes. I felt someone rest a hand on my shoulder. I wiped my mouth and looked up to see it was Katrina with puffy eyes. Thomas stared at the tragedy in remorse as Orion threw his head back and howled.

"They're gone," Katrina said quietly. "They were all killed."

"Not quite," Thomas said as he turned to stare down at me. "Sir Charles's and Bruce's spirits...do you feel them?"

I tapped into my gift, breathing for air. I felt for any sort of cord, a connection, a sense of familiarity with the death around us. I didn't feel Sir Charles or Bruce.

"No," I said in a relieved breath.

"Do you know what that means?" Thomas asked. "There's a good chance that they're both still alive somewhere."

Chapter 22

Caitlin

Nothing really happened after the kiss I shared with Captain Raina. We just went back to her room, had dinner, focused on spellwork and went to sleep. That was it, no fireworks bursting in the sky, no crashing waves.

That part in romance novels and movies is all made up. I mean, okay, there were fireworks, just not literally.

So what does that make us, then? Are we still just first mate and captain of the Crimson Kraken and it was just a one and done thing or are we more than that? I've never had this problem before, okay?

The next morning, I woke up in the hammock to find that Captain Raina was not there in the room with me. She wasn't asleep in her homemade bed and she wasn't at the table charting the map or looking up magic spells. I quickly got dressed, grabbed my sword, and went out onto the deck. There was no one at all on deck, only the dark sky and the sounds of the gentle waves. I tiptoed up the steps to avoid waking the rest of the crew and found Captain Raina at the wheel. I figured she'd be here anyway.

"Morning, Captain," I said.

"Indeed it is, Sullivan," she said curtly without even sparing me a glance.

'Sullivan'? Since when has she addressed me by my surname? It shouldn't be a big deal, but to me, it is.

"You're up early," I responded, trying to sound chipper.

"What, am I not allowed to be up and about on my own ship?"

I placed my hands roughly on my hips. "What is going on?"

Again, she refused to look at me. "What do you mean?"

"You're acting different, cold, distant," I told her as I crossed my arms. "Did I say anything? Did I *do* something? Is it about the kiss?"

Captain Raina turned the wheel slightly to the left. I sighed.

"It isn't about the kiss, Caitlin," Captain Raina finally said after a few minutes. "Not entirely, anyway."

"I don't understand."

Captain Raina gave me a sideways glance. Better than nothing, I guess.

"Within the next few hours, we will be at Asmund Rock," she explained. "Once I have what I need, I can begin to exact my revenge."

I shrugged. "I already knew that, so what?"

Captain Raina snapped her head to look at me. "The kiss shouldn't have happened, alright? Is that what you want me to tell you? My revenge comes first, not some silly witch with no memories of who she is falling from the sky and floating all alone in the ocean! I can't afford any distractions!"

I took a small step back. My mouth fell slightly open, forming a small 'o' shape as tears pricked at my eyes. What she just said felt like a slap to the face.

"I'm a distraction?" I asked in a small voice. "What happened was a mistake?"

I could tell by the look in Captain Raina's eyes that she instantly regretted what she said. That doesn't mean she was going to take it back. I sprinted down the stairs, not even bothering to be quiet.

"Caitlin—" Captain Raina started.

"As soon as you get Scathe's talisman, you can drop me off at another dock in the kingdom," I stated before she could finish.

"You don't know your way around, Caitlin," Captain Raina argued.

"I'm a water witch," I snapped. "I'll manage."

I opened the door to her quarters and violently slammed the door behind me. When I was inside, I grabbed a nearby pillow and slammed it against my face. I screamed into it before breaking out into a fit of sobs. I don't care if I seem childish! Maybe I am, but I never felt this way about anyone before! I

162

thought she was finally opening herself up to me, that she trusted me, that she maybe even liked me! All she did since I've been here, besides telling me what to do, was flirt with me whenever she could. That's *not* fair!

Was the kiss really one-sided? Was I really the only one in this relationship or whatever it is that actually felt something? God, I was stupid to think that maybe it *was* something more! If the captain wants to focus on her revenge, fine! She can do that while I find another boat. Once I do that, I can start searching for my brother and sisters. I couldn't do that before, but now I can!

The sky grew lighter after a while, not enough to see the light of the sun, though. Just another dull, dreary day on the open sea. I had calmed down a bit. I wasn't sobbing like I had been before, but instead I lay on my hammock quietly crying to myself and sniffing. My chest hurt a little, too.

Is this what the kids call 'heartache'?

I don't know how much longer I lay there alone in the hammock. It could have been hours. But I decided to get up and study the maps. Maybe I could do a tracking spell to find where my family went. I planted my feet firmly on the ground and took a couple of steps towards the table when all of a sudden, a pain shot through my head. It was so intense! It felt like someone had grabbed a needle and stuck it in the side of my head like a syringe! I hissed at the pain and grabbed both sides of my head. More pain followed after that: in my neck, my shoulders, my stomach, my back, and in my legs. I cried out in pain as I sank to the floor. The pain became so overwhelming—too much to bear. The room began to spin. No, not fast, but slow. My head rolled to the side and soon, I was unconscious.

When I woke up again, I was sitting at a table—a long rectangular table with a white tablecloth and a golden candelabrum in the very center. I was in a room with gray walls and a single paned window behind me. I felt younger, for some reason, like what I was seeing already happened. I tried standing up, but my feet wouldn't move. I wasn't paralyzed, but I *was* trapped in my own body. Out of my control, I reached down and picked up a cup of tea with my shaky hand. Tears fell down my cheeks and I was crying to myself, trying to stay quiet.

Why was I so upset? Why was I being so quiet?

Suddenly the door opened from across the room. A man stood in the dark doorway. His hair was long and wavy and red, same as his beard and goatee. His eyes were green and he had olive skin. This man was all muscle and wore only a black shirt with a vest and black pants. I gasped and pushed my chair out before getting to my feet. I cried harder, again all without my control.

This was a memory! I had already lived through this! A sinking feeling aroused in the pit of my stomach. Whatever was about to happen, I was going to be forced to relive it!

I cried harder as the man with red hair stalked slowly toward me. I wrapped my arms around myself and huddled into the corner as far as I could. The man with red hair stood before me and looked angrily down at me.

This was a grown man huddling me, a thirteen-year-old, into a corner. What was this about?

I looked down at my beige ballet shoes, flinching as the man slammed his meaty hands on the walls on either side of me, keeping me there. The door was shut. Even if I ran for it, he probably had us locked in here.

The man lowered his face to mine. I could smell his horrible breath, feel the hairs of his beard. I felt my heart racing so fast, I thought I might die at any second. A name went through my mind, something that was on the tip of my tongue.

Eluf. Eluf Helvig, my abusive stepfather, the father of my two sweet little sisters, my mother's husband and old flame, the King of Clover Talamh.

I flinched as Eluf caressed my cheek, which only made me cry harder.

"I was told you began your Red River last night," Eluf whispered in my ear. "That means you can bear children. You are a grown woman now."

I'm going to be sick! I'm going to be sick! I'm going to be sick!

I cried harder as his hand started moving lower and lower until…

I shot up screaming. I didn't know what had happened or where I was. I just couldn't take what was happening anymore! What I saw! It wasn't a nightmare at all! It was a memory, a memory I had forgotten about until now! Something so disgusting and despicable had happened to a little girl—to me!

I didn't hear the door open. I didn't see or hear who came rushing in and sliding across the floor towards me.

"Caitlin!" It was Captain Raina's voice. I felt her throw her arms around me and pull me to her chest. "Caitlin! It's me! What's wrong?"

Tears pooling down my face faster than I ever thought possible, I threw my arms over her shoulders and clung to my captain for dear life. I was safe. I was safe and I was back here with my captain. I didn't care about our fight earlier; I just needed her. I didn't want to be alone.

"He raped me," I sobbed into her neck. I squeezed tighter. "Jotnar *raped* me!"

Brigit

"It is out of the question, my son," Queen Valentina said forlornly.

"But it's *my* future!" I cried out, standing beside Salem. I held back the urge to stomp my foot like one of my sisters. "I should have a say!"

"You cannot change fate," Akoni said as he sat beside his mother. "Our marriage has been sealed for almost a century."

A century? I thought it was only a few decades! If that's the case, just how old is everyone in this room?

"If Brigit does not agree to this marriage, we should not force her!" Salem countered. "It is unethical! It goes against everything we believe in and have fought for!"

"It is not for you to decide!" Akoni argued as he shot himself up on his feet, staring daggers at Salem.

Salem's face reflected the anger on Akoni's face. "And it is not your wedding alone, Akoni! If one party does not accept, or feel happy, we shouldn't pressure her! Our kingdom is called Sanctuarium, a place of security and peace! Should we not uphold its name?"

Queen Valentina gave both her sons a considerate look. Then she did the same with me. I held my breath. I know she's the queen and she wants to do what she can for her kingdom and her oldest kid, but I hope she makes the right decision.

The Queen stood up and clasped her hands together. "I will discuss this with the council and we shall put it to a vote."

The three of us all gawked at her in disbelief. "A vote?"

I pressed my hand against my chest to keep from hyperventilating. A vote? Are you kidding me? A fucking vote? She's going to put the fate of my life and my future up to a vote?

"Do I get to be a part of this vote?" I demanded, keeping myself from shrieking.

"I also would like to know," Akoni stated.

"As do I," Salem said.

Akoni glared at his brother. "Why do you care what her fate of marriage is? This has nothing to do with you!"

Salem dared to take a step closer. "I care for the security and well-being of all who live in this Domain and our castle, not just because of who or what the individual *could* be."

I wanted to throw my arms around Salem and hug him right then and there, but restrained myself. That wouldn't look too good to everyone else here.

Queen Valentina raised both her arms. "Silence. Yes, you will all be part of this vote. Let me just speak with the council before we decide. We will meet back here in the throne room tomorrow morning before breakfast."

The Queen disappeared into another room as Salem and I turned to head for the courtyard.

"Stop. Right. There!" Akoni demanded.

We both did so on impulse before turning to confront Akoni. He angrily stepped in our direction. The guy was practically foaming at the mouth!

Akoni jammed a finger into Salem's chest. "How *dare* you talk to your future king in this manner!"

Salem aggravatingly slapped Akoni's hand away, much to his surprise and mine. "You are not king, yet, Akoni! Maybe if you, for once in your life, listened to reason—!"

"That is all I ever do! I am to be king and I always do what is structured! I do what is logical and correct!"

"Even at the expense of another's health and well-being? If this is you doing that, brother, then you are going to make for a *sorry* king indeed!"

"What did you just say to me?" Akoni demanded.

I stepped in between the both of them and pushed them apart. "Okay, both of you, stop!

This decision is going to happen regardless and—!"

"You should not be arguing!" Akoni interrupted, pointing a finger at me. "Every woman here accepts her marriage and you are no different!"

I turned on him. "The fuck you just say to me?"

"You heard me, girl."

G-Girl? I'm sorry, what? "Say that again."

Akoni looked at me, daring me to repeat what I had just said. I guess egos are bruised easily in this world, too.

"Watch how you speak to me, girl. I am your future king!"

"I am from Clover Talamh! You are not my king and I'd rather die at the hands of my parents than ever marry you!"

Akoni stared at me, taken aback as though I just murdered his cat right in front of him. I probably should've stopped, but since I was on a roll, I kept going. "Why would I want to marry—how could I marry or ever find myself loving a spoiled, whiny, horrible little bitch bag like you?"

Akoni's eyes widened and he pulled his hand back. I gasped and took a step back. He was going to hit me! I knew he was a dick, but I didn't think that he'd do this! Just before he could swing his arm down and finish the attack, Salem caught his brother's wrist and pushed him away. Akoni snarled, glaring with narrow eyes at the two of us. He looked like a wild animal, but as soon as he traded looks with Salem and I, it was obvious that something had clicked. He knew.

"This is not over," was all Akoni said before storming off after his mother.

Salem turned to me, breathing heavily, and cupped my face. "Are you alright?"

I nodded. "Yeah, I'm fine."

But something wasn't really fine, and I don't mean because of what just happened. My head suddenly felt like it was underwater. My words seemed to come out in slow motion. I've never been drunk or drugged before, but I wondered if this is what that felt like. My eyelids grew heavy and my balance went off kilter. I don't remember falling, but apparently I had, considering Salem had caught me and was laying me down on the floor. He was crying out to someone. I wasn't sure who; his voice sounded so far away.

Suddenly, I was in a courtyard, shooting arrow after arrow at the center of the target. I was wearing a short-sleeved mint green shirt, long brown pants, and was barefoot. My hair was messy, too, like I had forgotten to brush it earlier. This wasn't the courtyard I have been training in for the last few days; this was another courtyard.

Another castle.

It was completely made of stone with long thorny vines stretching all the way to the top.

The windows were made from stained glass and there was a barn in the opposite direction. People were hauling wagons full of either lumber or hay while others were at work feeding the animals or sharpening weapons.

In the corner of my eye, I saw a boy wiggle his fingers at a small dog. Orange sparks danced brightly atop his fingertips. Magic.

Then it dawned on me that I was in the Witch Domain.

It felt familiar somehow, like I really had been here before, like I already did this. I had no control over my movements. I just kept shooting arrow after arrow, not missing even once. Then I realized something else. I was shorter...shorter and ten fucking years old! Puberty was a fucking bitch, okay? I don't feel like going through that again!

"Brigit!"

I turned at the sound of my name. Caitlin was in the courtyard a few yards away with an old lady on her arm. Caitlin—as always—looked gorgeous with her long red hair and blue eyes. She was wearing a long-sleeved, sky blue dress and ballet slippers while the old lady had puffy silver hair and brown eyes and wore a long red cloak.

"Grandmother and I will be in the garden drinking tea with cakes," Caitlin said sweetly.

"Would you like to come with us?"

I felt myself smiling giddily. "Yeah!"

"Alright, well, go wash up, first," Caitlin told me. "We don't want to make work harder for our servants. They already do too much as it is."

Bossy Caitlin as ever. I ran as fast as my legs could carry me into the castle. I ran down the halls leaving dirty footprints behind me. I ran past servants carrying letters, trays, and laundry. Some yelled at me to stop, but did I listen?

Babe, I listen to nobody.

I threw the door open to my room and tossed my bow on the bed. I yanked the quiver of arrows off my back and tossed it carelessly next to my dresser. I slammed the door shut, eager to get back outside to hang out with Caitlin and our grandma when all of a sudden, the castle shook. It *shook*. I gasped and fell on my side. Portraits on the walls fell off the hooks, landing with a thud on the floors followed by vases and pitchers of water and wine. I felt myself panic as servants screamed and ran.

Get up! I thought to myself. Get up or you'll die!

With legs like Jell-O, I staggered across the long hallway, back in the direction I had come from. I tripped, falling a few feet from one of the windows.

What's happening? What's going on?

I crawled the rest of the way to the glass window and peeked my head out. Smoke was coming from the top of the castle. It was too high to see where exactly, but enough smoke had started to darken the sky. Everything looked a lot smaller from up here, but I could see that the barn had been set on fire and there were men in armor stabbing witches in the chests or through their backs. Animals were going crazy and I could hear the screams from up here. The castle shook again. Someone was throwing something at it, but what? Boulders? Magic?

Who would attack us? Why are we under attack? What was happening? What's going on?

A loud wail came from behind me. I looked over my shoulder to see Nora—who was only two at the time—standing there frozen with her face red from crying. I pushed myself up only to hear something snap. I looked up in horror to find that it was the long crystal chandelier falling right above Nora! She was going to be killed!

I ran faster, pumped full of adrenaline. I was only a few feet away. Knowing I wasn't going to get to her in time, I threw myself at Nora and tackled her to the ground just as the chandelier smashed into the ground. Sharp pieces of gold and crystalline material exploded, rocketing in all different directions. I wrapped Nora in one hand and shot my hand out with the other. Green light burst from my palm, creating a force field in front of us. The sharp objects bounced off my magic and shot elsewhere. Nora sobbed as she held me tighter in her hands. When it looked like the explosion had stopped, I put my hand down and the green force field vanished. I panted and held Nora closer.

Alison! Alison was all alone in her nursery! I had to get to her and get out of the castle with my sisters!

But that's not what happened. I was snatched up from the ground, ripped out of Nora's little fingers, by the back of my shirt. I screamed and threw my fists around aimlessly, only to be thrown across the room. Nora screamed again and when I looked up, it was something horrible: a knight with large bat wings on its back and its face—what I assumed was human—was mutilated and decomposing. It snarled at me, somehow able to produce drool. I raised my arms and shot green magic at the creature.

I'm not a religious person, but I've heard stories from other religions that we were formed from the earth and that when we die, our bodies return to earth. If that's the case, then c'est la vie!

The monster roared in anguish before exploding into a pile of dust. Nora ran to me and threw her arms around my waist, balling her eyes out.

"It's gonna be okay!" I promised. "Come on! We have to get out of here!"

I took Nora's hand and we ran out of the room and turned a corner. Alison's nursery was on the right side at the end of this hallway. The castle shook again as something else made an impact, but I forced the two of us to keep moving.

I just hoped that my brother and sisters were okay!

Nora and I made it to Alison's room, but the door had been shut. The nursemaid knows that is prohibited! Holding Nora with one hand, I pushed the door open with magic with the other and the two of us stepped inside. What I saw stopped me in my tracks. Alison was sound asleep, wrapped in her strawberry red blanket above her crib. Someone was holding her. The room was dark; the curtains had not been drawn and there was no light, but I could see a figure holding our baby sister. It was a boy, I think, a boy with dark armor and dark, shoulder-length hair. He was wearing an iron mask covering the lower half of his face. The boy held Alison, staring at her for a few seconds before lifting his head to look at me.

I recognized his eyes! I had seen him before, but—

Just as our eyes met, the ground beneath Nora and I shattered, breaking open like paper. From what I could see from the split in the ground, it led to a whole 'nother level of the castle, a much colder and darker part. Nora and I screamed as we were pulled through the cracks by gravity. I don't know how, but our hands managed to stay clasped together. Everything was in slow motion. And then—

"Brigit!" Salem cried. "Brigit!"

I sucked in a breath like I had been underwater too long and sat straight up. Salem touched my shoulder carefully as I got my bearings. It was just Salem and I in his family's throne room. I remember now; the two of us had just fought with Akoni when I passed out.

"Brigit, are you alright?" Salem asked, unshed tears in his eyes.

He looks so scared, like he thought I was going to die. In a way, it was like I had. Those visions were what happened before my family and I disappeared. That boy, whoever he was, had Alison. Why was he in our castle? Why was he in her room?

"Brigit?" Salem repeated.

I looked up at him before throwing my arms around his neck. He let out a surprised gasp before pulling me into a hug.

"You fainted," he explained. "I was calling your name. I thought you had been hurt or that this had become too much for you."

I buried my face in Salem's shoulder, letting the tears fall. I really fucking hate crying, but I admitted to myself that this was okay. Salem pulled away and brushed the hair away from my soaking wet face.

"What happened?" he asked tenderly.

I said tearfully, "I remember now. I remember everything."

Chapter 23 ´

Megan

"Are you mad?" Angus demanded.

I squeezed his arm desperately. "Angus, I need to draw some blood; I didn't say it was going to kill me."

Angus shook his head quickly. "No, I cannot—"

"I will be fine."

Angus stared at me incredulously. "What does making you bleed have to do with finding the children?"

"Angus, this is blood magic," I explained. "I can return their memories and find a way to locate them. I just need a secluded space to perform the ritual."

Angus sighed. "I don't like this."

I cupped his face. "I am not going to die, Angus. I won't even be hurting myself critically. I just need my blood to perform this ritual."

"At least tell me why..."

"Blood. As in my blood. My kin."

Angus rubbed his hands over his face and began to pace. I understand his worries and concerns, but this is something I have to do.

"They deserve to know the truth," I continued. "When we first arrived in the Other Realm—Connecticut—I was never able to figure out what had happened to their memories. We just woke up like it was any other day. I had tried dropping hints to the older three, but they only looked at me like I was bonkers.

There was no magic in that place, but now that I once again have access to my powers, I can perform the ritual to give those memories back to them."

Angus nodded, but took a few seconds longer before he would meet my eyes. "Do you know what restoring years of missing memories will do to them? Especially ones that are not so happy?"

"I know," I answered in an almost whisper. "They will have two lives in their minds, both real and fake. The memories of what happened to them and who they were will put them into shock, but we can't just go about doing this anymore. The lying, the secrets, the pretending, it all must end. They deserve to know what happened and who they really are."

Angus rubbed his forehead once before taking my hand. "Then let us get to this secluded space."

Angus and I walked as far as we could from the camp, walking farther and farther into the forest. The only sounds around were that of birds and the soft movements of the trees against the wind. I took a stand right next to a river-bank, away from Angus, with his dagger in my hand.

"I'm here if you need me," Angus said.

I looked at him and smiled reassuringly before sliding the blade across the palm of my hand. It stung, but I refused to make a sound or show any other sign of pain. I balled my hand into a fist and squeezed as hard as I could, and held it over the riverbank. Three crimson drops fell into the water.

From my bleeding heart to yours, I call upon you, Garrett.
From my bleeding heart to yours, I call upon you, Caitlin.
From my bleeding heart to yours, I call upon you, Brigit.
Together, our hearts and minds are one.
This curse of days and years forgotten undone.

The water came to life, almost as if it were boiling. I took a step back and watched as the clear water shimmered as bright as sapphire before the light extinguished and it slowed to a steady pace. A light filled my chest and a heaviness seemed to lift. I smiled and turned to Angus.

"It has worked!" I said. "They shall have their memories back."

Angus pressed his lips thinly together and offered me a small, sympathetic smile. "Do you truly think they're ready?"

I motioned to the river. "If I didn't, do you think I would have done this?"

"I'm not talking about regaining their memories," Angus corrected. "I'm talking about having to fight their parents? Not just the older three, but the little ones? They are all so very young."

I don't know why the question threw me off, but it did. I had known that the day would come when the children were going to have to fulfill their destinies to save this world, that they would have to defeat a great evil, but even so, I still am not prepared for it. These children I have come to see and love as my own. Just being away from three of them is heavy on my heart. I can't imagine what I would do if harm were to befall on them.

"I fought like hell to protect them and keep them safe," I said fiercely.

Angus smiled—a real one this time—and took my hand, leading me away from the river. "You raised them well, Megan. I know you fought hard for them to live, but now, they're going to have to fight for themselves in order to stay alive. They must count on themselves now."

"I know they will," I stated. "They're survivors...every single one of them."

· · · · ·

"A war is coming," Angus said that night in front of the group. "A war has been coming for a great many years. Jotnar, Nimh, and Scathe were the ones who chose to see that through. We can no longer hide. While Lady Megan and I are gone, continue training, gather whatever food you can, map out the area. It is time we end things."

I grasped the front of my cloak at Angus' words. No more hiding. As much as I loathe the Fey, I will not tuck my tail and hide. I will make them lower their shields and let Angus out of his contract.

As everyone dispersed to begin their tasks, Angus asked, "Are you prepared for this?"

"I am," I stated firmly. "I don't care what I have to do, we are ending this deal with the fairies."

Angus pulled his hood over his head so that it covered his eyes and walked me to my dark brown horse.

Hello, Lady.

"Hello there," I said kindly. "Pleasure to meet you, dear."

I grabbed the horse's saddle and threw one leg over on the other side right before I pulled my own hood over my eyes. "What is your name?"

Dawn.

"I am glad to be riding with you, Dawn."

"Auntie, wait!" Nora cried.

"Wait up!" Alison called, following her sister.

The little ones ran up to meet me with cloaks of their own; Nora wore a long yellow cloak while Alison wore a long red one that trailed behind her.

"Girls, what are you doing?" I asked. "You *have* to stay here."

"But we wanna help!" Nora cried.

"Yeah!" Alison shouted in agreement. "Please don't leave us alone!"

My heart hurt at those words. "Oh, come on! That is *not* fair!"

Angus coughed awkwardly beside me on his horse. "Megan, the Lady of the Fae is their aunt…"

I didn't forget that detail, I was just hoping to avoid it. The Lady of the Fairies will not harm the girls or let any harm of any kind come to them, but it is still too much of a risk. The Lady of the Fae, Freya, married Jotnar's younger brother, Sven, and had a child named Fell—a hybrid of witch and fairy, something that has been forbidden since the days of the first sun. I never knew either of them that well, only what my sister had told me in writing. However, Freya was a fairy, which was enough for me.

A few months before the siege, Sven died of heart failure and Fell soon went off to the Emerald Mountain in Sanctuarium. Still…

"They will also be safer with us, Megan," Angus added. "You will not have to worry so much about their well-being while we're away."

"Yeah! Let us come, Auntie!" Alison pleaded.

"Let us come!" Nora repeated.

I sighed and waved my hand up to a satyr. "Alright. Bring them up."

The satyr smiled, nodded once, and lifted Alison onto my horse, settling her in front of me and then did the same with Nora and placed her in front of Angus on his horse.

"Let us begin, then," Angus said with a smile. "Megan?"

Angus and I turned our horses to the border—and the world beyond. Once I get us through, that's it. No changing our minds, no going back. Angus and I will have to follow this through and watch each other's backs and the girls. We will face the dangers of Shadow Knights, human knights, monsters, and the animal spies of our enemies.

But this could mean ending this war once and for all. I can find Garrett, Caitlin, and Brigit. We can be together again, just as it has always been.

With that thought in mind, I smiled to myself and raised one hand. I thought of the barrier being as easy to pass as a curtain, a veil, of sorts. A blue light began to glow and formed into the shape of a door. Everyone watched as I snapped once on the reins, ushering my horse forward. I felt no difference as I passed through the light blue entryway and into the world. When I looked back, there was nothing. There were no tents, wagons, or survivors of the war. It was all just forest. Then the light blue doorway shimmered again as Angus and Nora came into view. I clenched my fingers and the light went out like a candle flame.

"This is it," I said.

Angus looked at me intently and said, "This is it."

Chapter 24

Garrett

Thomas flicked his wrist, summoning a ball of fire into his hand before throwing it onto the pile of bodies. The sky was dark and we had just finished gathering the fallen. Orion lifted his head into the air and howled in mourning once again. I stood at Katrina's side and took her hand. She lay her head on my shoulder. She didn't say anything, but I knew what she must have been thinking. She lost the friends and family she made. More innocents died at the hands of my father and his stupid war.

Thomas took a step back so that he was on the other side of me. He stared at the fire that swallowed up the bodies of the Defyers. Without looking away, I asked him, "You didn't know that he was going to do this, did you?"

"No."

Thomas turned away and walked towards Morrigan. After a few more seconds, Katrina and I did the same. Orion followed close behind as we rode into the forest. Thomas slowed so that we could catch up. I was on one side of him and his horse while Katrina rode opposite of us.

"What's the plan, Thomas?" I asked. "What do we do?"

Thomas was silent for a few seconds and his eyes stayed glued on the forest ahead of us. "The Dwarf Domain is Jotnar and Nimh's territory. It will be highly guarded by soldiers and monsters alike."

"So we'll have to be careful then," I said.

"What makes you so sure that Jotnar and Nimh took Sir Charles and Sir Bruce and not Scathe?" Katrina asked.

Thomas gave her a look. "Lady Katrina, we are closing in on the Dwarf Domain, that is their territory. Jotnar likes to torture and play with his prey before actually killing them. He'll want to torture them to find you, Garrett."

I ignored the sinking feeling in my chest as my fingers tightened around the reins of Pluto. "So we just sneak in, then?"

"We will have to do it carefully," Thomas explained. "Once when I was young, I tried sneaking into their castle to kill them—"

"What?" I interrupted. "You tried killing them?"

"Scathe sent me to kill them before the siege even happened," Thomas explained. "That's a long story and one for another day, but it didn't matter. Nimh found out that I had gotten inside and sent me away to Scathe's castle. We'll have to find a way to get inside."

"Don't you have to report back to Scathe soon, though?" Katrina asked.

"Not until I bring Garrett's dead body back to him, which I plan to do."

My head snapped towards my brother. "I beg your pardon?"

"Body double."

"Oh, you're still doing that?"

"Yes. He will give Petra and Muriel back to me and then I will find his talisman and kill him. That talisman is the only thing keeping him alive. Once I destroy it, he will die," Thomas explained.

"Okay, but what about Sir Charles and Bruce?" Katrina asked. "I don't mean to offend you or be the bearer of bad news, but what makes you think they'll help you after everything?"

"They will have to," Thomas said firmly. "Sir Charles Morgan is Muriel's father and Petra's grandfather."

Katrina and I shared a look of shock before Thomas snapped on Morrigan's reins. Jotnar has Sir Charles and our father has Sir Charles's daughter and grandchild who happen to be my brother's family—which I guess makes us family.

Family looks after each other, something Jotnar, Scathe, and Nimh know nothing about. I can never understand what made them do this, what made them turn out to be the way they are. I also don't care. It doesn't matter what you've been through, what has happened to you, you cannot take your rage out on innocent people—or your family.

We made camp on top of a slope just above a stream. I had no idea what time it was. All I knew was that emotionally, physically, and mentally, I was exhausted. Thomas volunteered to take the first watch, which I agreed to. As Katrina and I settled together beside a tree, she looked at me and asked, "How do you know you can trust him?"

I shrugged. "I just can."

Katrina stared long and hard at me for a few extra seconds, like she couldn't quite believe me.

"I understand why you don't trust him, but you have to trust me, okay?" I said. "Please?"

Katrina nodded and laid her head down on my shoulder. I looked at the back of Thomas's head before falling asleep and thought to myself, *I can trust him. I do trust him.* I trust him.

I woke up a few hours later to Thomas shaking my shoulder. "What's up?"

"Your turn."

I held back a tired groan and tiredly pushed myself up. Thomas walked over to another tree and nestled himself comfortably against it as I sat on the tree stump. I was so tired, and sitting on the stump in the middle of the night, not doing anything except keeping watch was not very exciting.

It's going to be a long night.

I was supposed to wake up Katrina so that she could take her turn keeping watch, but I didn't want to wake her, so you know what I did? I stayed up the rest of the night and kept watch. Because I'm just that guy.

Was I tired? Yes. Am I going to admit that to Thomas and Katrina? Nope. I heard Thomas stir as the sky got lighter. I shook my head and rubbed my eyes with the heels of my palms and stood up.

"Morning, Thomas," I said airily.

Thomas pushed himself up and stared at me as he shuffled his messy hair. "What are you still doing up, Garrett?"

I smiled sheepishly. "I decided to keep watch the rest of the night."

"What?" Katrina asked in surprise as she climbed to her feet. "Why?"

"Garrett," Thomas interrupted, "you do realize you have only gotten three hours of sleep, right?"

"I'll be fine," I said. "I couldn't really sleep and I didn't want to bother anybody and—"

A sudden pain hit me in my chest. I automatically felt like I was having a nervous breakdown. My breathing became heavy and tears stung my eyes. I bent down to my waist, pressing my hands over my chest as tears spilled out of my eyes.

"Garrett!" Katrina cried as she and Thomas caught me in their arms.

"Garrett, what's happening?" Thomas asked quickly.

I saw Orion rush to my side as my legs gave out. This wasn't my pain that I was feeling.

This was Caitlin's. She was in trouble!

"Cait…" I whispered weakly. "Cait…"

My head rolled to the side and I suddenly saw Graham standing behind Thomas and Katrina who were trying to keep me awake. How did he get here? I stared at him as my vision became blurry with tears and dizziness. I couldn't hear Katrina and Thomas anymore. I couldn't hear…

Caitlin.

Caitlin…

I rode on Pluto through the forest to the top of the hill as far away from the castle as possible. I felt younger, a lot younger. The sun was out, something I haven't seen in the past almost *month* since I've been back. You know what else is kind of insane to me? The fact that I haven't heard a single bird chirp at all in my time back and all of a sudden, I could.

Something didn't feel right with me. I was in my own body, but I wasn't in control. In a way, it's like I was trapped in my own body.

"Katrina?" I called. "Katrina, are you here?"

Why was I calling her name out in the woods? What's even happening? Why the bloody hell can I still not move?

Relax, Red. She's probably just running a bit late.

"Yeah, you're right, Pluto," I said while patting the side of his neck. "I just can't wait to see her. It's been almost a whole week and Eluf and my mother have been breathing down my neck."

Gee, it's like you're a teenager who needs privacy and you know, a life.

I chuckled. "Yes, strange, is it not?"

I climbed off of Pluto and started walking to the edge of the hill. The castle was in view, tall and dark as usual. Everyone else in the kingdom hears rumors that Eluf and my mother are horrible parents, but no one has the strength to confront them on it, not that I want them to. If someone got hurt because of me, I wouldn't know what to do or how to live with myself. For years, since Eluf took the throne, he has been overtaxing the people and terrorizing them. If anyone, no matter who they were, steps out of line, he'll kill them on the spot.

My mother knows this. She's seen it happen but she doesn't care. She's always been verbally and emotionally abusive towards us. She doesn't get her way, she screams at us loud enough to shatter glass. Only once in a while will she actually lay a hand on one of us.

I have been trying to find a way for us to get away for years now, especially with Alison having been born a few weeks ago. I have a few ideas of where we could run and hide, though I'm not sure if that would work a third time.

"Garrett?"

The sound of Katrina's voice snapped me out of my thoughts. She rode Heaven from the woods, looking like light at the end of a dark tunnel, like the moon shining in the darkness of a winter's night. She smiled as she climbed off her horse. I let my legs carry me to her before enveloping her in a hug and lifting her off her feet. She smelled like lavender and pine. I gently set her down and brushed a few strands of blonde hair out of her face.

"I'm so glad you're here," Katrina said. "I feel like it's been forever."

"I know, I'm sorry," I said. "My mother and her husband are quite literally...to put it nicely...the worst."

Katrina giggled. "I'm just glad to see you. And I'm glad to see that you're safe."

I took Katrina's hands and planted a kiss on her knuckles. "I will find a way for us to be together. I swear it."

Katrina's face turned to concern. "Why do they care so much about us anyway?"

I shook my head slowly. "I couldn't say. Eluf isn't even my father. The only reason I can come up with as to why he cares is because he lives for control, that he feeds off it."

Katrina pressed her forehead against mine. "I wish you didn't have to live with someone like that."

I caressed the side of her face. "I try to ignore him. And my mother. And my father, really."

"Quite a list."

"Isn't it?"

Suddenly, something came over me—a range of emotions that I've felt before: fear, sickness, and rage. I was so afraid that I felt like throwing up.

"Garrett?" Katrina asked fearfully. "Garrett, what is it?"

I began panting. My forehead and palms became sweaty. "Caitlin's in trouble. I'm feeling her pain again…"

Katrina's eyes widened, but before either of us could say anything, we heard an explosion. The ground shook, knocking us both over. I grabbed Katrina by her arm and pulled her up and shakily hurried to our frightened horses.

"An earthquake?" Katrina asked in fright.

I pulled on Pluto's reins and looked at the castle. I gasped. Dark clouds of smoke crawled up to the sky, floating up from the side of the foundation. We were under attack!

"The girls!" I cried. "Come on!"

I kicked Pluto's sides and we took off towards the castle. I could hear the screams of my people from the hill, but it was what I felt that was the most draining. I felt spirits surrounding me at a rapid pace, circling me like angry vultures. I shook my head, trying and failing to clear away my dizzy spell.

Help us…

Save us…

Avenge us…

Help…

Help us…

I pushed away the sounds of the ghosts echoing in my head as I rode faster into the streets of the Capital. Buildings were on fire and there were bodies in the streets, some were just laying there dead, others were laying there dead and on fire. Horses whinnied, throwing their front legs up in the air, knocking a few knights away. I jumped off Pluto and looked at Katrina. "Get my sisters and get out of here!"

"I won't leave you!" she shouted over the chaos.

"I'll find you, now go!"

I smacked the side of Heaven and they took off. I unsheathed my sword and ran headfirst into the battle. My heart stopped as mutilated corpses rose from the ground snarling and hissing. They grew large, bat-like wings and their eyes were cold and dead.

Bloody hell…

Suddenly, I heard a child's cry. Out of habit, I threw my head over my shoulder and found a young blonde boy with blue eyes standing in the middle of the street, his nose and eyes red and puffy. I didn't stop to think or second guess, I just ran towards the boy and snatched him up just before a knight wearing iron could swing his sword down upon the boy. I jumped out of the way with the boy in my arms and focused my attention on the knight. Purple magic shot out from the ground and sent the knight flying in the other direction.

"Lord Garrett!"

I looked up in time to see a woman in chainmail riding to me on a black and white patched horse. I handed her the child. "Take him and get out of here!"

"Reinforcements are coming, Milord!"

The knight rode off with the boy and I focused my attention on the fighting. Another knight in dark armor swung his sword at me, but I blocked his attack and threw him off. Then I shot different shades of purple energy at him, causing him to explode into dust. Then another knight in dark armor swung his sword at me. I flicked my wrist and the knight exploded into another pile of dust.

I spun around, ready to continue the fight when I saw *him*. Thomas was standing across the cobblestone street, staring at me. It was just like the nightmare I had! I couldn't believe what I was seeing! My own brother was here attacking me! I turned to run, hearing a whistling behind me getting closer at a rapid speed. I jumped to the side and looked up as Thomas's ax disappeared in a dark cloud of smoke. Thomas marched in my direction as his ax reappeared in his hands, coated in dark tendrils of smoke.

I jumped to my feet and swung my sword. Thomas blocked the attack and swung his ax. He then proceeded to slam his palm into my chest, which sent me flying into a stone wall. I hit the ground just as the lower half of my body was pulled into the earth like quicksand. I clawed at the ground, desperate to not get pulled in, but of course, that didn't work. The earth closed around my waist, leaving only my top half exposed. I tried pulling myself out, but it was no use.

I was stuck.

Thomas stared at me for a second before grabbing my sword and heading in the direction of the castle. I tried pulling myself up, more urgently this time, on the verge of a panic attack.

"Thomas, stop!" I screamed. "Why are you doing this?"

But he just kept walking calmly, despite the war that was happening around us. He was heading towards the castle! He attacked me! He led a siege here! He was killing people! What if he goes after our sisters next?

"Thomas!"

This isn't him.

"Thomas!"

This can't be happening!

"*Thomas!*"

Caitlin

Captain Raina placed a blanket over me as I sat at the table nursing a mug of tea. I finally stopped myself from sobbing, but I was still crying and sniffling. The captain took her usual seat across from me, her eyes full of sorrow and sympathy.

"You remember everything, Caitlin?" she asked softly.

The only answer I gave her was one very small and stiff nod. The tea was warming my hands, but I still shivered at the memories. I stared into my tea, ignoring all eye contact.

"He raped me every day since I was twelve," I said quietly.

I could feel the anger and disgust radiate off of Captain Raina. In the corner of my eye, I could see her hand ball into a tight fist.

"It wasn't your fault, Caitlin."

I don't know what it was: whether it was Captain Raina saying my actual name or the fact that she told me what happened to me was not my fault, but I started sobbing again. Captain Raina pushed herself out of her chair, walked around the table and gave me a tight hug. I didn't hug her back, though. I couldn't. All I could do was continue crying.

I remember since I was twelve, for a whole year, Eluf assaulted me and told me to keep quiet or my sisters and my brothers would be hurt.

That's right. I have two brothers, not one. Thomas. Thomas Sullivan. He would come visit us whenever it was possible and the four of us—him, Gare, Bridge, and myself—would go outside and have as much fun as we could away from the castle. We'd still have guards with us, but at least our parents left us alone.

It all came back to me at once—the abuse, the tyranny, Thomas, the siege. I remember having tea in the gardens with my grandmother, someone I have always been close with. She was someone I could confide in, yet I never told her or anyone what was really going on. I wanted to tell someone so badly, but I couldn't bear the thought of my brothers and sisters being hurt. Eluf, no, Jotnar doesn't deserve to be king. He shouldn't be able to get away with this.

"I will kill him," Captain Rain growled. "I will *kill* that bastard!"

This time, I did take her by the arm. For a few seconds, I had to compose myself. The tears still came, but not as rapidly as before. Something else came over me—not disgust, or fear, or tragedy.

Hatred and anger. I blinked once, squeezing my lids shut before opening them. My breathing was more composed, too, but barely. "Not before I'm through with him."

I snapped my head up at my captain, understanding and determination in her glassy eyes. "I want him to pay first before we kill him. I want him to suffer." I gave Captain Raina's arm a slight squeeze, my jaw set. "I want him drowning in his blood, begging me to stop before I watch the light leave his eyes."

The two of us stared at each other a few seconds longer before we heard a knock at the door. We both turned to see one of the pirates—the one who blocked my path my first day on this ship—open the door slightly.

"Land ho, Captain," he said. "We've made it to Asmund Rock."

As he left, Captain Raina looked back at me. I could see a fire in her eyes. To be honest, she always had that fire, that fury, in her eyes, one that could rival any storm, but this one was different. I've never seen something that could look both fiery hot and frigid all at once.

"It's time, Caitlin," she said.

She took my hand and pulled me up, our eyes still locked on each other's. I only had three words to say: "Let's fucking go."

Chapter 25

Megan

"I spy with my lil eye something green," Alison said.

"Everything is green, idiot," Nora snapped.

"Nora, be nice," I said. "Don't call your sister an idiot."

"Princess, what you see that is green, are they perhaps trees?" Angus asked with a smile.

"Yes, but which one?" Alison asked.

Angus coyly rubbed his chin in thought before turning his head this way and that way, looking around in wonder. He pointed to a random tree that we passed. "This one, perhaps?" Smiling gleefully, Alison shook her head. Angus pointed to another and then another.

"Yes!" Alison grinned.

Nora rolled her eyes. "God help me."

I burst out laughing at the comment. "Nora, you sound just like Brigit!"

"I miss her," Alison said as she looked down at the horse's mane and started fiddling with a few strands. "I miss Gary, too, and Caity."

I set my chin on top of her head and rubbed her arm. "So do I, honey. So do I."

We continued riding for a few more hours in between moments of silence and games of I Spy until the girls complained of their 'rear ends starting to hurt'. We chose a spot to dismount; Angus helped the girls down first and then myself as the horses started eating leaves off of trees and some grass.

"I shall go find us some wood," Angus said. "Soldiers usually make camp in these woods, so if they see a fire, they'll likely think of us as their own."

"Be careful," I warned him.

Angus smiled, planted a kiss on my forehead, and walked a little ways in another direction, his hand on the hilt of his sword. I watched him go until he was out of sight.

"Does this count as camping?" Alison asked as she and Nora took a seat next to each other on a fallen log.

I smiled and rubbed the top of her head. "Sort of."

"Cool!" Alison cheered. "This is my first camping trip, then! Can we sing some songs when Lord Angus gets back?"

I opened my mouth to answer before shutting it again. I have to be careful when I explain this to her and Nora.

"Well, no, my sweets," I said as I crouched in front of them. "I'm afraid we cannot. We are not only camping, but we're playing hide and seek."

Alison tilted her head to the side and looked at me in confusion. "Hide and seek?"

Nora gazed from Alison to me. "She means from the bad guys."

I sighed. "Yes, from the bad guys."

"Like our mom and dad," Nora added.

I stared at Nora, my brows furrowed. "How did you know?"

Nora shrugged. "You're not very good at keeping secrets, Auntie Megan."

I continued to stare, urging her to continue on.

"I can hear your thoughts," Nora said. "They're loud. I heard you blocking someone out the other night: the lady whose voice sounds like growling."

Alison looked up at me. "Is that true, Auntie Megan?"

I slowly nodded. "Yes, we are trying to hide you two from your mother and father, Jotnar and Nimh. They're the bad guys who have torn this world apart."

"Are they gonna hurt us?" Alison asked.

"No," I said firmly, taking each of them by their hands. "I will not let that happen to either one of you. I will protect you both as well as your brother and sisters until the day I die."

"You're not gonna die, though, Auntie Megan, are you?" Nora asked tearfully.

"Of course not!" I exclaimed as I pulled them both into a tight hug. "I promise we will all be okay. No one else is going to get hurt, okay? I promise."

I pulled away from the girls and wiped away their tears. I smiled, trying my hardest to not break down crying as well.

"Come on, then," I said to them softly. "Chin up, both of you. We have to keep a stiff upper lip right now. We have to be brave and strong right now, okay?"

The girls nodded before I kissed each of them on the forehead just as Angus returned with wood piled up in his arms. "I have been thinking: Would you girls like to try hunting? It will come in handy, including how to build a fire."

"That sounds like a great idea," I agreed as I stood up. "What do you two think?"

"I guess," Nora shrugged.

"Sure," Alison answered quietly.

Angus stared at the girls in concern before turning to me. "Have I missed something?"

I tucked my hair behind my ear. "They know, Angus."

"Ah," Angus said in a small voice. "Well, your Majesties, I...I do not have the right words..."

"When do we start hunting?" Nora asked without looking up.

"Whenever you would like," Angus answered.

Nora nodded. "Then let's go."

Angus set the wood down as the girls stood up. Angus and I linked arms and followed the girls who walked a few feet ahead of us hand in hand.

Thomas

"Garrett? Garrett, wake up!" I said as I shook him. "Garrett!"

"What's happened?" Katrina asked close to tears. "Why won't he wake up?"

Almost as if on cue, Garrett shot right up gasping for air. Katrina and I both took hold of his shoulders, assuring him that he was safe.

"Are you alright?" I asked him.

His sweaty hair stuck to his head and his deep blue eyes stayed glued to the forest floor.

He was shaking. I pressed my hand to his forehead, looking upon my brother with concern.

"You're burning hot, Garrett," I said.

"Are you okay?" Katrina asked as she pulled out a handkerchief and dabbed his face. "What happened?"

"It must have been a spell of some sort," I concluded. "Garrett?"

Garrett lifted his head up to look at me, his shirt stained with sweat. "I remember everything. I remember it all."

"You do?" Katrina asked.

Garrett continued to stare at me. "The spell that sent us away and made us forget...that was you, wasn't it? You sent us away."

No point in hiding it now. Letting out a small sigh, I said, "Yes. It was my doing." He and Katrina stared up at me, silently telling me to go on.

I pressed my eyelids shut before explaining. "I cast a spell to send you and the others away. I have discovered a world where magic is weaker, where Jotnar, Nimh, and Scathe would not be able to harm you. They would not be able to reach you or kill you. You would all be free from the torment of this world. All I wanted was to protect you five. This was the only way I could, but your memories being wiped was actually not part of the plan. That was most likely a side effect of the spell. I knew that even if you all grew older, the three of them would only continue to harbor you as prisoners. They would never allow you to leave. All of you are very powerful, and you are part of the prophecy."

"Prophecy?" Garrett asked. "What prophecy?"

"They call it the Prophecy of the Star," I explained. "The five points of the star would end the blight: water, spirit, air, earth, and fire. It has been in the making for centuries. Once Jotnar discovered exactly what that meant, he planned to kill you five. I couldn't allow that to happen. But I knew I couldn't risk getting caught in their castle a second time, so I convinced our father that Jotnar and Nimh would always be a threat as long as they lived because of their power. He sent me to lead the siege, not bothering to shy away from the possibilities of what might happen to Muriel and Petra if I failed. So I led the siege, I cast the spell to send you away, and I told

Scathe that you five had died—that Nimh and Jotnar had let you all die in order to escape."

Garrett pushed himself up, taking Katrina by the hand and looked into my eyes as a few tears fell down his cheeks.

"You put yourself at risk for us and you suffered for it all this time?" he asked.

Tears stung my eyes. "I would rather miss you all and never see you again than have you near and in danger."

Garrett stared at me before doing something that surprised me. He grabbed me by my shoulder and pulled me in for a hug. I didn't know how to act or how to respond for a moment, but somehow I managed to wrap my arms around my brother and embrace him in turn. The tears pooled from my eyes, but I didn't care as I buried my face into Garrett's shoulder.

I patted his arm and pulled away sniffling. "Come on. Let's go get Bruce and Charles."

Garrett smiled at me and took Katrina's hand. "Together."

I smiled back at him. I finally have my brother back. "Together."

Chapter 26

Brigit

Salem helped me to my bed and pulled the covers over me. He hurried to find some tea as I continued to cry and shake. All those memories had come rushing back to me all at once.

I remember bits and pieces of my early childhood, but what kid doesn't? I was always able to practice earth magic; I always had a connection to it. I could grow plants just by looking at a pot full of dirt. And any tree stump that I found immediately grew long and tall with a snap of my fingers. I would go outside and play dolls with my friends and Caitlin under a shaded tree, even with our cousins, Kaylee and Shauna. The four of us had always been close. Before my mother left my father, we'd visit Uncle Varian and Auntie Eve. Garrett was never one to play dolls with us, so he'd just stay home and ride his horse or practice with his sword.

I remember sneaking into the kitchens with the twins and taking some food before making a run for it. I remember the smells of cooked ham or roasted duck, the smells of spices and vegetables and soup. I wouldn't get in trouble because I was the baby, but the twins on the other hand, well, that's another story.

We had tutors, which wasn't horrible. We all learned math, science, geography, history, and grammar, but I was more interested in going outside. That's all I could think about during those lessons: for them to hurry the fuck up so that I could go outside and play. I'd make my brother and sister go with me otherwise I would scream my head off until they did.

Now that I think about it, that's not so different from how Nora and Alison acted back in Connecticut.

Usually on sunny days, I'd collect bugs, or try to, at any rate. Of course, my mother was not too happy with me showing up dirty with bugs in my hands, but she'd never scream at me, or not that I can actually remember. I think it's because everyone had told me she had lost a few children before having me, so she was extremely attached to me. Not to mention, I was also told growing up that my mother almost lost the twins in childbirth: Their heartbeats were very slow and their breathing was extremely shallow, but a nurse from the Elf Domain had arrived and saved their lives.

Then my mother started to change. No. She was always a crazy narcissist, I was just too young to realize that. I remember certain times she'd scream at the twins for seemingly no reason at all, and when…

Thomas. I had another brother! No, a half-brother! Oh, for fuck's sake! What difference does it make? He's still my brother! He was there! He was there in the castle! He had picked up Alison in her room during the siege and we made eye contact! But why was he there in the first place?

He was there with us playing outside. He would give me advice on how to better my magic. He'd give me piggyback rides and call me 'flower'. I remember this one time, we were hosting a party and a few young boys had their eyes on Caitlin (who was completely oblivious) and not me. I remember running away to the outside of the barn and crying to myself when Thomas had found me. I wasn't sure why he was there or how he had found me. He wasn't even allowed to visit when we had guests staying with us. Thomas took a spot beside me and studied me with concern.

"What's wrong, flower?" he asked.

"Nothing," I snapped as I scooted away. "I'm fine. Leave me alone."

"Well, first, you're not fine," Thomas stated. "Second, I'm your brother, so I will never leave you alone. You can tell me what's wrong. I won't say anything to anyone."

I hesitated, but I was just so angry that I had to let it out, so I did. "All the boys like Caitlin, but not me!"

"Sweetheart, that's because Caitlin and those boys are older than you," Thomas explained as he wiped away my tears with a hanky, "of course they won't pay attention to you."

"It's because she's prettier than me, isn't it?" I cried. "It's 'cause her hair is all pretty and looks like daytime and she has those stupid eyes that look like the sky! It's not fair!"

Thomas patted my head and smiled at me. "Don't you get it, flower? Those things are what make *her* special. She may look like daylight with her bright eyes and lighter hair, but your dark eyes and darker hair make you look just as pretty. Caitlin is the daylight to your starlight; you look like all the mystery and wonder of the night sky with your hair and your eyes resemble that of the earth, which you can actually bend to your will. If you really wanted to, you could make the earth tremble. You're strong and tough, Brigit. Remember that."

He and I had always been close, huh? Garrett always had Caitlin and Alison was always close to Nora. I was the middle child. It's not exactly the best. Sometimes I had to be the one to break up the fights with my siblings back in Connecticut, which wasn't often, but it did happen. Other times, with how close the others were to each other, I felt out of place. No, they didn't ignore me, they all showed me love, but it could sometimes be a little lonely. Garrett's best friend in the family was Caitlin and Nora's was Alison because of their closeness in age. I didn't have that. Now that I remember, even though Thomas was older than me, we always had this bond. He was the one I always went to for advice or if I just wanted to play or talk to someone.

Eventually, Nora came around, but I was not happy about it. I thought she was going to be getting all the attention because I was no longer going to be the baby. Turns out, I was totally right. Nora got all the attention and I was brushed aside like yesterday's news.

I kept to myself most of the time after that. I went outside more and stayed away mostly because I wanted nothing to do with any of this. I couldn't handle the changes. It was all just too much. I just lost the ability to see my dad as much as I used to as well as my best friend in the family, Thomas. My mother had married someone else—someone I didn't even like to begin with—and she had a new baby with him. I was scared, so I stayed away, and in doing so, I had gotten better with my powers. Hell, I got better at schoolwork. I don't remember the abuse as much, though. I remember screaming and cursing and things being thrown, but other than that, not much else.

"Milady?" Salem said.

I looked up to see him carefully entering my room with a cup of tea in his hands. He crossed the room and gently set it in my hands which I was grateful for.

"Thank you," I said as I sipped from the mug.

"My pleasure, Lady Brigit," Salem said as he sat at the foot of my bed. "How's your head?"

I shrugged. "It's a little sore, but I'm okay."

"And your memories?"

"All there." I took another sip. "I have another brother, huh?"

Salem sighed. "Yes."

"Thomas Sullivan is his name."

"Yes, Milady."

"Did he lead the siege?"

"Yes."

I took another long sip of my tea before settling back against the headboard. Thomas, the one I used to be so close with, led a siege to my home and attacked my family and friends. I just wish I knew why. Why had he done something so awful? How could he just turn on us on a dime? Could something have been done to stop him?

"I will leave you to rest, Milady," Salem said. "You have had a long day." Salem got up and pressed a kiss to my forehead before heading for the door.

"Wait," I said.

Salem stopped and turned to look at me. I fought back the urge to break down crying.

"Please don't leave me alone."

I've already lost everyone and everything I loved and knew. I didn't want to be alone anymore, not with what I learned. Salem made his way back to my bed and lay down next to me as I sat there drinking more of the tea. Once I finished the rest of it, I set the mug on my bedside table and set myself flat against the mattress and pillows.

"The council will announce their decision tomorrow," Salem stated. "I know it seems like I am just adding more to your stress—"

"You're not," I interrupted. "Thank you for telling me."

Salem clasped our hands together, looking me in the eye. "Either way, we're going to find a way to settle this. We'll find a way, Milady. You will not be forced to marry anyone you deem unsuitable."

Especially since that rat bastard tried to hit me. I let out a long, exhausted sigh. "How do you get through most days?"

I huddled closer to Salem, resting my head on his shoulder.

"I pray," was his answer.

I snickered. "I'm not exactly religious."

"And that is alright, Brigit," he said softly. "You do not have to believe in any Gods, if that is what you choose. I will not force you to do such. My customs, my people, we believe in the Gods, especially the Gods of nature. I pray to them for fruitful harvests or for answers. I pray for the health of others. Because sometimes that's all we can do."

Megan

"Okay, spitfire," I said, taking Alison by her shoulders and placing her in front of the logs piled up, "go ahead. Start a fire for us, okay?"

I took my hands away and took a few steps back. Alison stood for a few seconds just staring at the logs not doing anything. She instead whimpered and hid her face into my leg. I rubbed her head sympathetically.

"It's okay, honey," I reassured her. "You don't have to if you're not ready."

I turned to Angus who nodded his head once and grabbed two small rocks from the ground and knelt beside the firewood. Nora came around and took Alison's hand and led her away to their tent that Angus and I set up for them.

"You two stay in the tent and rest," I said. "Angus and I are going to start cooking dinner."

The girls said nothing as they crawled inside their tent. When I turned my head, I saw that Angus had started the fire. I helped him skin the rabbits and we began roasting them over the fire, turning them around and around as the scent of their flesh rose into the air.

"The princesses took the truth better than I initially thought," Angus said.

"Indeed."

Angus turned the rabbits around on the stick. "They are strong, good young ladies who have been through so much, but they are so resilient—so adaptable."

"They really are," I agreed. "I do think they're in some shock, though."

"Of course," Angus said. "Princess Nora was too young to remember her parents and her life before all this, and Princess Alison was much too young to remember anything."

"Yes, Alison was only a few weeks old," I stated.

I took out one of our canteens and placed my hand a few inches over the lid. Blue magic shimmered off my palm and I could feel the canteen becoming cooler and cooler. When I removed the lid, there was water inside. I took a sip and handed it to Angus.

"I can understand their fear and frustration," Angus went on as he took a swig from the canteen. "They don't remember their parents, but they must have fantasized what they must have been like. All they know is the world they grew up in. This all must be so overwhelming and confusing and now, after years of imagining and wondering about their parents, they learn that they are evil to the core."

"Yes, well, it didn't help that I lied to them," I pointed out as I flipped my hair over my shoulder.

Angus turned the stick once more. "I do not usually condone lying, Megan, but sometimes, it is okay to not tell the complete truth in order to protect another and their feelings."

"It all should never have happened, though," I whispered, leaning closer to him so that the girls wouldn't hear. "And it's not like I could tell them—any of them—when we were dropped in the Other Realm. That's not how things worked over there! They would have thought I was mad!"

"You did what you thought was right," Angus countered. "You were transported to the Other Realm with the children for a reason and you had to raise them the way you thought best."

Blinking away tears, I stared deeply into the love of my life's eyes. "Do you think I did okay with them?"

Angus smiled at me. "You did better than okay."

I smiled at him and leaned in closer, kissing him. His beard tickled my skin, but I leaned in closer, deepening the kiss.

"Stop," Nora said.

Startled, Angus and I parted ways and turned to find Nora and Alison taking seats on the log next to me.

"Ew," Alison said simply.

Angus and I chuckled. "Sorry, girls."

"Are we gonna eat soon?" Alison asked, kicking her legs nonchalantly.

"It is just about done, Your Grace," Angus told her.

"Can I have some water?" Nora asked me.

I smiled at her and surrendered the canteen. "Absolutely."

"So tomorrow," Angus began as he pulled the rabbits away from the fire, "after breakfast, we will pack our things and continue on with our journey. Lady Freya is your aunt, but she is very dangerous and not to be played with. You two will be safe with us, but you can't say a word or do anything unless Megan and I say otherwise, okay?"

The girls nodded in unison as Angus prepared their plates.

"Then after we break the deal, are we gonna go find Gary, Caity, and Brigit?" Nora asked.

Angus and I shared a look as I passed their food to them. "Hopefully, yes," I answered, "we will."

"I can't wait to see them all again!" Alison exclaimed.

I smiled at her and pressed a kiss to her brow. "Me neither."

Chapter 27

Thomas

We rode on horseback after some time walking. We were fortunate enough to not get spotted or attacked. We had yet to run into any of Jotnar or Nimh's soldiers, which set off some alarms in my head. Usually their territory was crawling with them. *You know this has got to be a trap, right?* I scratched Morrigan's ear. "Yes, I figured."

"Figured what?" Katrina asked.

"Usually entering this territory is complicated," I explained. "All of a sudden, only hours after capturing Sir Charles and Bruce, does it seem barren."

"Yeah this definitely has 'trap' written all over it," Garrett agreed. "We're literally almost at the castle and haven't gotten into any kind of brawl."

"Which means your mother and stepfather *want* you to come and save Bruce and Sir Charles," I stated. "They know we're coming."

"Great," Katrina muttered.

After a bit more riding, we stopped by the side of a river to wash up and refill our canteens. Well, Katrina and Garrett refilled their canteens their own way while I used magic to refill mine.

Garrett snickered, "Showoff."

"Don't be jealous, brother."

We clinked our canteens together and sipped the water as Orion and the horses lapped it up with their tongues. I wiped my mouth and turned to Garrett and Katrina.

"One thing," I said, "if we are going to fight, you will not go in unprotected, either one of you."

I flicked my wrist and black smoke poured from the ground and floated up from beneath their feet. The two looked down to see what the smoke was doing—and they finally did—once it had cleared. Their simple wardrobes changed into something else entirely. Garrett was wearing a suit of armor that was purple from head to toe: from the pauldrons to the breastplate to the greaves and the gauntlets. His sword was slung over his shoulder resting on his back and he had a dagger with a silver hilt strapped at his hip. Katrina was also wearing purple armor, much like Garrett's, only she was wearing a medallion around her neck made from gold formed in the shape of a wolf's head.

Katrina lifted the golden wolf's head by her fingertips to better see it. "What's this?"

"An extra layer of protection," I answered. "If you are ever separated from Garrett, that medallion will send a telepathic message to him. It will glow as he gets closer to you."

The two glanced at each other before looking away. It's adorable that they think I can't see what's between them like that. Garrett shifted his shoulders and snickered humorlessly.

"This armor's heavy," he said.

"Then we will have to train you to fight in the armor after we rescue the others," I said.

"Until then..."

I waved my hand over his breastplate. Purple energy reflected off my palm, allowing Garrett to stand straighter and taller. "We don't have the time to train you in the armor now, so making it lighter will have to do."

"Thanks," Garrett said.

"Yes, thank you," Katrina said with a kind smile.

I smiled at the two of them before pushing a leafy branch aside. Just down the slope from where we stood was Jotnar and Nimh's castle. It was just as big as I remembered, if not much darker and cloaked in shadow. Dark cyclone-like clouds hovered over the tallest tower and lightning struck the mountains miles across the land.

"Welcome home, Garrett," I said in jest.

Garrett bumped my shoulder with his fist. "It never felt like home, Thomas. You know that."

I nodded once. "I do."

"What's the plan exactly?" Katrina asked, standing beside Garrett.

I jerked my chin towards the castle. "Gare, you remember where the dungeons are?"

"Yes, I do," he confirmed.

"Good," I said. "That's likely where Sir Charles and Bruce are. You two will be disguised with a charm I am going to place over you. The only one who will see it's actually you is me. Get them out and meet back here."

"What are you going to do?" Garrett asked.

I moved the branch out of my way and descended down the slope. "I am going to kill

Jotnar and Nimh, little brother."

I heard a twig snap behind me and I could tell based on the sound that it was Garrett stopping himself from tripping and falling the rest of the way down the hill. "Wait," he said. "What?"

Muriel

I heard something that sounded like the crackling of a small fire followed by a quick *pop!* That sound was what woke me out of a dead sleep. At first I thought it was Thomas, but then I remembered that he can't break the spell Scathe put on the cell door. Only Scathe can do that. With that thought in mind, I gasped and threw myself up in time to see the horned monster himself yank the door open before stepping inside. I took quick steps backwards until I hit the wall trying to get away from him. He wasn't in my face, but he was close enough that I could smell his rotting breath.

Scathe grabbed me by my arm causing me to recoil and pull back to no avail. His claws dug into my skin but I didn't show any sign of pain. I refused to do so after everything he's done.

"Let go of me!" I demanded.

Scathe ignored me and dragged me out of my cell and up the stairs. I tried pulling harder but it didn't matter. He had the high ground.

"Get off me!" I growled.

We stopped suddenly in the dark hallway and Scathe forcefully pulled me in closer so that I was inches away from his face. His eyes were dark and cold like the depths of the darkest, coldest sea and empty like that of a sea monster's.

"Keep fighting me, child," Scathe dared me in a whisper, "but wouldn't you rather see your daughter?"

I stopped fighting and stared at him in shock. "You're lying, you miserable bastard!"

"Am I?" Scathe grinned. "True, I am not an honest man…"

"You are no man!"

Scathe growled, his claws drawing some blood from my arm. "I am granting you your wish to be with your child once more, human. I still need you both alive, after all."

Scathe raised his other hand; dark, inky tendrils appeared in his palm and crawled in between his decaying fingers.

"And what of Thomas?" I demanded.

Scathe smiled at me again. Each time he did that, I felt the need to punch him. "He will be reunited with you both, but he has to find you first."

Before I could say another word, Scathe covered his hand with the dark tendrils over my nose and mouth and everything went dark. When I woke, I found myself in bed. A *bed*—one with a big, heavy white quilt and red sheets. The walls around me were completely gray and barren. There were two white wardrobes— one big and one small—on the other side of the room and next to my bed…

A small gold-framed bed!

I threw the covers off of me and desperately looked around. I started sobbing as a painful smile crept over my face. Wrapped comfortably in a forest green blanket softer than the clouds was Petra asleep next to the stuffed dragon my father had given me all those years ago. I carefully caressed the side of her soft little face. I started crying even harder. I never thought I'd see Petra again, but now…

"I found you," I wept. "My sweet Petra, I found you!"

Chapter 28

Megan

I helped the girls in their tent before quietly crawling out and into the tent that Angus and I had been sharing. I snuffed out the lantern in the center and tucked myself into my bedroll, laying my head on Angus's shoulder.

"I miss them," I said after a few minutes.

Angus rubbed my shoulder and kissed my brow. "You will see Garrett and the girls again, I'll make sure of it."

"Not just them," I said while trying—and failing—to not croak. "I mean my parents, Varian, and my sisters, even Amelia. I miss who Amelia used to be. She's always been spoiled and always had a temper, but she and I could always talk, or at least I thought we could. Only years later did I find out it was all a lie. She doesn't love anyone but herself. There's nothing inside of her but a cold, dark abyss and she took our family from me."

I wiped away my tears only for Angus to give me a light squeeze and pull me in closer.

"I miss my father every day," Angus told me. "I know someday soon I'll see him and my mother again just as you will see yours and your siblings again."

I sniffed once before pulling my head up to kiss Angus's cheek. Those were the words I needed to hear. They didn't exactly make me feel better completely, but it helped. I know that I'd see my family again, that we'd soon be reunited, but that will not be for a long time.

Angus planted another kiss to my lips which immediately set something off between the both of us. The two of us sat up, pressing kiss after kiss onto each other's lips feverishly. I pulled away just long enough to watch Angus's fingers unfasten his belt and then his pants. I excitedly helped him remove his shirt in between kisses along with his pants and undergarments.

Underneath it all was his long, turgent member.

He growled, pulling my shirt over my head and tossing it aside as we both sat up on our knees. I pulled my belt off and pushed my pants down before Angus roughly grabbed me by the back of my head and brought me in for a deep kiss. I moaned, pressing another kiss on his mouth as my hands grazed his bare chest and torso.

I took his face in my hands, bringing Angus in closer. He hissed and slipped his tongue into my mouth. Angus leaned over me, pressing me against the cool bedroll as two of his clever fingers slipped inside of me.

We remained as quiet as possible, but it was nearly impossible. I gasped as his touch grew more and more urgent. I arched my back and let out a quiet moan.

Our tongues crashed against each other as Angus's second hand cupped one of my breasts. I moaned his name like a silent prayer, my body slowly contorting in rhythm of his hand between us. I shivered as the nerves between my legs exploded. Still groping my breast, Angus gave me a longing, mischievous stare before lowering his head and taking my breast into his mouth. I clenched the sheets in one hand and Angus's hair in another. He let out a quiet groan, whether it was from pain or pleasure or both, I couldn't tell. His tongue swept over my nipple before moving on to the second one.

"Angus…" I whispered.

Angus lifted his head and planted a kiss against my jaw and then my lips. Seconds later, he planted himself into me, forcing another gasp out of me. I dug my nails into his back, feeling him bury himself again and again inside of me.

I wanted to scream so loudly that the creatures who lived in the deepest depths of the sea could hear, but I managed to control myself.

It was torture as Angus pulled himself out a few inches before slowly thrusting himself inside over and over and over again. Angus planted a trail of kisses down my neck and collarbone as I wrapped my legs around his waist. I savored his touch, his scent, his strength as he whispered my name against my skin. Angus shuddered as he climaxed. As he released, I could see nothing, rising to my own.

As he finished, he pulled himself out of me and lay next to me, the only sound being our rasping breaths.

"Bring back memories of when we were younger?" Angus asked between breaths.

I chuckled. "I wasn't even thinking about any of that. I couldn't think at all because of you."

Angus let out a quiet laugh before rolling onto his side, resting his cheek on the palm of his hand. "You have no idea how happy I am to have you back in my life."

Smiling, I planted a gentle kiss on his lips. "Actually, I've got a pretty good idea."

"Time to get moving," Angus announced as he put the last bag on his horse. "We don't have much of a journey left."

The girls trudged across what was our campsite yawning and rubbing their eyes. I grabbed Alison from underneath her arms and lifted her onto my horse as Angus did the same for Nora.

"Are you alright, Princess?" Angus asked.

Nora sleepily rubbed her eyes and nodded.

I smiled. "You two can rest while we ride on. We'll wake you when we get there." I took Angus by the crook of his arm and led him a few steps away from the horses and the girls. I bent my head down a bit and lowered my voice. "It's time."

Angus nodded his head. "Are you ready to face Lady Freya?"

I scoffed. "I'm not afraid of her. I may not like her, but we need her to lift the spell over the camp. We have to break this deal with them. You know the fae cannot be trusted, they're demons."

"And the girls?"

"They will need to stay behind us the entire time. I know for a fact that not even the Lady of the Fairies, their aunt, will spare them."

Angus took my hand and led me back to the horses. "I pray to the Gods that we succeed."

As I mounted my horse I sighed, "You and me both."

Garrett

As we got closer to the castle, I became more and more anxious. Thomas is going to try killing my mother and stepfather *alone*. I know he's crazy, but still.

"Thomas, this is insane!" I snapped.

"Keep your voice down!" Thomas hissed. "Just get inside and get Charles and Bruce out. I'll meet you back on top of the hill afterwards. Don't do anything suspicious and whatever you do, don't get caught. Either of you do, you're as good as dead."

"One problem," Katrina pointed out. "How are you going to get inside this time? Last time you tried, you were caught immediately."

Thomas threw a sly grin over his shoulder. "I've picked up a few things since then."

Katrina and I threw each other a confused look and, in unison, asked, "Like what?"

Thomas didn't answer. Instead he *transformed* into a blackbird and flew away in the direction of the castle. I shook my head smiling.

"Damned showoff."

Katrina playfully elbowed me. "Well, he is *your* brother."

I snickered as we walked further down the hill.

"Is it easier to control your powers now that you remember how?" Katrina asked.

I shrugged. "That's a yes and no answer. I can control my powers, but I can't control when and where spirits choose to contact me. I could be asleep in the middle of the night and all of a sudden, I'll hear someone talking to me, like they're whispering a secret in my ear, but when I open my eyes, I see the apparition at the foot of my bedroll. A few weeks ago, before I got my memories back, I was training with Sir Charles and I had a full on conversation with a man. I swear to you, Katrina, he looked like a real flesh and blood guy. He said his name was Graham and—"

Katrina immediately stopped and grabbed my arm to keep herself steady. "What? Wait—what did you say his name was?"

"He said his name was Graham," I answered awkwardly. "Why?"

Katrina lifted her head showing me that her eyes were full of unshed tears. "Because Graham was the name of my father."

I stopped myself from stumbling and stared at Katrina who had started crying. "Katrina, I didn't know—"

"No, no, no," Katrina said quickly as she took both my hands. "It's okay that you didn't know. It's just that I haven't spoken or heard his name in so long and when he died…I was all alone and…"

"Katrina," I said gently as I squeezed her hands, "you don't have to explain yourself to me, okay? He was your father. I'd react the same way. You never need to apologize to me, especially for your tears."

Katrina nodded as more tears slid down her face. I quickly brushed her tears away and grabbed her by her shoulders.

"Once we're done here, we can talk to him, if you want," I offered.

"You'd do that for me?"

"I'd do anything for you."

Katrina gave me a wide smile, one so wide and big, it had to hurt. She wiped away her remaining tears and gave me a fierce nod. "Down with the King and Queen, then." I smiled back at her. "Down with the King and Queen."

Chapter 29

Caitlin

We all filed down the rope ladder and planted our feet on the sandy beaches of Asmund Rock. The only thing within sight was a giant rocky mountain as gray as the clouds. There was no breeze, no sounds of birds, nothing.

"Are you alright?" Sheila asked as she walked beside me.

I pressed my lips together angrily. "Not really."

Sheila looked down at our boots and then back to me. "We heard you screaming; it woke us up."

"I'm sorry."

"I didn't tell you that so you could apologize, Lady Caitlin," Sheila stated. "I only told you that because we were all worried about you. Are you alright? And don't lie."

Thankfully, I didn't have to answer because Captain Raina caught up with us and jerked her head forward, dismissing Sheila. I like Sheila, but right now, the last thing I need is a therapy session.

"Don't worry, Caitlin," Captain Raina said, "once we kill Scathe, Jotnar will be next and it will not be painless. After what he did to you, he will pay."

I said nothing as we walked towards the entrance of a dark cave.

"Scathe's talisman is in there?" I asked.

"Aye," Captain Raina confirmed.

"So Scathe sent it here to protect it?"

"Aye, right under Jotnar's nose," Captain Raina replied. "You see, Fenrir-Himinn is the home of Jotnar's family."

"So Scathe hid his talisman in plain sight."

"Exactly."

I looked back at the ship anchored in the dark waters. A mist had started to appear, making it look mysterious. The fact that I was so scared and confused when I first arrived here still boggles me. I wasn't sure what my purpose here was or if I would even make it. Now I find myself to be the First Mate among all these pirates—and a water witch, too. Even when I was younger, before the siege, I wondered if I'd live long enough and overcome my trauma. I had almost no faith in my survival. Even when I lived in Connecticut, even though I had no memories of my parents, I often wondered how I'd survive without them, how I'd live the rest of my life without them.

Now I know that I am a survivor. I have made it this far and I don't need them in my life. Because kids like me, especially those who have experienced something similar to what I went through, never forgive and we never forget.

I may have forgotten before, but I will carry that trauma with me for the rest of my life. When I regained my memories, it all came back so fast and I hated—*hated*—that I could remember any of it at all. My parents and my step-father stole everything from me, but I will be damned if I let that trauma define me. I will use my pain and put it to good use. I will put an end to the tyranny of this world and make sure that the ones responsible pay for their actions.

Because how screwed up is that? I was abused in more ways than one, I suffered, and the ones who did this to me are still alive and they're literally ruling the world. They're getting away with it just like they have in the past.

Doesn't seem right to me.

I swear on my family's name that they will all pay. I will not stop until all three of them die.

One by one, we filed into the cave. Actually, it was more of a long tunnel that led into a wide cave. There was a giant hole miles above us, revealing the cloudy sky outside. The sand beneath us became muddy and I realized the ground wasn't actually sand, but instead a watery trench that was a few inches deep.

Captain Raina held her arm out and stopped me from continuing. The rest of the crew behind me stopped in their tracks. Captain Raina looked up. There were rocky steps spiraling towards the top of the cave. Floating high above us was a blood red crystal attached to black wire.

Scathe's talisman.

"Alright, Treasure," Captain Raina said. "This is your time to shine."

"What do you mean?" I asked.

"His talisman is protected by blood magic," she answered. "Only you, Lord Garrett, or Lady Brigit will be able to take it."

Understanding, I walked through the murky water until I made my way to the bottom of the steps. I looked up, staring at the talisman. That object is the only thing my father cares about. He never cared about me, Garrett, or Bridge. When he and my mother were married, he never cared about her either. The only thing he cares about is himself.

With that in mind, I took one step up and then another and another. I remember my other brother, Thomas. Every time he came to visit, it was like the four of us had normal lives, as normal as it could get in this world. He was one of my best friends and I loved him.

He saved my life more times than I can count. I knew he was dealing with something, though I was never really sure what. I thought that if he could survive and find a way to reach happiness and overcome his darkness, then I could, too.

Finally, I reached the top of the steps. There was no cliff or bridge for me to stand on. It was literally the top of the staircase high above the crew. The talisman was only a few yards from me floating all on its own.

I reached my hand out, keeping my eyes completely locked on the talisman. I imagined a string of red tying around me and through the talisman. We are connected. I am Scathe's blood, but that is all. His blood. He is not my heart or my soul. He is just blood. The crystal began to glow brighter and brighter, nearly blinding me, reminding me of a rocket when all of a sudden, it vanished in an explosion of light. I opened my eyes and looked down, letting out a small gasp.

The talisman was in my hands.

I ran down the stairs, not slipping even once, and held up the talisman in triumph. The crew cheered, raising their swords and clapping their hands.

Captain Raina smiled and sprinted the rest of the way towards me. She took my hands and gave them a friendly squeeze.

"Well done, Caitlin," she praised. "Now we can kill him."

"Not quite," a strange, eerie voice hissed.

My skin crawled. I knew that voice. Captain Raina spun around and I froze. The crew had been thrown into the air, flying across the cave, slamming their backs against the cold walls.

A pale, bony figure with a needle and thorny crown stood in the shadows, her eyes sewn shut. The air suddenly became colder. I knew all too well who this was.

"Mother," I murmured.

Brigit

Salem and I hadn't moved at all for hours, not even to go down to dinner. I wasn't hungry, but I told Salem that he shouldn't go hungry because of me. He refused.

Less than a day until my fate would be decided.

There's some good news.

I don't care what the council decides. I. Am. Not. Marrying Akoni! Aside from not letting others choose my future for me, the son of a bitch tried to slap me! That's a fucking red flag right there and if you can't see that, you're blind!

There's no way in hell I'd marry someone like that! If he acts like this already when he doesn't get his way, I'd hate to think what could happen if the council forces me to marry him. Fuck, did Akoni have girlfriends at all before me? Did he hurt them? Did he abuse them? Did his family know about if he did? Look, I'm not saying he did actually abuse someone, but I wouldn't put it past him at this point, either. If he did have girlfriends and he did hurt them, because he's a prince, he probably forced them to keep their mouths shut.

I've heard stories back in Prospect about stuff like this: when a woman is so afraid to leave that she stays with her abusive boyfriend or husband; she may love him so much despite the abuse and chooses to stay even though she hates him. The man will put up a front and act like God's gift to the world outside of his home, but when he is alone with her, he is the shittiest person alive. He will beat her down and build himself up, then blame her for putting his hands on her in the first place. He'll cry and play the victim, maybe even promise that he will be better and that he'll change and never hurt her again.

That never happens. Then she does leave or she breaks up with him despite her fear. You know what happens then? The man hurts her, violates her, and kills her.

But it's always the woman's fault, right? It's because she "stepped out of line". I fucking hate people like that. Yes. Damn. I know! Not all men. I get it, okay? But just because you have a dick doesn't give you the right to act like one or think with it. No real man would hurt a woman.

Yet another reason I never chose to get into a relationship: I didn't trust anyone.

The sky was getting darker and darker and a light breeze came in from the balcony, causing the curtains to drift lazily in the air. Salem had fallen asleep, his dark hair swept over the pillows. He looks pretty even when he's asleep. It's almost unfair considering when I wake up, I look like Garfield the cat.

I gently pressed a kiss to his forehead and pulled the covers to our chests. I feel safe with Salem, just like he was family. He promised to help me get out of this arrangement with Akoni, and I know he will, but what's that going to do to him and his family?

I woke up hearing screaming outside the castle. At first, I thought it was another nightmare or another memory, but when I smelled smoke, I realized that it wasn't either of those. Salem and I both shot out of bed to see orange and yellow flames licking the balcony curtains.

"Run!" Salem yelled.

He jumped out of bed and grabbed my hand. We booked it to the door, ready to open it.

Salem yanked the door open only for more flames to swipe at us like the claw of an angry lion. The warmth of the flames touched my skin and we weren't even a foot in front of the flames! The heat was so strong that it overcame me and clouded my lungs. I started coughing. Everything was so disorienting, and I didn't know how, but Salem managed to pull us away from the actual line of fire and into the hallway. I covered my nose and mouth with my sleeve, but when we turned the corner, we found that portraits of his family, his plants, and even more curtains had been set ablaze. It looked like we were running right through hell.

Elves screamed and ran through the castle. Some—the ones who were warriors—ran through the flames carrying blades, crossbows, and quivers of arrows on their backs. I knew exactly who was attacking us. Thomas told me the story years ago before the siege: a story of the beast who guarded the Emerald Mountain. Salem and I ran past a stained glass window and I turned my head to look outside, which confirmed my suspicions. It wasn't exactly a victorious feeling, considering the sight scared the shit out of me.

Flying high above the castle, swirling past one of the towers covered in green scales with golden eyes was a fire-breathing dragon.

I let out a small scream as Salem and I sprinted down the stairs, jumping past the last few. I let out another scream as Salem pushed me against the wall to avoid one of his soldiers running past, completely engulfed in flames. Still holding on to my hand, Salem pulled me along and we ran out the entrance to the castle. Everything was on fire. The trees, the bushes, the barn, it didn't matter. Screams and shouts of commands could be heard from all around; so much so, it was hard to figure out exactly who was where and doing what.

Salem grabbed me by my shoulders and turned me to face him. "I need to find my family and get them out!"

I opened my mouth, ready to agree to go with him, but... "I need you to run!" he shouted over the chaos.

If my heart wasn't already bursting from my chest, it was at that point. I shook my head furiously. "No, I—!"

"Go to the hideaway in the forest!" he ordered. "The one I showed you days ago and stay there until I find you! Run, Brigit!"

Salem let me go and ran back into his fiery castle. I called out to him, my eyes stinging from unshed tears.

"*Run!*" Salem shouted before disappearing into the castle.

I didn't know what to do! My heart was racing and I felt sick! It was happening again!

The attack, the panic, everything! It was all happening again!

I wanted to go after Salem, but I couldn't risk him getting hurt trying to help me and his family escape.

Deciding to listen, I ran off in the direction of the woods. Somehow, they had been spared from the flames of the dragon. I looked up at the sound of a deep, guttural roar. The dragon was closer now, its massive wings creating huge gusts of wind that only spread the fire further. I studied paleontology for a while when I was younger as a hobby. The T-Rex could grow to be forty feet in length and twelve feet in height. The dragon looked to be about the same size as that, with each wing probably being the size of its body. The last thing I saw before running into the dark forest was the green dragon spewing clouds of orange and yellow from its mouth towards the castle.

Chapter 30

Megan

After a few hours passed, we stopped to make camp. Angus went to hunt some rabbit for us to eat while I took the girls to gather firewood. The girls each collected smaller sticks and twigs in their arms while I piled on larger, thicker sticks and branches. We wouldn't be staying long, just enough to eat, feed and water the horses, and then leave. When we arrived back at our new camp, Angus hadn't returned. I wasn't worried. Sometimes hunting just takes a bit longer. The girls and I set our firewood in one spot and dusted our hands off. As I went to my horse to grab the pot, I heard Nora whisper something.

"What was that, sweetie?" I asked.

"Lord Angus is coming back," she said louder.

"Oh, well, alright."

We waited another few minutes before Angus returned with his full sack slung over his shoulder. We watched as he skinned and prepped the rabbits for cooking, though the girls were less interested and more disgusted.

"I know it is not a pretty sight, Princesses, but learning how to hunt just may come in handy for you one day," Angus said.

I started a fire which allowed Angus to cook our lunch. I fed the horses and gave them fresh water, staying silent until…

"We should stay here until tomorrow morning," Angus said.

I turned to him. "Why?"

"We've been traveling for hours, Megan and we still have almost a week to go," Angus answered. "The horses need rest, the girls need rest, and so do we."

I nodded. "Good point. Alright. We should be safe enough, anyway."

"Yes, not to mention it gives the princesses more time to learn how to hunt and track."

"Can never go wrong with that."

"Especially in these times."

We all gathered together and ate lunch, tossing jokes and telling some of our favorite stories of when we lived in Connecticut. Nora told one story of when she and Alison discovered how to make water balloons from a children's magazine and threw them at Brigit while she was sleeping. I remember being in the garden watering the plants when I heard screaming. The girls came running out with Brigit furiously running after them and cursing.

"My, my, what little tricksters you two are," Angus laughed.

"You have no idea." I smiled.

Angus took a sip from his canteen, the smile disappearing. "Would you ever want to go back?"

I stared at him in surprise. Did he really just ask us that?

"No," I said simply. "That world is not home. There may have been some good things about it, but it will never be home."

"Yeah," Nora agreed. "I miss things like TV and Hot Pockets, but this world is cool! It's got magic and really nice people and talking animals!"

Angus tilted his head to the side in confusion at her. "Teevee?"

"I like this world better," Alison stated. "The other one is so boring."

The smile on Angus's face reappeared. "Well, I am glad to have you all back. It truly hasn't been the same without any of you."

I smiled at him and took a bite of my stew. I could never be the same after everything I've seen and lived through. Nothing makes me happier than the fact that we are back where we belong.

That night, Angus took the girls and I out into the woods to hunt for deer. Alison was against it at first, because ever since she saw *Bambi*, she freaks out when a deer is in sight. I told her that the deer would not be female, but male, and that the deer would give his life so that we may live.

That only made things a bit more complicated because Alison started saying how Bambi would be an orphan: no mother and no father. Then she accused Angus of being the hunter who killed Bambi's mom.

So instead of deer, we decided to hunt rabbit again, which also surprised me, because I swear, Bambi had a rabbit friend in that movie and Alison was completely fine with that.

"I'm getting kind of sick of rabbit, though," Alison said as she climbed on top of a fallen tree and started balancing herself on it.

"Well, you won't eat deer…" I started.

Suddenly, Nora stopped in her tracks, eyes as big as saucers. The rest of us stopped and looked at her.

"Nora?" I asked, bending down and grabbing her arms. "Nora, what is it?"

For a second, Nora couldn't say anything. She was in so much shock that it was impossible for words to come out. Until finally, she croaked, "Someone's coming."

Before I could ask who, an axe came whistling past my head and landed with a loud *THUNK!* in a tree behind me. Alison screamed as men and women in chainmail armor charged towards us. Angus drew an arrow and pulled it behind his ear, shooting at them. I turned, summoning my magic. I threw my hands out in front of me and the soldiers gasped before exploding into water. More knights jumped out of the woods, raising swords and daggers. Again, I raised my hands, blue magic cooling my palms and fingers. I threw my hands out, and they, too, all exploded into puddles of water.

"Back to the horses!" Angus yelled as he shot one more arrow at a knight.

I took Nora by the hand and Angus lifted Alison into her arms. We took off back to the direction of the horses, but quick footsteps were closing in on us from behind. I spun around, ready to turn these creeps into puddles just as I had done with their friends when Nora shot her hand out. Wind blew from her palm and shot into their chests, knocking them all backwards.

"Well done, Nora," I gasped as I pulled her along. "Come on!"

The horses were going wild and when I saw why, I almost let out a startled cry. Corpses were crawling out of the ground like something out of a horror movie! Some didn't even have legs! They growled and made gurgling sounds, drool dripping out of their decayed mouths. Most were just skeletons!

One of them had almost reached the horses when a ball of fire shot at it, sending it flying through the woods. I had no idea where it came from at first until I looked over at Alison. She was holding onto Angus with one hand and held out the other towards the Shadow Knights. She clenched her little hand into a fist, causing the line of fire to spread, setting the corpses ablaze. I shuddered at the sight, holding Nora close to me.

Alison was using her magic.

"On the horses," Angus said in disbelief. "C-Come on now."

Legs shaking, Angus and I lifted the girls on top of our horses and grabbed our satchels. We only slung them over our shoulders and threw ourselves over our horses, not bothering to pack. A disgusting smell filled my nostrils and I forced the bile down. With Nora in front of me, I pulled on the reins and we all rode as fast as we could away from where we had been attacked.

Those were both Scathe and Jotnar's men. They all knew where we were. We hadn't even been here that long. How did they know?

They'll keep coming and coming and they won't stop until we're all dead. That much is clear.

Garrett

One of my favorite movies growing up was *The Wizard of Oz* and the scene that both cracked me up and had me on the edge of my seat was that scene where the Lion, the Tinman, and the Scarecrow stole the guards' uniforms and disguised themselves to sneak into the castle of the Wicked Witch of the West to save Dorothy. That doesn't mean I didn't criticize it a little as I got older, though. You mean to tell me those three stooges snuck into the castle undetected? They weren't even green!

We were using magic to disguise our faces; the only ones who would recognize us would be each other.

Did we sneak into the castle in a straight line much like that scene from *The Wizard of Oz*? Yes. Were we successful? Absolutely.

When the soldiers turned a corner and disappeared in another room, Katrina and I ducked into a corridor.

"Left," I whispered.

Katrina nodded and we crept as silently as we could in that direction until we came upon a doorway. Standing a few meters away were two guards. Actually, they weren't even standing guard. They were sitting in a corner playing cards.

Nice job, guys.

I cleared my throat and motioned for Katrina to follow me. The two guards stood at attention immediately, acting one hundred percent guilty.

"We are to relieve you of your duties," I said confidently. "Jotnar's orders." The two guards looked at each other and then at the two of us.

"That can't be right," said one.

"Yeah, even if it were true, why would that be?" asked the second.

I gave the two guards a look that said 'AUDACITY' in neon red across my forehead. "Maybe it is because you two are the worst guards I have ever seen in my life! You are supposed to be guarding the prisoners! Jotnar and Nimh could see you and have you killed in the most torturous ways possible and you're sitting over here playing cards! We are relieving you of your duties as of now on their orders. If you have issues with that, take it up with them if you're bold enough."

The two guards stared at the two of us a bit longer, looking like caught children with their hands in the cookie jar. They walked past us, their heads hung with shame. They didn't even bring their deck of cards with them.

"Nice," Katrina whispered as soon as the two guards had gone.

"Thanks."

The two of us hurried down the stone steps, feeling a change in the air. It was colder the further down we went. I felt so much energy, too. There has been so much death here, so much pain and torture.

Save us...

Avenge us...

Kill them...

Help us...

He violated me…

He took my tongue…

She clawed my eyes out…

The spirits around me were telling me exactly how they died and it was sickening. My mother and stepfather hurt and killed so many innocent people like it was as easy as riding a bike. They felt no remorse. The spirits here—some were so young—felt sad and angry.

Very angry.

I stopped in the middle of the staircase, hissing in pain. Katrina quietly called my name, resting her hand on my burning arm.

He took my arm…

Run…

You shouldn't be here…

"Garrett?" Katrina said.

Get out of here…

Get out of here…

Evil lives in the shadows…

Not safe here…

Get out of here…

"Garrett?"

I shook my head and the pain and the voices disappeared. I could still hear the voices, but they sounded distant. It was almost like radio static; some were trying to warn me, telling me to get out and others were telling me what they went through.

"I'm fine," I said. "Let's go."

We finished our descent down the stairs into the dark dungeons. There were a few cells with cast-iron bars making up the structure. There were no windows or torches lit, either. "What was that?" someone whispered.

"I don't know."

Katrina and I ran towards the cells. The first one was empty, as was the second one, but the third… Sir Charles was on his feet holding onto the bars with a look of defiance on his face. No blood or bruises on him. That's good.

"More of you?" he asked.

"Not quite," Katrina stated.

I waved my hand over my face like I was pushing away a curtain, purple magic shimmering in my hand.

Sir Charles's eyes lit up. "Lord Garrett!"

I smiled, waving my hand back over my face. I turned to Katrina. "This is Katrina. We're here to break you guys out of here."

I looked past Sir Charles to find Bruce laying on the ground staring up at me in complete shock.

"I wasn't about to leave you two at the mercy of these monsters," I said. "I look after my own and that includes you."

I took a step back, gently nudging Katrina behind me. I flicked my wrist in front of the large iron lock which snapped and fell to the floor. The door swung open on its own and Sir Charles and Bruce stepped out.

"How did you get here?" Sir Charles asked.

"We had some help," I stated. "We have to be careful, though. Something tells me that getting out of here is not going to be easy."

Sir Charles smiled and bowed his head. "We are with you, Milord."

I smiled at him and placed my hand over his shoulder. "I'm with you, too, and I'm never going away again."

Thomas

Flying in the sky—soaring—was something I learned to do a few weeks after Muriel and Petra had been taken. I concentrated hard enough, thinking about when I was a child, how I'd daydream about flying away with my family.

Turns out, shapeshifting was a knack of my mother's. Now I'm using it to my advantage. I perched myself on the windowsill in one of the towers. I stayed there for a few seconds, not daring to move. You see, this tower in particular belonged to Jotnar and Nimh. I remember on my visits I was never allowed in this part of the castle. I was never explained as to why, but I was too nervous to ask.

It was dark, not freezing like Scathe's but drenched in shadow. The door to the room was open, allowing me to see some of the light of one of the torches. A shadow was creeping against the wall, getting closer to the room.

The door opened up a bit more to reveal Jotnar in his tattered brown cloak. He spun around the door and stepped in front of his wardrobe, his back facing me.

Now was my chance.

I willed myself to transform. My feathers and wings and beak vanished, returning me to who I really was. I silently pulled my ax from my side and raised it over my head.

Somehow Jotnar was a step ahead of me, because he spun around and threw darkness at me. I jumped out of the way and threw my ax. Jotnar side-stepped my weapon as gracefully as a stag and threw another cloud of darkness at me. I snapped my wrist, sending wind towards the cloud. The cloud vanished and I charged. I leapt into the air, summoning Spirit. This room was too small, so with Spirit, I teleported us to what used to be the ballroom, but not before landing a punch to Jotnar's face.

How I longed to do that!

Jotnar threw dark magic at me with each pump of his fist. I deflected each attack with the elements: Spirit, water, air, fire, and earth. Ever since Nimh caught me all those years ago, I had trained to better myself. I trained myself to become more agile and more aware of my surroundings.

I would not fail.

I shot one arm straight out and summoned all the elements at once. In a blinding flash of purple, red, blue, green, and yellow, the elements catapulted into Jotnar's chest, sending him flying across the ballroom shrieking in anger. His back slammed into a pillar and he landed on his stomach. It was pitiful.

"Too slow now, old man," I said to him. "You're one of the tyrants of this land? You're nothing. This is pathetic. I expected more of a fight from you."

Jotnar shakily raised his head, his eyes narrowed in anger. "You're just as arrogant as your father."

Jotnar raised his hand and flexed his taloned fingers. A dark mist appeared, covering the entire ballroom floor. When the mist dispersed, Garrett and Katrina were standing there in their normal forms with Sir Charles and Bruce. They all looked around in confusion, not quite sure how they had gotten here. Sir Charles's eyes landed on me.

"You!" he growled.

"No, Sir Charles!" Garrett shouted, taking him by the arm. "Thomas is the one who helped us find you!"

Garrett turned his head, finally noticing Jotnar push himself up off the ground. His eyes widened in fear and he took a step back. I don't blame him. This was the monster who abused him and his family for years, who tormented them and terrorized them.

Jotnar chuckled. "So you are back. You didn't run away like a coward, did you, Garrett?"

I stepped in front of my brother. "Don't you talk to him!"

Jotnar smiled, shooting a ball of darkness at Garrett and then at me. I blocked each attack with fire and then with wind.

"Come on, Garrett!" I said. "We can take him together!"

"Me?" Jotnar chuckled. "You can take me? You two are worthless! You two are nothing but unloved, worthless piles of nothing. You're both weak and spineless."

"No..."

I turned my head to see Garrett. His eyes were fierce and he stood straighter. A purple cloud energy was forming around him.

"We are not nothing," Garrett growled. "You may have ruined my childhood, but I'll be damned if I let you take away my present and my future!"

Garrett's eyes changed from blue to purple. Violet energy came to life, looking similar to fire, encasing him like a cocoon. I saw something on Jotnar's face that I'd never seen before.

Fear.

"I am *not* afraid of you anymore!" Garrett growled. "I am not the one who is unloved and spineless. That's all you."

Garrett shot his fist straight out, sending a cloud of black and purple at Jotnar who tried to block the attack only to stagger backwards. I stepped aside, nudging Katrina behind me. I'd never seen Garrett so angry before. Garrett was breathing heavily, looking like an angry bull. He raised his hands, curling his fingers. The ground began to shake and dust fell from the ceiling. Suddenly, corpses were rising from the ground—from beneath the marble floor!

They growled and snarled, pulling themselves up and crawling towards Jotnar. I heard something crack and shift. I looked up and realized it was from the ceiling. The castle was falling in on itself.

"Garrett!" I screamed.

I let my legs carry me, ignoring everything else that was going on. I grabbed Garrett and threw him over my shoulder.

"Thomas!" he shouted.

"We need to get out of here!" I protested.

Sir Charles, Katrina, Bruce, and I ran across the ballroom floor, barely missing the rubble that fell and shattered into several pieces. I didn't look back, for it was most likely not a pretty sight, and we didn't stop running until we were halfway up the hill. We did stop to catch our breath and looked back at the scene. It looked like the end of the world. The castle had fallen.

Nobody could have survived that.

"Is it done?" Bruce asked.

I set Garrett down and nodded. "I think so."

I hadn't even caught my breath when Garrett gave me a side hug. "We did it," he panted.

I chuckled. "Well, you did, anyway."

Garrett smiled. "Now, let's go find our family."

I nodded, pulling Garrett even closer for a hug. There's still so much that I have to make up for and so much we all have to set right. We indeed have a long journey ahead of us, but for my family, it'd be worth it.

Chapter 31

Caitlin

My mother was standing before me looking terrifying. I have never seen her look like this.

Like a monster.

I remember my mother looked like Brigit and Alison a long time ago. Now she looked like she was on the verge of death and that crown...were those needles? How was she not bleeding? And her bones...she looks so hollow. I had to swallow my breakfast once I realized that I could see her heart beating from within her chest.

Nimh stepped out of the shadows, no smile or anything. It terrified me to see that her eyelids were stitched shut and that her nails looked as long as butcher knives.

"So you are alive," Nimh said nonchalantly as the crew got up and pulled out their swords, stepping between me and Captain Raina. "Here I thought you died in the siege."

Nimh said it so...bluntly...like she couldn't care less that her five children could have been dead for the past five years. I shouldn't be surprised or hurt, but I was. I don't know how that could be possible.

Sheila fearfully took hold of my arm. "It's her," she whispered.

I covered her hand protectively. "I know, just stay back."

Nimh turned to me. It's ironic. She can't see me but I feel like she's looking right into my soul.

"I see you've also chosen to associate yourself with the ocean trash," Nimh spoke.

Captain Raina drew her own sword and aimed it at Nimh. "Watch who you speak to, tyrant."

"They're not trash," I stated firmly. "They are the best pirates who ever sailed the seas."

Nimh's thin lips tightened. "And you are among them. Tell me, dear, are you proud to consider yourself one of their own? Are you proud that you, too, are a thief, a cheater, and a killer?"

I tightened my fists at my sides and took a meaningful step forward. "I only killed *your* men who were chasing after *us*! I only kill because we are at war with *you*. You kill because you get angry when people don't bend the knee for you. You kill because you are a heartless skank who turned her back on the children who needed her!"

Nimh scoffed. "Right, *I* am the monster, not you five ungrateful little parasites. You were never abused, Caitlin. You are just complaining like the brat you've always been."

"KIDS AREN'T SUPPOSED TO BE GRATEFUL, YOU BITCH!" I screamed.

My cry echoed in the dark cave and the water around us began to ripple. Still holding Scathe's talisman tight in my grasp, I continued to yell. My own mother was trying to play mind games with me, just like she did when I was younger. I tried telling her of the abuse. Hell, she witnessed the physical and verbal abuse by her second husband! She was verbally and sometimes even physically abusive herself! I remember one time when Brigit got "mouthy" just because she finally chose to stand up for herself, Nimh slapped her. I knew that Nimh was always aware of the sexual abuse I was forced to endure, but she didn't care. She never stood up to Jotnar, she never sent him away, left him, nothing! She did *nothing*!

"YOU FAILED AS A MOM!" I screamed as tears drenched my face. I was breathing heavily, but I continued. "I NEEDED YOU! WE NEEDED YOU AND YOU FAILED US! MOMS ARE SUPPOSED TO LOVE AND PROTECT THEIR CHILDREN! I WAS A CHILD JUST LIKE MY

BROTHERS AND SISTERS! YOU TURNED YOUR BACK ON US OVER AND OVER AGAIN ALL BECAUSE YOU WERE AFRAID OF BEING ALONE! You didn't love us enough to stop the abuse! Kids need their moms from day one simply because they have no other option but to put their trust in them! But you took advantage of that! When you were so 'busy doing queenly things', I was the one raising the others! 'Don't bother me, kids! Get lost, kids. Do I have to beg? You kids can entertain yourselves! I don't have time for you kids! I'm the only one that does anything around here! You'll never make it in the world! Especially on your own!' How dare you treat us like that!"

My hand began to glow warmly, the one with Scathe's talisman. I could feel my power building up like a storm in the middle of the sea. No lighthouse or island in sight, just a ship struggling to stay afloat in the darkest night of the storm. I didn't even need to think. I threw my hands out and sent a huge wave of water at Nimh. She grunted, trying to block the attack with wind.

"Caitlin!" Captain Raina shouted.

"Get everyone back to the ship!" I shouted.

Not waiting for an answer, I marched forward and sent another massive wave at Nimh.

"MOTHERS ARE SUPPOSED TO HAVE YOUR BACK! THEY'RE SUPPOSED TO PUT THEIR CHILDREN'S NEEDS BEFORE THEIRS!"

Nimh grunted, stumbling backwards. I threw deep blue magic at her. Her golden magic bounced off my powers and hit the cave walls. The area around us started to tremble, but I didn't care. I didn't care anymore!

"YOU TRAUMATIZED ALL OF US AND YOU PLAY THE VICTIM! YOU MAKE EXCUSES FOR WHY YOU DID WHAT YOU DID!"

Nimh growled, throwing air in my direction, but I smacked it away with the back of my hand and kept marching forward. The water beneath her feet slowly cracked, turning into ice. Nimh yelped and fell flat on her back. With Scathe's talisman warm in one hand, I summoned a long icicle in the other. It was long and freezing cold to the touch, so cold it stung, but I ignored the pain. I sat on top of Nimh's chest and raised the icicle above her bony throat.

"THE ONLY PARASITE—THE ONLY MONSTER HERE—HAS ALWAYS BEEN YOU!" I screamed. "You will not terrorize anyone in this world *ever again*!"

I raised the icicle over my head, ready to end it all. Nimh blasted me in the face with golden energy. I hit the water, completely soaked.

"I am your mother," Nimh hissed. "Show me respect! I am queen!"

I pushed myself up, standing firmly on my two feet. "I see no queen! And you are not my mother! The only mother I had was my grandmother and my Aunt Megan. They were the only mothers I needed. And people like you don't deserve children!"

Nimh growled, raising her clawed hand, summoning air. "I should have drowned you when you first came out of me! I should have left you at the mercy of your father just like your worthless brother!"

Nimh threw air at me, but I raised my hands, creating a wall of ice so thick you couldn't see through it. I clenched my fists and the wall melted. Once Nimh was in sight once more, I summoned the icicle and threw it straight at her. Nimh let out an agonized scream as the icicle pierced her shoulder and pinned her against the wall of the cave. Blood trickled down her raggedy black dress and her breathing turned shallow, followed by wheezing.

"Thomas isn't worthless," I panted. None of us are. As for killing me, yeah, you probably should have. Guess another mistake you can add to your list was having kids in the first place."

Nimh's legs went numb and her breathing was slowing down. She wasn't going to last very long.

Captain Raina walked up beside me, sheathing her sword. "You okay?"

I slowly nodded. "Sort of. Feels better to have gotten all that off my chest."

Captain Raina snickered. "Everyone is on the ship. We should..."

I stared at Captain Raina. She looked frightened. "What's wrong?"

"The talisman," Captain Raina answered. "Where is it?"

I looked down at my hand, ready to reveal where it's been this whole time, but it wasn't there. It must have fallen when Nimh knocked me down. Nimh let out a wheezy gasp, snapping her fingers. The cave started the shake; rocks tumbled from above. The cave was going to fall and kill us in the process!

"Run!" Captain Raina shouted.

"But the talisman—!" I started.

"Isn't as important as our lives!" Captain Raina argued. "Move out!"

She grabbed me by my hand and we ran, more heavy rocks and boulders crashing down behind us. We almost tripped a few times, running through the cave tunnels. The entrance was only yards away, but by the looks of it, we weren't going to make it.

"Climb on!" Captain Raina shouted.

Before I could ask her what she meant, she had jumped forward, landing on all fours in the form of lioness with brown eyes. I cursed and threw myself on her back. She took off at a speed so fast it made my head spin. The cave was falling to bits behind us just as she leapt out of the entrance and onto the sandy beaches. I gasped and fell off Raina, landing on my back facing the starless sky. I heard panting in sync with my own and realized Raina had transformed back into her true form. She lay down beside me, gasping. We stayed there for a few minutes, ignoring the irritating sand and catching our breaths when... "Neat trick," I said.

Raina chuckled. "Thanks."

"I'm sorry I lost the talisman."

"Don't be. We'll find it."

"How do we know it wasn't destroyed?" I asked.

"Because every day since the siege, it has been nothing but cloudy days and starless skies," Raina answered. "Which means that not only did the talisman somehow make it out, but so did Nimh."

I sat up. "How could she have survived *that*?"

Raina sat up, brushing some sand off her coat. "The worst types of people, even with magic, tend to find ways to cheat death."

"Then we'll just have to fight her another day," I said.

Raina nodded. "Yeah."

She pushed herself up to her feet and offered me her hand, which I took. She pulled me up and planted a kiss on my lips. It was quick and unpredictable, but it made me smile.

"Together next time, okay?" she said.

I giggled. "Together."

Raina planted another kiss on my forehead and linked our hands together. As we walked back to the Crimson Kraken, I asked, "Where to next?"

Raina playfully bumped my shoulder. "How about we look for your family?"

I smiled. "Yeah! That'd be perfect! I can't wait for you to meet them! Especially Brigit. I have a feeling you two would get along."

Raina brought our linked hands to her lips and kissed my knuckles. "I look forward to it, Treasure."

Brigit

Have you ever run in the woods by yourself at night? It's no easy task, especially when there's a literal fire-breathing dragon flying in the sky atop a blazing castle. A lot of the trees looked exactly the same: healthy and normal-looking, unlike the trees that were on fire by the entrance to the castle. I remembered the path that Salem took me on, the one with the hideaway in the forest floor. It was by a gnarled tree with thick and knotted bark. I dropped to my knees and searched the ground, frantically sweeping dirt, moss, and leaves away until I found something hard and long.

The latch.

I got to my feet, pulling the door up, revealing the dark hideaway. Ooh, boy. I fucking hate the dark. Always have, but I'd rather take my chances in here than out there with a dragon. Besides, Salem said he'd find me soon. I wouldn't be hiding here for long. I hurried down the steps, careful not to trip, and pulled the latch down with me. The hideout was spacious enough to fit a bathroom in, so my claustrophobia wasn't kicking in. There was a long table in the far corner with a wooden chair tucked in. There were a few bowls and a candelabrum sitting on top of the table and a shelf full of bottled herbs, crystals, and stones. Behind the staircase was a hammock and a big heavy blanket folded neatly in the center with boxes of jarred food and water on the side.

It looked pretty nice.

At last, I was safe and sound in the underground hideaway. That's when I chose to let myself cry. I crouched on the bottom step, hugged myself, and started *bawling*. I'm trying to stay strong, but I need to be honest with myself. I'm so afraid. I'm afraid of dying before getting to finish growing up. I'm afraid for Aunt Megan, my brothers, and my sisters. I don't even know if they're alive or where they are. I'm afraid for Salem and his people. I care so much about him and this kingdom; I don't want him to lose his family or his home or his life!

I'm afraid for this world. I'm afraid for the people here.

Praying, huh? I've never been one to pray or believe in God, or the Gods, I guess. But something is out there, right? The Universe has to hear me, doesn't it? There has to be something. *Something.* I lifted my head up and wiped away my tears.

"I'm not one to pray," I said out loud. "I don't even know if you Gods exist at all. I don't even know how to really pray. I've been rediscovering who I am; just a little girl born into misfortune, but if the stories I've heard about the Gods are true, then maybe we aren't so different at all."

My palms started to glow green—lime green. An energy circled me and filled my heart. I heard voices, calm and soothing names like a mother I never had. I felt hands rest on my shoulders reassuringly. Names entered my head: Geb, Gaia, Demeter, Danu, Sif, to name a few. I felt energies surrounding me, getting bigger and bigger; some were like parents, some felt more like teachers and mentors. I continued on.

"I pray, Gods save our Earth. Prove you have humanity, that we all have worth. Gods save our souls. We hold you in our hearts. Gods, please hear my call. Return what was stolen from us. It's not my soul I pray for. So far, I've survived, but I've seen those who struggle just to stay alive. Gods hear our prayers, from the lost and the scared. I pray you won't let your children fall."

I felt more hands touch my shoulders. They were all Earth deities, re-assuring me that I wasn't alone, like everything was going to be okay.

"I used to wonder why some are more favored," I went on. "Why those who seem to rule the world...they hate us, they beat us, maybe even turn a blind eye on us. Gods, please, I beg you, help the hurt and the abused. We're all seeking the purpose for why we exist. Warfare and tyrants brought us all to our knees. Many of us are taught from birth to pray to you, please don't let our words go unheard. From the torn and the scarred, to the harmed and the branded, hear my prayers, and don't let this kingdom fall."

The light in my hands vanished and so did the Godly energy. They were here. They heard me. I know they did.

Just as I thought things were starting to calm down, I heard something outside. It sounded like movement.

Salem!

I climbed up the steps and threw open the latch. When my eyes landed on the one making the noise, I screamed. It was the green dragon that had set the castle on fire. It was looking right at me. Its eyes alone were the size of my head! It stared at me curiously. I didn't move. I just froze. It's like everything inside me just shut down. It was terrifying but at the same time, I was in awe. I've never seen something so powerful and incredible in my life!

"Such a small little witch, aren't you?" the dragon asked.

It—he can talk? And his voice is *so deep*!

"So little, yet so powerful already," the dragon spoke. "The Gods have brought me here to you, High One."

It took me a second to find my voice. "Y-you destroyed the Elven castle! You attacked this Domain!"

"Not in my right mind, High One," the dragon explained. "Only the Dragon Tamer can control me and my kind."

"Who's the Dragon Tamer?" I asked. "And who are you?"

"I am Veles," the dragon stated. "As for who the Dragon Tamer is, that would be Jotnar."

My heart sank. "He's the Dragon Tamer?"

"As was his father before him," Veles explained. "To be a Dragon Tamer, you have to be born with fire magic. Jotnar has no fire magic, none that he was born with, anyhow."

"He stole it, you mean?"

"From when his brother died, yes."

I took a deep breath, considering my question. "So why are you here talking to me?"

"Because you and your kin have a great future. I can speak to you because you were born with magic, and my kind is magic. The only one in your family who will be able to control, tame, and protect the dragons of this world will be Alison, the Noble One."

I struggled to say something. *Alison?* Alison is going to be a Dragon Tamer?

"Your siblings have already tried to kill the monsters who rule with fear in this land, but failed," Veles explained. "They tried with strength and valor, but one does not fall easily when they are as poisonous as them."

I blinked away the tears in my eyes. "So they're all alive?"

"Indeed, High One," Veles nodded. "You each have a great destiny to bring the monsters in this world to their knees, as they have done to you and countless others. Alison's destiny will be to protect the dragons, new and old. Nora—the Honorable One—will one day rule Clover

Talamh as its rightful heir, bringing peace and prosperity back to the world."

Nora's going to be queen. That's a lot to put on a little girl, adding to that the fact that she's seven and one of the Saviors. No pressure or anything, right?

"Garrett—the Spear—will rule as Lord of a great land someday, being the bridge to the living and the dead, reuniting loved ones and helping those in need of sanctuary. Caitlin's destiny—the Pure One—will be to rule the seas beside another, finding trade routes and exploring the world, whatever it may hold."

Hearing what everyone else was going to be doing in the future was incredible but unbelievable. It's not that I didn't believe Veles, it's just...wow.

"As for you, High One, your destiny will be to rule beside an Elf King for all eternity, bringing fertility and restoration to the kingdoms." An Elf King? Does that mean—?

"What about Thomas?" I asked.

Veles looked upon me like he wanted to answer but was searching for the right words.

Why? What does Thomas's future hold?

"Brigit!" I heard Salem call.

Veles and I both looked in the direction of the castle. He was coming! He was okay!

"I must go now, High One," Veles stated. "The Earth Gods protect me, but there are many more dragons to come. Your magic along with the elves' will be strong enough to keep out anyone and anything. Remember to stand your ground and hold your head high. You are like a mountain, High One. Many will try to move you, to bring you down, but no one will be strong enough to do so."

Veles spread his massive, powerful wings, lifted his head, and took off into the darkness of the night sky. I had a feeling I'd be seeing him again. When he was out of sight, that's when Salem finally came into view.

"Brigit!"

I climbed out of the hideaway and threw myself into Salem's arms. He picked me up by my waist and spun me around, happily kissing my neck and cheek.

"You're okay!" I cried as he put me down. "Is everyone else okay? Is anyone hurt?"

"My family is fine," Salem explained, cupping my face. "My parents and Akoni have sustained minor injuries, but my family is alive and well."

"What about the castle and the rest of the forest?" I asked.

"Nothing that can't be fixed," Salem answered. "Parts of the castle indeed need repair, but it still stands."

I leaned closer to Salem and kissed him. I was so relieved! Everyone and everything was going to be okay!

Salem is the family that I found when I returned to this world. At the time, I had no idea who he was or even who *I* was. I had no idea what was going on. Then he found me. He helped me and gave me a home.

Because of Jotnar and my parents, I almost lost another family. Another home. If my destiny is to rule and bring back what belonged to this world, I don't care what I have to do. I'm not losing anyone else ever again. I have hope, love, and family, and I'll be damned if I let *anyone* take that away again.

So bring it on. They wanted war...they've got it.